Praise for Steve Frech

'I absolutely LOVED this book … An unputdownable page turner of a read'

'This book just pulls you right in … I couldn't put it down!'

'One of the best thrillers I've read this year'

'So gripping, I just could not stop reading'

'Like riding a rollercoaster … Should be on everyone's reading list'

'I burned through this'

'I was hooked from page one'

Nightingale House

STEVE FRECH

ONE PLACE. MANY STORIES

HQ
An imprint of HarperCollins*Publishers* Ltd
1 London Bridge Street
London SE1 9GF

First published by HQ 2020

This edition published in Great Britain by
HQ, an imprint of HarperCollins*Publishers* Ltd 2020

ISBN: 9780008372194

MIX
Paper from
responsible sources
FSC™ C007454

This book is produced from independently certified FSC™ paper
to ensure responsible forest management.

For more information visit: www.harpercollins.co.uk/green

Printed and bound in Great Britain by
CPI Group (UK) Ltd, Melksham, SN12 6TR

Thank you, Deborah.

Nightingale House was not born with secrets, but they were made here.

They were sealed into the walls and buried beneath the floorboards.

Most of us don't know what happened in the rooms we live in before we arrived. We never hear of the tragedies that occurred in the room where we sleep or the unspeakable acts that took place years ago in the basement.

And while the secrets of most houses are eventually forgotten, Nightingale House won't allow that.

Its secrets remain, hiding in the shadows at the top of the stairs, in the whispers at the end of the hall, and in the sound of a little girl crying on the other side of a door to a room that's empty.

They are still here, waiting …

1

With one hand, I reach up and press my fingers to my chest, feeling the ring that's hanging from my neck, under my shirt. With my other hand, I reach out to my eight-year-old daughter, Caitlyn, who is standing by my side. Gusts of wind kick and swirl around us.

"Ready?" I ask.

She takes a deep breath and grasps my hand. "Ready."

The Queen Anne-styled Nightingale House, sitting on the shore of Willow Lake, stands before us.

"Let's do it," I say.

We begin slowly walking up the stone path. The gables of the house, with its Turret Room, loom above as we approach. The wind does its best to knock us off course, but we eventually reach the wrap-around porch step up to the heavy, oak door.

I fish the key out of my pocket and offer it to Caitlyn.

"Care to do the honors?"

She stares up at me with those big, blue eyes. She looks so much like Nicole it hurts. I know Caitlyn is missing her mother right now just as much as I am.

"Okay."

She takes the key and attempts to slide it into the lock, but her hands are shaking.

"You want some help?" I ask.

"No," she stubbornly sighs.

I smile. She's so much like Nicole.

She finally gets the key into the lock.

"There. See? I did it," she says, giving it a twist. She pushes down on the handle and leans against the door. The hinges sweetly groan as it swings open.

We step inside out of the wind and are greeted by the smell of polish from the gleaming hardwood floors. To the left is the living room. The sofa and coffee table are surrounded by unpacked boxes. Directly in front of us are the stairs to the second floor. The door to our right leads to the study.

No.

I forgot.

We were going to call it my "Writing Room". It's where I'm going to write the sequel to *In the Shadows of Justice.*

*

A couple years ago, I was a struggling writer, working as a substitute teacher, trying desperately to support a wife and child. We were living in a cramped, two-bedroom apartment in Portsmouth, New Hampshire with this dream that one day, my little stories would become best-sellers. So far, all I had to show for it were two books that hadn't gone anywhere. I felt like this third one, a political thriller, was my last shot.

Nicole and I had a routine; I would get up at four in the morning and start writing. Nicole would get up at six and get Caitlyn ready for school. Then, over a cup of coffee, Nicole and I would sit at our thrift-store-purchased kitchen table and I'd read to her what I had written. I loved it. I knew that if by some miracle, my political thriller became a best-seller, this would always be my favorite part; just me and Nicole, sitting at the kitchen table, her eyes widening as the story unfolded. She was my best critic, cheerleader, and editor. I'll never forget the day we were sitting at the kitchen table, rain beating against the window, and I read the words 'the end'. I looked up from the page and she had tears in her eyes. Nicole took my face in her hands, kissed me, and said, "This is it."

We got an agent, there was a bidding war, and we were off to the races. And I keep saying 'we' because I mean 'we'. No Nicole? No book.

Fourteen months later, after a year of editing, tweaking, and finally, publication day, came 'the call'.

The book had been out for two months and sales were strong. The reviews were great. My publisher had already offered a two-book extension to my contract along with a handsome advance. Nicole and I tried not to talk about it too much, out of fear that we would jinx it.

Then, one morning while we were getting Caitlyn ready for school, my agent, Lana Gifton, called.

"Have you seen the *New York Times* best-seller list this morning?" she asked.

It took me a second or two, but I gradually grasped her meaning.

"… no way."

"I really think you should," she said, and hung up.

I flew from my chair and raced for the computer. I pulled it up on the browser because, of course, I had it bookmarked.

My heart stopped.

"Nicole!" I yelled.

She ran over and stood behind me.

"What's going on?" she asked.

I pointed at the screen.

8. *In the Shadows of Justice – Daniel Price*

"Oh my God!" she screamed.

I leaped up and we held each other as we both started crying.

"Mom? Dad? What's wrong?" Caitlyn asked from the doorway.

I ran over and gave her a fierce hug.

"Oomph …"

"Pumpkin, how would you like not to go to school today?"

She eyed me suspiciously. "What would we do?"

"Whatever you want."

We spent the rest of the day bowling, going to the movies, and eating ice cream.

That night, after Caitlyn passed out in her bed from exhaustion, Nicole and I went to our room and made love more passionately than we had in years. It was a celebration of everything we had worked for.

Afterwards, we lay side by side, sweating, and in total bliss.

"Hey, Shakespeare?" she whispered. It was her favorite pet name for me.

"Yeah?"

"I think it's time we start looking for some new digs."

"Way ahead of you."

"Oh, yeah?"

"Yep. What were you thinking?"

She playfully bit her lip. "Hmm … anything?"

"Well, we may have to skip the helipad and twenty-car garage, but other than that, name it."

"I want to live on the water. Doesn't have to be the ocean but maybe a lake."

"Done." I nodded.

She laughed. "I like this little fantasy."

I took her hand. "It's not a fantasy anymore."

I think that was the first time we both realized that it was finally happening. No more dreaming to take our minds off our desperate situation. No more trying to hide how broke we were from Caitlyn.

"I want to live in an old house," Nicole said, before quickly adding, "Not ancient, but something with character."

"Perfect."

"What do you want?"

"Me?"

She nodded.

"I want round two."

She laughed as I pulled her to me.

*

It took Nicole all of thirty-six hours to find the Nightingale House.

I was in love from the moment she showed me the pictures online and told me the house had a name. It was also within our price range, only an hour away in the town of Kingsbrook, Maine, and we had four hours until Caitlyn would be home from school.

"Let's go!" she said, grabbing my wrist.

The excitement on the drive up Highway 16 was too much for conversation. The house. The town. It was all too perfect.

We exited at Kingsbrook/Willow Lake and drove down Main Street, which lined with stately homes, all of them at least a hundred years old. The town square was rimmed with coffee-shops, antique stores, and cafés.

The directions took us into the outlying forests. It was autumn and the trees were splashes of red, orange, and yellow. One last turn and Willow Lake came into view. The road, which ran parallel to the shore, was dotted with houses, the last one being the Nightingale House.

The pictures hadn't done it justice. They couldn't have. To see the porch, the gables, and the Turret Room looking out over the lake on a computer screen was one thing, but to be standing in front of it was something different, entirely.

Walking up the stone path, Nicole appeared to be in some sort of trance. A realtor with a spindly frame and glasses that required him to constantly push them up the bridge of his nose greeted us on the porch.

"Mr. and Mrs. Price?" he asked.

"That's us," I replied, since Nicole was incapable of speech.

"Pleased to meet you," he said, offering his hand. "I'm Mark Stelowski."

I shook it and he made a grand, sweeping gesture towards the house.

"Well, here she is. Built in 1893 by—"

"Uh, Mr … uh …?" I interrupted.

"Stelowski."

"Stelowski, great. I'm going to need you to do me a favor."

"Uh … of course."

"I'm gonna need you to sit this one out."

He blinked. "Oh … um … sure, okay."

"Thank you."

Nicole and I stepped inside.

It was my turn to be speechless but she suddenly came out of her trance.

She glanced into the room on our right, which contained a large bookcase built into the wall. "That's your study." She was about to go into the living room but stopped. "No! Correction. That's your Writing Room."

"Love it," I replied.

She quickly resumed her path into the living room. "Couch, recliner, television," she said, pointing around the room.

"Awesome."

I followed her into the dining room. A large window offered a stunning view of the lake. A wooden pier jutted out into the water.

"We're eating dinner here, every night," she said.

"I'll cook!" I offered.

She grimaced. "Eh … we'll see."

We moved into the kitchen. A back door led to a deck and the backyard. While the house had kept its old charm, the kitchen had all the modern conveniences with updated appliances and an island counter. There was a small alcove with a window overlooking the lake.

"Coffee, right there, every morning," I said.

"While you read to me," she added.

Nicole went over to a small wooden door and opened it.

"Pantry?" I asked.

"… No."

She went through and I heard her footsteps descend creaky wooden stairs. I crossed the kitchen and followed her into the darkness. I kept my hand against the cool stone wall to my right for balance. Once we reached the bottom of the stairs, Nicole went to the middle of the room and pulled the chain of a small, bare lightbulb that was barely visible in the darkness, hanging from the ceiling. The lightbulb had to be decades old and weakly glowed, barely illuminating the space.

"And … the basement …" she said.

"Yeah," I weakly offered.

There wasn't much to say beyond that. Wooden shelves rested against the walls and planked floors.

"Upstairs?" I asked.

"Upstairs," Nicole confirmed and snapped off the light.

We bounded back up the steps and hurried through the house like children having a race.

"Almost done!" I called out through the open front door to the realtor as we passed. He had to think that we were crazy as we charged up the stairs to the second floor.

At the top of the stairs, the hallway stretched out before us. To the right was the Turret Room. The windows offered an almost panoramic view of the lake. The ceiling vaulted to a point and a closet was near the door.

"Caitlyn's room?" I asked.

"I don't know. You think it might be too much of a change for her?"

I shrugged. "We'll ask her."

"We're gonna spoil that kid."

"Damn right, we are."

We went into the blue guestroom across the hall from the Turret Room. I stood behind Nicole in the doorway.

"Guestroom?"

"Until we give Caitlyn a sibling," Nicole replied.

I wrapped my arm around her waist, playfully growled, and nibbled her neck.

She laughed and spun away from me. "We're not done yet!"

We went down the hall to the master suite.

I opened the door and we both gasped. The walls were paneled in rich, rose-stained wood. A fireplace was nestled into the far wall and a door in the corner led to the bathroom.

"Our bedroom would have a fireplace?" Nicole whispered.

"Our bedroom would have a fireplace."

We walked back downstairs in a daze. It didn't seem possible that this house could be ours. We stopped in the living room and faced one another.

"Do you want to live here?" I asked.

"I know it sounds weird but, I feel like I'm supposed to be here ... Do you want to live here?"

I nodded.

We kissed and held one another with our foreheads pressed together.

"Nicole ... we're home."

We kissed one more time and then I called towards the front door.

"Mr. Kowalski?"

"It's 'Stelowski,'" Nicole corrected me with a giggle.

"Sir!" I yelled, playing it safe.

The realtor stepped inside and stopped at the image of Nicole and I holding one another in the living room.

"So, um ... do you have any—"

"We'll take it," Nicole said.

*

Two months later, once the papers had been signed, we brought Caitlyn to the Nightingale House.

Nicole was still unsure if Caitlyn would go for the Turret Room, but I never doubted it for a second. She walked through the bedroom door and fell in love. We had a hard time pulling her away from the windows as she looked out over the lake. Her bedroom in Portsmouth didn't have a closet, so she even viewed that as a luxury. She ran into the middle of the room, stared up at the ceiling overhead, and began spinning around.

Then we showed her the blue guestroom and the master suite. She dutifully paid attention but I could tell her heart was still in the Turret Room. We went back down the hall and stopped in between the doors to the Turret Room and blue guestroom.

"Are we really going to live here?" Caitlyn asked.

"Yep," Nicole said. "And you can have your pick. You can have the blue room or the other—"

Caitlyn dashed into the Turret Room.

"This one! This one! I want this one!" she cried as Nicole and I watched from the doorway.

"Why this one?" I asked.

"Because I'll be like a princess in a castle!"

It was so damn cute, I almost had to sit down.

Afterwards, we drove back into Kingsbrook and had milkshakes at a place called 'Murphy's'. Well, Caitlyn and I had milkshakes. Nicole had hot chocolate. Murphy's was like a soda shop out of the 1920s. The namesake was the owner's black lab, who was sleeping in a bed on the floor by the register. The place was packed but we were lucky enough to grab a booth. Caitlyn watched people passing outside the window and began making up stories for them.

"That's Mr. Teffelbottom. He's a scientist that does experiments in his basement," she said. "And there's Mrs. Longshanks. People say she's a witch."

Nicole and I exchanged a glance. This had been a little bit of an issue with Caitlyn. She liked to tell stories. Most people would have said she had a problem with lying, but since she was our kid, we preferred to call them stories. She also tended to tell them when she was overexcited. We viewed it as mostly harmless. If pressed, she would usually admit that she was just making stuff up. Still, there had been problems at school. After the amazing day we had, neither one of us felt like correcting her. Instead, we tried to steer her back to conversations about the new house.

After our milkshakes and hot chocolate, we got back in the car for the drive back to Portsmouth. No one was anxious to return to the apartment.

We were halfway there when we pulled up to a red light.

"When we move in, can we play hide-and-seek?" Caitlyn asked. "At Sarah's birthday party last year, we turned off all the lights in her house and played hide-and-seek."

"You bet," I said.

Caitlyn beamed.

Nicole twisted herself to look at Caitlyn in the back seat.

"A princess in a castle, huh?"

"Yep."

Nicole gave me a wink. "Maybe we should get you a princess bed for your room."

I watched in the rearview mirror as Caitlyn's eyes widened.

The light turned green.

I pulled forward and smiled at Nicole.

Our eyes met.

12

That's when I saw the blinding headlights in the window over her shoulder.

There was a sickening crunch and the sensation of every bone in my body flying apart.

Then, nothing.

*

Caitlyn lets go of my hand and I follow her as she walks through the living room and into the dining room.

When she stops, I can see the angry red scar on the back of her neck.

Her shoulders sag.

I feel it. I can feel Nicole's absence starting to overwhelm Caitlyn. It's starting to overwhelm me, too. It's been overwhelming me for months but I have to be strong for Caitlyn. I can never let her see me like that.

"Hey, you know what?" I ask.

She turns to me. "What?"

"I think there's something in your room."

She cocks her head. "What is it?"

I playfully shrug. "I don't know."

"Then, how do you know th—"

"Pumpkin, you should go see your room."

She gives me one more quizzical look and then starts slowly walking back to the stairs as I follow. The closer she gets, the faster she goes. By the time I reach the stairs, she's reached the top and turns into her room. I take my time catching up.

Halfway up, I hear her squeal with delight from her bedroom.

I reach the top of the stairs. All the doors in the hallway are open. A steady, rhythmic sound emanates from Caitlyn's room.

I round the corner into her room and find her bouncing on her new, four-poster canopy bed.

"My princess bed!" she happily sings.

"Hey! You're gonna break it!" I warn her but not too sternly.

She falls onto her back, laughing hysterically.

"All right, enough of that, you little monster." I point to the cardboard boxes in the corner. Each one has "Caitlyn" written in black marker on the side. "Start unpacking. Set up your room however you want. If you need me, I'll be down the hall, okay?"

She nods.

I go to leave, but hear her hop off the bed and run towards me. I turn just in time as she throws her arms around me in the strongest hug her arms can manage.

"Thank you, Dad."

I return her hug. "You're welcome, sweetheart."

"I love you," she says.

"I love you, too."

We hold each other, both missing Nicole.

I kiss the top of her head. "Okay. Get to work."

She goes to the boxes as I turn and leave. I hear her ripping the tape to unpack as I walk down the hall to the master bedro—

Huh.

This door was open a moment ago.

There has to be a draft, somewhere. I can hear the wind battering the house.

Oh well.

I open the door and go inside.

14

April 7th, 1900

I love it. I simply love this journal.

I've never kept a journal, but I will try to do so, especially because of who gave it to me, but more on that in a little while.

The party was fine but I'm much too shy for public gatherings. Besides, while it was my seventeenth birthday, the party wasn't really for me. It was Father's way of "introducing" us to Kingsbrook before we open the pharmacy. I know Father is excited, but he's been excited for every other business he's put his hand to, like the grocer's or the launderer, and they've all been disasters. This time, though, I heard him promise my stepmother, Carol, that it would be a success.

The party was held at the house we're renting in town. We can't afford to buy a house, but Father wanted us to appear successful because it will give people more confidence in the pharmacy. Father also wanted the party to be as elegant as possible but since we don't have the means to buy a house, we certainly don't have the money to hire caterers or planners. Everything fell to Carol and she was stretched to the limit. I felt horribly for her and tried to help as much as I could, but Father insisted that I was to be the centerpiece of the party.

As the party began and the guests arrived, I did my best to be cordial as Father introduced me, but after the introductions, he would forget all about me and go on and on about the pharmacy. It became so embarrassing that I had to step outside to get away, just for a moment.

I went to the backyard and hid out of sight behind one of the oak trees. I thought I was alone but there was someone else there, hiding from the party, as well.

He was tall with dark hair and striking blue eyes. Those eyes stopped me in my tracks. You can imagine my surprise when I saw that he was drinking from a flask. He was just as shocked to see me as I, him. He then got this little smile on his face and held out the flask. He was offering me a drink!

Unable to speak, I walked away, back to the party, but I couldn't stop thinking about that vicious little smile and those piercing blue eyes.

Later, at dinner, while Father was giving an overlong toast, in which he thanked everyone for welcoming us to Kingsbrook, and extolled the virtues of the soon-to-open pharmacy, I saw the man seated next to a tired-looking blonde woman a few tables away. While everyone else was politely listening to Father ramble on, the man and I locked eyes. He still had that little smile.

Once dinner was over, we moved on to the presents.

It was so uncomfortable, people I didn't know giving me presents, but I did my best to be truly appreciative. There were some pieces of jewelry, a book of poems, some things called 'crayons', and other knick-knacks.

When it came time, it was the blonde woman who stood and presented the gift, which was wrapped in tissue paper. She wished me a happy seventeenth birthday and handed it to me. I unwrapped the tissue paper and inside was this journal! The engraving on the front is so wonderful and the lock is so clever! The man, who I assumed was her husband, sat in his chair, and nodded in my direction. I nodded back.

After presents, I tried to keep my eye on the man as he mingled with other guests. He appeared charming and engaging. Those eyes sparkled every time he laughed. Everyone seemed to enjoy his company. I would say more than myself or Father's attempts to promote the pharmacy, he was the center of attention at the party. I did find it odd that he rarely spoke to his wife and I began to feel as though he was deliberately avoiding me, even though we continued to exchange glances.

At one point, Father grew frustrated and tried to wrestle the attention away from the man to talk about the pharmacy. Again, I was so embarrassed that I had to escape to the kitchen. There,

I found Carol desperately setting up a tray of desserts for the guests.

"What are you doing in here?" she asked.

"Father's being unbearable about the pharmacy," I replied.

She rolled her eyes in agreement. "Well, don't stay away too long. It is technically your party." She took the tray and went out into the living room. I stayed out of view as the door swung open, and waited for it to close.

It was hot in the kitchen. Carol had opened the window and I could hear voices outside.

I glanced out, and just below the window I saw two girls talking. I couldn't make out their faces, only the tops of their heads.

"Can you believe they're here?" one asked the other.

"Why not? From what I understand, it's not the first time it's happened," the other replied.

"What have you heard?"

"Stories mostly. Except this last one. I know for a fact he was caught with a young woman."

"Who told you?"

"Someone who knows their valet ... Can you blame the young woman, though? He is handsome."

"Patricia, stop it."

"What? He is. There's no denying it. Lots of women fancy him, and as I said, I've heard stories. He's even told me that he fancies me."

"You really are a terrible gossip."

"It's not gossip if you know."

Just then, the door to the kitchen swung open and Father poked his head inside.

"Darling, you're being rude. People are asking where you are."

At the sound of Father's voice, the girls below the window hurriedly walked away. The one named Patricia glanced back and our eyes briefly met before they rounded the corner of the house.

"*Come on,*" Father insisted.

I went to join 'my' party.

Once the party ended, Father and I waited at the end of the drive to see the guests off and individually thank them for coming. When I spotted the man towards the end of the line, I pretended as though I wasn't anticipating our formal introduction and farewell. That blonde woman hung on his arm. I tried to concentrate on the people to whom I was saying 'goodbye', but my attention kept flicking back to him.

At last, they reached Father and me.

Father shook their hands and said, "Mr. and Mrs. Carrington, thank you so much for coming."

The woman thanked him for the invitation to the party and again welcomed us to Kingsbrook.

Then, they turned to me.

I thanked them for coming and for the journal.

She took both my hands and said, "It was our pleasure."

She let go and I offered my hand to Mr. Carrington. "Thank you for coming, Mr. Carrington. So nice to meet you."

He locked me with those eyes and gently took my hand. "And you," he said.

No one could see it, but when he said 'you', he applied the slightest pressure with his finger to the palm of my hand. It was distinct and deliberate. "You should come visit us some time at the Nightingale House."

Unable to help himself, Father suddenly jumped in. "Well, if there is anything you need from the pharmacy, don't hesitate to contact us. We'll even make deliveries."

His attempt to casually insert business into the conversation went over like a stone, but the Carringtons remained polite. I couldn't prevent my eyes from rolling as Father rambled. Mr. Carrington shot me a sideways glance and gave me a sly wink. Afterwards, Father and I watched them ride off in their carriage, driven by a man I heard her address as 'Theodore'. Then, we saw the rest of the guests off.

I'm in bed now, and I can't stop thinking about him. This journal is such a perfect gift. Although I only shared a few words with him all night, I feel like he gave me the most attention. This town may not be all bad.

Good night.

2

Through the open door of the bedroom, I can hear Caitlyn singing to herself down the hall as she unpacks.

My unpacking is relatively easy. I hang my clothes in the closet and I tuck away the rest in the dresser. I'm not much of an interior designer, so the walls are going to remain bare. The only 'decoration' is a photo on the mantel over the fireplace of Nicole and I on our wedding day. Now, I'm sitting on the corner of the bed with the last thing that needs to be put away: a small cardboard box. I stare at it for a moment, then flip open the lid to reveal the small, snub-nosed pistol resting inside. I purchased it at a pawn shop a few months earlier, during what was my lowest point after Nicole's death. It was an impulse buy that I immediately regretted, but I can't bring myself to get rid of it. I keep the bullets in the drawer below the top drawer in a pretense of safety. Nicole would be furious if she knew I had a gun in the house.

"But Nicole's not here, is she?" I mumble to myself and instantly feel ashamed.

I close the lid, go to the dresser, tuck the box into the back of the top drawer, bury it behind pairs and pairs of socks, and push the drawer closed.

The wind blasts across the top of the chimney, filling the room with a soft wail.

I take in my new bedroom.

It feels cold; like the room doesn't want me here. The shadows on the walls don't seem to match what's around me.

It's a ridiculous thought, of course. The room feels unwelcoming because this isn't the same room as before. I was supposed to share this room with Nicole and now, she's not here. That's all. I'll get used to it. I really don't have a choice, do I?

The wind gusts again, causing a louder wail than before.

But not right now, I think, and head out the door.

*

A gust of wind rattles the window above the sink.

"Bowl," Caitlyn announces.

She hands me the bowl and I place it on the shelf in the cabinet.

She takes another paper-enclosed item out of the box marked 'kitchen' and unwraps it.

"Little bowl," she declares.

"Thank you," I reply and place it next to the stack of other bowls in the cabinet.

After unpacking our rooms, Caitlyn wanted to help with the rest of the house. I wasn't going to say no and figured that the kitchen would be the room with the most objects she could help with. At first, she delighted in unwrapping the items, like she was unwrapping Christmas presents. She would take them out of the box, tear away the paper, declare what they were, and hand them to me to put away in the cabinets she can't reach. However, that was an hour ago and for her, it's no longer like Christmas.

She lifts another item out of the box and unwraps it.

"Bowl," she sighs, disappointed.

"Thank you," I say, repeating our process.

"We have a lot of bowls," she says.

"Well … maybe."

I guess we do have a lot of bowls but the real problem is that she's getting restless. The novelty has worn off.

Caitlyn looks at her hands and claps them together.

"Gloves," she says.

"What's that, pumpkin?"

"I need gloves. The movers had gloves. I should wear gloves."

She abruptly turns and walks away into the dining room, out of sight.

"Caitlyn?"

"Be right back!" she calls out, her voice heading upstairs.

I lightly laugh, bend down, take another object out of the box, and remove the heavy wrapping paper.

A bowl.

Caitlyn may have a point.

Another gust of wind rattles the window, drawing my attention, and I glance out across the lawn towards the lake.

Nicole is standing by the shore.

She's staring right at me, unmoving, with a fearful, anxious expression. The wind whips her hair about her face.

The window continues trembling in the frame.

Behind her, the surface of the lake ripples from the wind.

She looks so worried, so scared. It's as th—

"Okay! I'm ready."

I drop the bowl. It crashes to the floor and shatters into countless shards of sharp, ceramic pieces.

Caitlyn is standing just inside the kitchen doorway, wearing her big, bulky, red snow gloves. She looks just as startled as I am.

"Pumpkin, you scared me." I exhale, clutching my chest. "I'm sorry."

We stare at the broken pieces.

"It's okay, Dad. We have a lot of bowls." She stares at the pieces a moment longer and then has an idea. "I'll go find the broom!" she proclaims, like she's going on a new adventure, and stomps away.

I turn back to the window.

Nicole is gone.

*

A few hours later, I'm in the living room, working on that most essential of projects: the entertainment center. Caitlyn is reading a book on the couch. I've already hooked up the television. It's resting on the floor while broadcasting a Cubs game. They've brought in their "ace" relief pitcher who has promptly blown a two-run lead.

"Oh, you jerk!" I say as the runner crosses the plate.

Caitlyn raises her head to look at me, but goes back to reading.

The wind has died a little bit, but short gusts will occasionally rake across the house.

I've gotten over the shock of seeing Nicole. Honestly, it's nothing new.

I've been having dreams about her. They started the day after the accident. Sometimes, they're nightmares. Other times, they're wonderful visions where we're living our lives, like nothing had happened. I'll wake up right in the middle of the dream and try to fall back asleep as quickly as possible, in the hopes that I can pick up right where I left off, but whenever I fall back asleep, we have really big heads and are watching sumo wrestling fish or something equally bizarre.

I'll admit that this was different. It was the first time I've seen her while I was awake, but I'm not too bothered by that. After she died, I used to feel like she was around all the time at the apartment, and today of all days, when I was missing her more than I thought possible, of course I would see her in my mind's eye. I've come to grips with the idea that the next few weeks and months are going to be tough with moving into a new house without Nicole. I don't know how I'm going to react, but I'm just going to have to roll with the punches.

There's a knock at the door.

"Hello?" a sing-song voice rings from the porch.

I stand up and walk to the door.

I open it to find a woman in her early sixties with short, dyed hair that remains almost motionless against the wind. Her cheeks are creased in laugh-lines. Her eyes sparkle, as does her jewelry. In one hand she has a plate of cookies. In the other, she's holding a bottle of scotch. She is clearly in a class by herself.

"Are you my new neighbors?" She smiles.

"I believe so," I reply. "Come on in."

"Thank you." She steps inside and I close the door behind her. "I'm Mildred Johnson. I live next door."

"Hello, Mildred Johnson. I'm Daniel Price and this is my daughter, Caitlyn."

Caitlyn gets off the couch and joins us.

"It's a pleasure to meet you," Mildred says with, of all things, a curtsey to Caitlyn.

Caitlyn loves it and tries to return the gesture. "Nice to meet you, Mrs. Johnson."

"Oh, you can call me Mildred. I wanted to welcome you two to the neighborhood." She offers the plate of cookies to Caitlyn. "These are my legendary 'Twice-Spanked Cookies'. The trick is, just as they start to rise when you're baking them, you spank them down with a spatula."

Caitlyn takes the plate. "Thank you, Mrs. Johns— I mean, thank you, Mildred."

"You are so welcome. And this is for you," she says, extending the bottle of scotch in my direction but stops. "You're not on the wagon, are you?"

I laugh. "Nope."

"Oh, thank God," she sighs, and hands it to me.

24

I don't recognize the label, but I do notice that the bottle has been opened and some of the liquid is gone.

Mildred reads my mind.

"I had to know if it was any good," she offers without a hint of shame.

"And now, it's my turn. Care to join me?"

*

We spend a little while talking in the kitchen while Caitlyn enjoys one of Mildred's 'twice-spanked' cookies. The wind has finally died down to a gentle breeze and we head outside.

Mildred and I sit on the back porch, sipping our scotch, enjoying the sunshine, and watching Caitlyn stand knee-deep in the water and attempt to skip rocks. Occasionally the wind will kick back up for a second, grab hold of one of the flat stones Caitlyn just threw, and send it sailing to the left.

"So, Daniel Price. What do you do for a living?"

"I'm an author."

She raises an impressed eyebrow. "Really? What do you write?"

"Novels."

"Anything I would know?"

"Maybe. *In the Shadows of Justice*? It's a political thriller."

She shakes her head. "Nah. I only read the steamy stuff. If I'm not going to blush, I want nothing to do with it."

I chuckle and take another sip. It is good scotch.

"Is there a Mrs. Price?" she asks, hesitantly.

"There was. She passed away eight months ago."

"Oh … that sucks."

"Yes, it does."

She contemplates her scotch and shrugs. "Still. A sexy, single, successful author? The women of this town will eat you alive."

She catches me mid-sip and I erupt in a fit of laughter and coughing.

I've found that there's a ritual to disclosing Nicole's death. I'll be having a pleasant conversation with someone. They'll ask. I'll tell them. There's a moment of awkward shock. They'll offer their condolences and then a shadow hangs over the rest of the conversation. It's refreshing for someone to take it in their stride and I'm oddly thankful for it. Besides, I knew Nicole's sense of humor, and she would have found it hilarious.

"What about you, Mildred Johnson?" I ask, after the coughing subsides. "Is there a Mr. Johnson?"

"Yep. That's how I bought that thirty years ago," she says with a wave towards her house, which is about a hundred yards down the shore. She then looks back at the Nightingale House. "You'll love this place."

"Did you know the people who lived here before us?"

"The Thompsons. Wonderful people. They were getting older and the house was getting to be too much for them. They moved to some God-awful place in Florida. But if you ask me, all of Florida is God-awful."

We watch as Caitlyn tries to sidearm another rock. She gets two skips before the rock disappears below the surface.

"How is she handling it? Her mom and all?" Mildred asks.

"It's rough. We were all in the car together. T-boned by a drunk driver. My wife died instantly. Caitlyn was out for a few days."

"… That *really* sucks," she says, eyes still on Caitlyn.

"Yes, it does."

"And the drunk driver?"

"He died at the scene."

"That's too bad." Mildred looks down into her scotch and then adds, "They should have kept him alive so you could finish him off."

"… I'd be lying if I said that thought never crossed my mind."

Mildred nods, as if I passed some kind of test. "Well, let me know whenever you need someone to look after her. I'll spoil her rotten."

"Mildred Johnson, you are my kind of woman."

We clink glasses.

*

Our inaugural dinner for our first night in the Nightingale House is pizza.

While I pay the delivery guy, Caitlyn sets the table. I know it's pizza but I feel that we should observe some sort of ceremony and actually eat at the table. As I carry the pizza towards the kitchen, I see that Caitlyn is setting out three plates on the dining-room table.

"Who's the extra plate for?" I ask, suddenly worried that she's setting a place for Nicole, like she's forgotten that she's not here.

"The pirate," Caitlyn responds.

"I'm sorry—the pirate?"

"Yeah. I met him outside when I was throwing rocks. You didn't see him. You and Mrs. Johnson were talking."

Honestly, I'm a little relieved.

"Is he joining us for dinner?"

"He said he might stop by," she replies, completely unfazed.

"Do pirates even like pizza?"

"Everyone likes pizza, Dad."

I suppose she's right. I'm weary of the story, though.

Since Nicole's death, Caitlyn's lying has become much worse. She would tell me things about her friends at school that alarmed me, but a little investigation would show that she had made it up. I tried to get her to stop. Each time, she said that she understood that it was wrong and promised to stop, but she kept doing it. Finally, I took her to a child psychologist. He said her fantasies were a normal coping mechanism for Nicole's death. Caitlyn's reality had been shattered and her active imagination had been providing an escape. He added that I should only worry if she

27

started believing the stories she was making up. As it stood, she never insisted they were true if I questioned her about them.

I know I'm not supposed to let her get away with these little stories but it's been a long day, we're starving, and if I'm going to allow myself some room to process things and not freak out, I should probably do the same for Caitlyn.

*

After dinner, we both get ready for bed and crash on the couch to watch a Disney movie we've seen a hundred times before. By the end, Caitlyn is already fast asleep in her nightgown, drooling on my shoulder. I'm not too far behind.

The movie ends. I reach over, pick up the remote, and hit the power button. The screen goes dark.

There's a man standing next to the television.

I throw a hand over Caitlyn, and quickly turn on the lamp on the end table, nearly knocking it over in the process.

The shadows are obliterated.

"Dad?" Caitlyn mumbles, rubbing her eyes. "What's going on?"

I'm still shaking. I glance around the room. Caitlyn and I are alone.

"It's okay, pumpkin. Sorry. Daddy was having a bad dream."

She sits up, more asleep than awake. "About what?"

I finally take a deep breath and settle myself.

"Nothing. Come on; time for bed."

Instead of getting up, she leans over and falls back asleep on my arm.

I smile. "That's the way it's gonna be, huh?"

She doesn't argue as I gently lift her up. She only wraps her arms around my neck and rests her face against my shoulder.

I carry her to the foot of the stairs. I can't help but look back one more time to the spot where I had seen the figure.

There's no one there.

3

This is the worst night since the night Nicole died.

I'm lying in bed, sleeping on the left-hand side, because that's where I always slept when Nicole and I shared this bed, staring at the darkness overhead, and I can't stop crying. My muscles ache from the sobs that have been wracking my body. I'm worried that I'll wake Caitlyn, but I can't stop. I grab a pillow, go into the bathroom, and close the door. Using the pillow to stifle my cries, I sit on the cold floor and weep. I don't care how this looks. Ego is nothing in the face of crushing grief.

When they told me Nicole was gone, it was surreal. I couldn't process it. I still can't. I've spent the past few months thinking that somehow, at any moment, she'll walk through the front door and life will go on the way we planned, the way we worked so hard for, and finally achieved. After the accident, Caitlyn and I lived in the old apartment and it always felt like Nicole was nearby, but now, in these new surroundings, I don't feel her anymore. For the first time, it feels like she's truly gone.

After I don't know how long I've been sitting on this floor, sobbing, I press my face into the pillow and scream with every fiber in my body. I scream again, and again, and again, until my lungs finally give out. That's it. I lean back against the wall and take deep breaths that catch in my chest. The sobs stop because I no longer have the strength.

The bedroom door creaks open.

Damnit.

Despite my efforts, I must have awoken Caitlyn with my crying. I quickly wipe my eyes, expecting to hear her call out to me or her footsteps approach the bathroom, but once the hinges of the bedroom door stop, there's silence.

"Caitlyn?"

No answer.

I pull myself up off the floor and go out into the bedroom. The door is open, but the doorway's empty. I grab my phone as I cross the room and check the time. 2:42 a.m. This long night just got longer.

I poke my head into the darkened hallway.

The only light is coming from the night-light in Caitlyn's room which is spilling out from the crack under her door.

I quietly move down the hall towards her bedroom. She must have gotten scared when she heard me crying and went back to bed. I get closer and my suspicions are confirmed. I can hear whispering coming from behind her door.

I carefully press my ear against it.

"I can't sleep … I can't sleep …"

I tap against the door and gently open it. "Caitlyn, I'm sorry. I didn't want—"

The night-light casts a soft glow around the room. Caitlyn's asleep. She's contorted herself into a ridiculous position with one leg off the bed and her butt up in the air.

"Caitlyn?"

Maybe she's pretending to be asleep to avoid talking to me.

I get closer and see that she is out cold.

I quietly turn, step out of the room, and close the door behind me.

I'm way more tired than I realized because I'm hearing things. I need to get back to my room, crawl into bed, and try to sl—

Drip … drip …

I spin around.

It came from somewhere on the stairs. I pull up the flashlight app on my phone and scan the stairs. They're dry. There are no water spots on the ceiling, either.

Drip … drip …

It's coming from downstairs.

As quietly as the stairs will allow, I creep down to the first floor. I wait at the bottom of the stairs, searching everywhere with the light from my phone. Unconsciously, I steal a glance to the television where I thought I saw the figure earlier, but there's no one there.

Drip … drip …

Wait … now it's coming from the dining room.

My blood begins to boil. I believed Stelowski when he said that all the pipes had been inspected. Now, I'm going to have to pay what will probably turn out to be thousands of dollars to fix it.

I go into the dining room and wait … and wait … and wait.

I continue searching the ceiling and the floor but everything is dry. My heartbeat begins to slow. My breathing returns to normal. This is pointless. There's nothing I can do about it tonight. I'll look tomorrow in the daylight.

Since I've come all that way, I'll check out the kitchen, just to be thorough. I walk through the entranceway and sweep the light over the stove, counters, and fridge. I check the door leading to the backyard to make sure it's locked, which it is. Through the window in the door, I can see the moon's reflection in the black water of the lake.

I have to get back to bed. Tomorrow, I'll call Stelowski and have him send someo—

Drip … drip …

31

It's right behind me.

I swing around, sweeping the light in a wide arc across the floor. It sounded so close, I'm surprised that I didn't feel the water on my bare ankles, but the floor is dry. I check the ceiling. No water marks. I stand absolutely still, holding my breath, until my muscles begin to cramp and my lungs start to burn. The stillness wins out. The tension flows from me. A new house, way behind on the next book, stress, grief, lack of sleep? Of course I'm hearing things. I tell myself that I have to take it easy and roll with the punches. It's time to get back to sleep.

I creep back through the first floor and up the stairs. I tip-toe past Caitlyn's room and down the hall.

I quickly hop into the bed, getting my freezing feet off the floor and slide them under the covers. I punch the pillow, fluffing it up, smooth it out, lay my head back, and wait for sleep to come … and wait … and wait … and wait … and wait …

May 3rd, 1900

Today was the grand opening of the pharmacy.

For the last month, Father's been talking about the crowds that were going to show up. In the end, there was only a handful of people. Most of them were other merchants from the town square and were more polite than enthusiastic. Father gave a ridiculous speech about how the pharmacy would provide for all of Kingsbrook's medical needs. He boasted of the tonics from the East and powders from Africa. Then, he announced that he would be giving away samples to prove their effectiveness. Carol was livid. Afterwards, they disappeared in the back and left me to work the register. The machine jammed and I needed Father's assistance. I went through the curtain to the storeroom and found them arguing.

Carol was furious and said he was throwing money away. Father said that once everyone sees how well the products work, they'll be back for more. Carol said that they didn't work and that Father knew it back in Boston. That's when they saw me standing by the curtain. I told them about the register.

Carol said she would take care of it and left us.

"Isn't it wonderful?" Father asked with a forced smile.

"Isn't 'what' wonderful?"

"The store!" he replied. "It's going to do such wonderful things for our family."

He's said that before about the grocer's we had in Boston and the launderette. And now, this.

Father and Carol continued to be hostile to each other and arguing in the storeroom. The stream of customers dwindled, and Father decided it would be best if I ran the store and the two of them went home to talk. I was fine with the idea; anything to get them out of the store.

There were some customers throughout the rest of the day, but nothing of the magnitude Father had predicted. Some of Kingsbrook's elite who couldn't be there earlier for the opening stopped in later.

They seemed relieved when I told them that Father was gone for the day. Then, they beat a hasty retreat, promising to return another time and congratulate Father on the pharmacy's success.

One of the latecomers was Mayor Fleming. To my surprise, he was followed by the young woman I had seen under the window at my party—the one named 'Patricia'. We recognized each other immediately. She smiled with false politeness as he introduced her as his daughter. He asked to speak to Father and I told him that Father had gone, but that I would tell him that he had stopped by.

As they turned to leave, you'll never believe who walked in … Mr. Carrington!

He exchanged pleasantries with the Mayor and a few words with Patricia before making his way over to the counter.

Those eyes.

"Ms. Harker," he said.

"It's good to see you, Mr. Carrington."

He was pleased that I remembered his name and winked at me, again.

I glanced over his shoulder and saw the Mayor speaking to his daughter. I couldn't hear what they were saying, but it was clear that he was leaving and she wanted to stay.

"Are you working here by yourself?" Mr. Carrington asked.

"Father needs me to work," I told him.

"Can't he hire someone?"

"Not yet, but hopefully soon."

He looked around at the almost empty store. "How is the grand opening going?" he asked with a smirk I didn't like.

I also noticed that Patricia Fleming had drifted closer to the counter. I couldn't believe it, but she was unmistakably eavesdropping on our conversation.

"Father says once we're established, it'll get better," I answered.

"Do you believe that?"

"I … I hope it will."

I was shocked that he would speak so bluntly but admired his honesty.

"Well, he needs to hire someone," he said. "A shop girl is no position for a lovely creature like yourself."

Yes, he did! He called me a 'lovely creature'!

I could feel my cheeks flush and I faltered for something to say. Then, I remembered the present they gave me for my birthday. "Thank you for the journal," I said.

"It was my wife's idea, but I'm glad you enjoy it."

"I do. I've been writing in it almost every day."

"Is every day worth writing about?" he asked.

I told him it was a good outlet for my thoughts, to which he replied, "And your deepest, most secret desires, I hope."

I know it may have been a little inappropriate but it was also fun. I have never met someone who is so intimidating, so clever, and so handsome. I was also enjoying the look of shock on Patricia Fleming's face that she was trying to hide.

"And how is your wife?" I asked.

"She's fine. She's at her mother's in Boston, along with our valet. They'll be back for the Fourth of July Celebration. Which reminds me, we have a picnic at the Nightingale House on the Fourth of July as part of the celebration. The whole town is invited, but it would make me particularly happy if you would attend."

I could think of nothing I wanted more but told him that I may have to work.

He said that was nonsense and that all the shops are closed on the Fourth of July. "And who knows?" he said. "Maybe business will be such that your father can hire someone else to waste their life behind that counter." He picked up a tin of lip balm from the display next to the register and laid it on the counter. "How much is this?"

I told him it was twenty cents.

He pulled out his billfold, removed a five-dollar bill, put it on the counter, and said, "Keep the change."

"You want my father to open an account?" I asked.

"I didn't say give it to your father. It's for you, on one condition."

"Yes?"

"You have to buy something for yourself. Something pretty."

I was speechless.

"Thank you," I finally managed to say.

He gave me that sly wink, again. "See? Business is already looking up."

He took the tin and walked out the door.

I never took my eyes off him until he disappeared out of view of the window. Then, I turned to Patricia Fleming. She was pretending to look at a shelf of tonics.

"Can I help you find something?" I asked.

She gave me another insincere smile. "No, thank you," she said. "It's all a little expensive for my tastes."

I tried to match her insincerity with a false smile of my own.

"Best of luck with the pharmacy," she said, then turned and walked out the door.

I was upset at her rudeness but then I remembered; he called me 'a lovely creature' and that I should buy something pretty for myself.

As I watched Patricia walk away, my gaze drifted towards the jewelers across the square.

I think I shall have to pay them a visit.

Good night.

4

I'm awoken by the sickening crunch of metal slamming into metal and glass shattering, just outside my bedroom door.

Then, silence.

I open my eyes and sit up.

The room is filled with a faint black fog.

I climb off the bed and listen at the door. There's a faint noise on the other side.

... *tick* ... *tick* ... *tick* ... *tick* ...

I open the door and walk through.

The black fog blankets the intersection. The pavement is littered in broken glass and bits of metal. Small wisps of steam and smoke escape from the crumpled hood of the pickup truck that slammed into our car. The force of the impact has melded the two vehicles together into one disfigured, twisted heap.

The traffic light above the intersection blinks red.

... *tick* ... *tick* ... *tick* ... *tick* ...

The black fog seems to guide me over to the wreckage. The bits of glass puncture my bare feet as I walk across the pavement, but I don't feel it.

I can't see inside the truck, but I know what's in there: the body of the driver, pressed against the steering wheel.

I don't want this. I don't want to see this, but the black fog urges me forward.

I get closer to the car.

Through the remains of the shattered window, I see Nicole's mangled, decimated body. Her head is twisted at an unnatural angle. Her face is covered in blood. Her eyes are open. They stare straight ahead but see nothing.

Why? Why did this have to be the last image I have of her? It's the image that has been burned into my mind: Nicole, my wife, the woman I loved, the mother of our child, broken, lifeless, grotesque. After I regained consciousness moments after the accident, I saw her and screamed, pleaded with her to wake up, knowing it was useless. Why did this have to be how I remember her? It's the cruelest trick, added to the cruelest joke of being hit by a drunk driver.

I look past Nicole's mauled body to the back seat.

Caitlyn.

She's strapped in by her seatbelt, her body laying back. Like Nicole, her head is at a nauseating angle. Her eyes are open. Lifeless.

No. No. It wasn't like this.

She was alive. I tried to help her. She was breathing but I couldn't touch her because I was afraid that if she had a spinal injury, I would paralyze her. So, I had to sit there, pleading, begging her to wake up. Those minutes between when I called 9-1-1 until the ambulance arrived were an eternity. I couldn't touch my daughter. I couldn't do anything. The EMTs had to drag me away screaming towards the ambulance as they began cutting into the door. Caitlyn was alive.

But now, she's dead in the back seat.

It wasn't like this!

"Caitlyn?!" I scream and frantically try to open the crushed door. The handle won't budge. Through the remains of the window, I grab the edge of the door and pull. The shards of glass slice into my hand and work their way under my fingernails.

I grunt, curse, and scream.

"Caitlyn! Somebody help me, please!"

In between my efforts, there's a faint whisper.

"It's your fault …"

I stop and peer into the black fog. A thin layer of snow lies on the ground among the black trees, but I don't see anyone.

"It's your fault …" the whisper says again, somewhere near me.

"Why didn't you see the truck? It's your fault …"

I slowly turn back to the wreckage.

Nicole's eyes stare lifelessly in front of her but her lips move. "It's your fault …"

"No … No … Nicole … Please … I'm sorry."

The rest of her body remains motionless except her lips. "It's your fault … Why did you let this happen?"

"Nicole. I didn't see—"

"It's your fault …"

Her whispers grow louder. Her voice is accusatory, sad, and terrified, all at once.

"It's your fault … It's your fault … You did this … You killed me … You killed us …"

"Stop! Please!"

Hot tears begin stinging my eyes.

"It's your fault. It's your fault. It's your fault—"

"Nicole, I love you. Please, please, stop it …"

Her voice and lips tremble, but her eyes and body remain lifeless.

"It's your fault. It's your fault. It's your fault."

I can't take this. I turn away from the accident but I still hear her.

"Why, Daniel? Why did you let this happen to us?"

The door to my bedroom is sitting there, just off the road. The fog parts, clearing a path for me.

"It's your fault. It's your fault. It's your fault."

Her voice follows like she's walking right behind me.

The doorknob feels like ice in my hand as I twist it open. I step into my bedroom and close the door behind me.

The black fog blankets the floor.

I can still hear Nicole's voice, as if she's standing just on the other side of the door.

"It's your fault. It's your fault. It's your fault."

I crawl back into bed.

Her voice trails away to nothing.

I lie there in the silence of the room.

Suddenly, the fog comes crashing into me. It races from every part of the room and every corner of the house. It enters my body through the pores of my skin, turning my blood into an icy, black sludge. I feel nauseous, like I'm rotting from the inside and I'll never be clean again.

Nicole's face appears right in front of me; not the mangled image I've just seen in the car, but the concerned, fearful Nicole I saw through the window of the kitchen earlier today.

"Daniel, wake up!"

*

My eyes fly open.

I sit up in my bed.

There's no fog or the voice of Nicole, accusing me through the door. It's just a room but the tears on my cheeks and the thudding of my heart are very real.

I swing my feet off the side of the bed.

I've never experienced anything like that. Yes, somewhere deep inside, I've always felt like it was my fault. I should have seen the truck. I should have made sure. I've gone over all the things I could have done differently, but to see that, to hear Nicole …

I'm not going back to sleep. No way. Not after that. I need out of this room. I need some television; something to erase what I've just seen.

I get up and go to the door.

I grab the knob but stop, fearful of what might be on the other side.

I twist the knob and pull the door open.

There's no intersection. No wreckage. No fog. No Nicole. Just an empty hallway.

I quickly go back to the bed and grab my pillow.

For the second time tonight, I go back down the stairs to the living room.

I turn on the lamp and go to the open box of Blu-ray discs sitting on the floor next to the television. I select a title, one that is sure to help clear my head, and pop it into the player. I stretch out on the couch, pop the pillow under my head, and pull the throw blanket on top of me.

The movie starts and I'm asleep in five minutes.

5

Tap. Tap. Tap.

The intermittent pressure on my forehead causes me to snort awake.

Caitlyn is standing next to the couch, hunched over me, her finger poised from tapping me on the forehead.

Sunlight is pouring through the windows.

"Why are you sleeping down here?" she asks.

I stretch my aching, cramped muscles. "I fell asleep watching TV," I reply.

Caitlyn turns to look at the television.

The menu screen for *Sleeping Beauty* has to have been repeating the same fifteen-second clip for hours, waiting for a response.

She turns back to me, very confused.

"I … I couldn't remember how it ended," I say.

She shrugs. "Whatever." She walks to the kitchen. "Can I have breakfast?"

*

I still haven't been to the store to do a proper grocery shop, so the options for breakfast are limited to cereal and Pop Tarts, which we're fine with. It's only the responsible parenting part of my brain that is uncomfortable, and it can wait.

"Okay," I say, sitting across from Caitlyn in the alcove. "The objective for today is to finish unpacking. We're going to try to get everything done."

"Everything?"

"Well, at least all the big stuff. Between the two of us, it shouldn't take too long."

"I wanted to play outside."

"You can, after you help me."

She pouts, apparently less eager to help than yesterday.

"Hey. That's what you get for waking me up by poking my forehead," I say with a wink.

She tries not to laugh.

*

And she does help.

We take care of the last two boxes in her room that need to be unpacked and put them away. Then, we head to the guestroom.

It's almost laughable that we're trying to fill this house with the stuff from a two-bedroom apartment. We don't even have a bed for the spare bedroom.

I can't help but think of the plans Nicole had for this place.

In the weeks before the accident, she had been looking at furniture and asking my opinion on whole sets. I told her all I wanted was a big, comfy monstrosity of a recliner. She had webpages of furniture sets bookmarked but we didn't pull the trigger, deciding that we would pull the trigger once we were in the house. After all, we would have so much time, right? The pages are still bookmarked on the computer, but I can't bring myself to look at them. Maybe one day.

Once we finish, I break down the cardboard boxes, and we carry them down to the basement.

"Watch your step," I warn Caitlyn as we navigate the stairs down into almost total darkness.

I make my way to the center of the room and pull the chain, snapping on the old lightbulb. It illuminates the immediate area but can't reach into the corners of the basement. We walk over to the heavy wooden shelves. I take my armful of collapsed boxes and set them down on one of the shelves. I reach out and Caitlyn hands me the two collapsed boxes that she was struggling to carry.

"Thank you."

I put her boxes on top of mine and start to walk back towards the stairs.

"Since we're coming back down, I'll leave the light on," I say, mounting the stairs.

"Hi …"

I stop and look back.

Caitlyn isn't following me.

She's standing in the middle of the room, under the hanging lightbulb, staring into the shadows in the far corner.

"Caitlyn?"

She turns to me, smiling.

"Pumpkin, what are you d—?"

Pop.

The bulb flashes, illuminating Caitlyn and the thing that's standing in the corner, before plunging the basement into darkness.

"Caitlyn?" I frantically try to get my phone out and turn on the flashlight app.

"I'm okay," she calmly replies.

I'm finally able to get the app up and find Caitlyn with the beam of light. She's still there, looking into the corner. I shine the light in the direction she's looking, but it's empty.

"You sure you're okay?" I ask.

"Yeah," she says, not turning around.

I point the beam at the lightbulb, half of which is now gone.

44

"You didn't get any glass on you?"

"No."

I swing the light around the room. It's just us.

"Come on, pumpkin. Let's go upstairs. I'll get another bulb."

She doesn't move. She's still fixated on that corner.

"Caitlyn, come on."

Reluctantly, she turns and I light her way back to the stairs. She climbs the stairs up to the kitchen.

I swing the light back to the corner.

It has to be lack of sleep, but when that bulb flashed, I thought I saw someone in that corner where Caitlyn was looking—someone Caitlyn said 'hi' to.

*

Caitlyn's waiting for me at the top of the stairs in the kitchen.

The spare bulbs are in the kitchen. I grab one and return to the stairs where Caitlyn is staring down into the darkness.

I hand her the phone with the flashlight app still on. "Here. Light the stairs for me, okay?"

We head back down. I'm holding the bulb. She's holding the phone.

We reach the bottom and I walk across the floorboards to the hanging, spent, ancient lightbulb. Caitlyn stays by the bottom of the stairs.

As I reach up to change the bulb, the light drifts over to the corner.

"Caitlyn, keep the light here, please."

She moves it to illuminate the bulb.

I carefully remove the old lightbulb, careful not to break any more of the brittle glass. I screw in the new bulb. As soon as it's in, the bulb blinks on. It fills the room with a much more powerful glow than the old one. I can't help but sneak a glance at the far corner, but it's empty.

I pull the chain, turning off the light, and walk towards Caitlyn.

"Let's go," I say, shepherding her up the stairs.

"Why did you turn it off?" she asks. "Aren't we coming back down?"

"Nah. Not today."

By the time we reach the top of the stairs and emerge back into the sun-flooded kitchen, I already feel slightly stupid. It was a shadow, nothing more. I had an atrocious night of sleep and an exhausting day of unpacking. Yes, Caitlyn is helping, but I am literally doing the heavy lifting.

And this house.

I love it. I do, but it's going to take a while to get used to it. It would be different if Nicole were here and my subconscious knows that too. Why else would I be seeing visions of her? I'll get used to this but I'm starting to worry about how long this adjustment will take, and not only for my own sanity, but for Caitlyn's sake, too. I have to stay strong for her, because I'm worried that soon, she'll start going through that same adjustment, if she hasn't started already. I have to accept that I'm a grieving widower, who is all of a sudden raising a daughter on his own, and we've just moved into a big, old house. This is going to mess with my head a little bit, and if we're being completely honest, the basement's creepy. All basements inherently are. There's something about them that suggests isolation, or even a grave.

"What's next?" Caitlyn says, clapping her hands like she's all business.

"Living room?" I suggest.

She turns on her heels and points commandingly to the entranceway.

"Living room!" she calls out and stomps away.

Okay. She might be adjusting much better than I am.

6

We've conquered the dining room and the living room.

It took less time than I thought, and that's including the times we stopped to have a "popping fight" with the bubble wrap.

But that was all that Caitlyn's concentration could take, and I'm unpacking the Writing Room on my own.

Since I'm not a big fan of going back into the basement, the large cardboard boxes remained in the living room and Caitlyn has found a million uses for them. Sometimes, they're spaceships that she'll pilot around the galaxy and suddenly cry out, "Asteroid field!" which is my cue to come over and shake the box. Other times, they're race cars and she's flying round the track. Last time I poked my head out of the Writing Room to check on her, they were laid end-to-end across the floor, creating a vast system of underground caves. From the Writing Room, I can hear her loudly announce her encounters with bats, lava, and trolls as I place some treasured paperbacks on a shelf in no particular order.

It used to drive Nicole nuts.

My books covered almost an entire wall of our apartment in Portland. One night, we were sitting on the couch with a glass of wine after Caitlyn had gone to bed.

"Alphabetically? By year?" she asked, waving her glass at the wall of books. "Ranked in order of your favorite? Is there any method to your madness?"

"Nah," I replied.

"Then how do you expect to find any particular book when you need it?"

"I won't need to find any particular book. They're just there."

"Then why have them?"

"You know how hunters have the heads on their walls, like trophies?"

"Yes, and they're assholes."

"Well, there you go."

"So, that would make you an asshole?"

"Yes, but I'm your asshole."

She gave me a look. "No other way we can phrase that, huh?"

I laughed. We kissed and—

Thump.

What the hell was that?

It was soft, almost inaudible, and sounded like it came from the bookshelf, and not in my memory with Nicole but here, in the Writing Room.

Maybe it was just a book sliding to the back of the shelf after I set it down.

I transfer the books in my hand to the shelf and wait to see if it'll happen again. When it doesn't, I bend down to grab more books.

Thump.

I stand up and stare at the bookcase.

It definitely sounded like it was in the bookcase. I know it can't be behind it. The bookcase is built into the wall. I step out of the Writing Room and inspect the wall on the other side, but there's nothing remarkable about it.

Maybe Caitlyn is playing a prank on me. After all, I don't hear her playing "caves" anymore.

I stick my head into the living room.

The boxes still span the floor.

I'm about to call her name when I hear her whispering from inside the box at the far end of the room.

"… No … I don't want to play with you, right now … You have to move. You're blocking my cave … Why? Why is he upstairs?"

"Pumpkin, who are you talking to?"

She doesn't answer.

"Caitly—"

"Nobody!" she answers in a chipper voice. "It's okay, now!"

I'm about to ask her what she means when she says that it's okay "now", but she suddenly cries, "Arr! There be treasure in these caves, me-hearties!"

The boxes begin shaking as she crawls through them.

I shrug and go back to the Writing Room to finish unpacking.

*

After our productive day, it's Chinese food for dinner.

Just like last night, Caitlyn sets the table while I pay the delivery guy, and also, just like last night, Caitlyn has set the table for three.

"Is your pirate friend going to join us this evening?" I ask.

"No."

"Then, who is the plate for?"

"My friend. She might come down for dinner."

"Oh …"

I take a spoon and start filling her plate with noodles, rice, and orange chicken. I know I said that I was going to give her some space with the 'stories', but I do want her to tone it down before she starts going to school. "Caitlyn, pumpkin, you know we really can't do that once school starts, okay?"

"Do what?" she asks.

"The made-up stories."

49

She stares at me as if it was an offensive suggestion and then shrugs.

We sit down and dig in.

Caitlyn struggles mightily with her chopsticks. I offered her a fork but she flatly refused. Towards the end of the meal, she's finally starting to get the hang of it, once again proving that she's inherited Nicole's stubborn streak.

"How is your friend enjoying the meal?" I ask.

"Dad, she's not here. She didn't come down."

"She doesn't like Chinese food?"

"No. She's hiding."

I wait for her to elaborate but she goes back to struggling with the chopsticks.

"Listen, this is our last night of junk food," I say, hefting the last of my sweet-n-sour pork from my chopstick to my mouth. "Tomorrow, we're going to go to the store, explore the town, and visit your school, okay?"

She barely nods, concentrating on keeping her mouth steady as she inches her chopsticks towards her mouth. The bit of orange chicken slides back to her plate. She huffs in frustration and grabs the plastic fork on the table to finish the last of her food.

*

Once dinner is finished, we head outside to the backyard to enjoy the warm evening. She spends the better part of an hour at the water's edge, walking in the water and playing with the fireflies, while I enjoy an after-dinner scotch in a chair on the deck. It's worth the mosquitos. My gaze drifts through the star-pocked sky, down to the trees, and to the other houses along the shore. Nicole would have loved this. Thinking about her gives me a sense of warmth, which is completely different from last night, but that's grief for you. Sometimes it makes you inconsolable, sometimes it makes you enraged. Other times, it makes you feel at peace, and you never know which one you're going to get. But Nicole would also point out that it's getting late.

I push myself out of the chair. "All right, Caitlyn. Time to get ready for bed."

In the moonlight, she suddenly whips around to look at me, keeping her hands behind her back.

"Pumpkin, did you hear me?"

"Yes."

"Okay ... well, come inside."

She stands motionless, as if she's trying to make a decision. Then, she suddenly brings her hands to her chest and begins running towards me.

"Don't forget to brush your teeth," I say as she races past me.

She's clutching something. It glints in the light from the porch as she runs past.

"Okay!" she says, running through the back door, leaving me to clean up our plates from dinner.

*

After depositing the dishes from dinner in the dishwasher, I go upstairs to say good night.

At the top of the stairs, I stand next to Caitlyn's open bedroom door and there's the sound of the sink running in the bathroom down the hall. I glance into her room and see the collection of empty cardboard boxes in the corner. I begin to make my way towards them when a reflection of light catches my eye from her nightstand. I go over and bend down for a better look.

This must have been what was in her hand.

It's a brass medallion, about the size of a half-dollar. It's scratched and worn. I pick it up and turn it over in my hand. On one side are three small pegs of different lengths. On the other side is an inscription in an elegant font.

It's suddenly snatched from me.

I look up to see Caitlyn staring at me, holding the medallion. Her eyes are a mixture of anger and fear.

"Sweetheart, where did you get that?" I ask, a little unnerved that I didn't hear her approach.

"She gave it to me."

"Who gave it to you?" I gently ask.

She grows more fearful. "I mean … I …." She clutches the medallion tighter. "I found it in the water."

"Hey. It's okay. You found it. It's yours."

She hesitantly replaces the medallion on the nightstand and crawls into bed.

"Good night, sweetheart," I say, pulling the covers up to her chin. "Big day tomorrow. Get some sleep." I kiss her forehead and go to leave.

I step into the hallway and begin to close the door behind me.

"Dad!"

I quickly push it back open. "What? What's wrong?"

"The night-light," she says, pointing at the outlet by my feet.

"Oh. Right. Sorry." I flip the little switch and the light softly glows. "There."

She slowly lies back down and turns away from me.

"Good night, pumpkin" I say, closing the door.

*

"DADDY!"

I'm awake in an instant.

Caitlyn is screaming. They are the desperate, terrified screams that fill every parent's heart with panic.

I spring out of bed and race into the hallway.

52

Caitlyn's door is open. I sprint down the hall and into her room.

Her bed is empty. She's not here, but her screams continue.

"Caitlyn?!"

I take a step towards the bed and my foot lands in a small puddle of water.

Her screaming stops.

In the light from the night-light, I can see that there are wet tracks, like footprints, leading back out into the hall.

I follow them down the stairs, through the living room and dining room and into the kitchen. The back door is open.

"Caitlyn?"

I rush out the back door and onto the deck.

It's unnaturally quiet. The night air is perfectly still.

The tracks lead off the deck and into the grass. I follow their direction towards the water and stop.

I see her. Caitlyn, clad in her nightgown, floating face down in the lake.

"Caitlyn!"

I sprint across the yard and crash into the water, kicking up my knees to fight the resistance. The water is up to my chest when I reach her.

I grab her and turn her over. She's ice-cold and her lips are blue. She's not breathing.

"Caitlyn? Sweetheart?"

Panicked, I seal my mouth over her lips and breathe. I feel her chest rise and fall but she doesn't respond. I do it again with the same result.

"Caitlyn, please! Please, don't leave me!"

Her eyes stay closed. Her body is cold and stiff.

She's gone.

I cradle her in my arms and press my face against her cheek.

"Now, we can be a family, again," a voice next to me whispers.

I turn my head.

The bloody, broken Nicole I saw in the dream last night is standing next to me. Her eyes are still lifeless, unseeing. Only her lips move.

Suddenly, her eyes focus on me. "Just like you wanted."

I stare at her in horror.

The bottom falls out from below my feet and I'm pulled under the water by a terrible weight. Caitlyn's body is gone. It's only me, plummeting down into darkness.

I try to scream but icy, black water fills my lungs. I fight to get back to the surface, but I continue to sink. I can't breathe. The vile, black water is filling my lungs. I'm losing control of my senses. My efforts grow weaker. My arms slow. My eyes remain open, but my vision fades.

Everything is a dark fog.

Through the void, there's a whisper. "I can't sleep …"

I thrash in my bed, flailing my arms against the water that isn't there and fighting for air. I can still taste the black, briny water in my mouth. My sanity slowly returns.

"Goddamnit," I sigh, wiping the sweat from my eyes.

It takes several minutes to calm my breathing before I can sit up and look around.

I'm still not used to this room.

Why does it feel so claustrophobic? It's not huge but it's not a cage.

And what is with these dreams?

Last night, it was Caitlyn's shattered body in the car, and tonight she was floating in the lake. Why is my subconscious doing this?

If I'm going to get any sleep tonight, I need to see Caitlyn. I need to see her safe in her bed. It's the only thing that can counter the lingering image of cradling her cold, dead body.

I climb out of bed and make my way down the hall.

I open the door to Caitlyn's room and my heart starts racing. Her bed is empty.

"Caitlyn?" I go over to the bed and throw back the covers. She's not there.

No. Oh, please, no. I start searching the floor for wet footprints.

"Caitlyn?!" I cry out.

There's a noise behind me.

Snoring. It's coming from the closet.

I tip-toe over and open the door.

Relief washes over me.

There she is, curled up into a ball, wrapped in a blanket, her head on a pillow, and sawing logs.

"Sweetheart, what are you doing in there? You okay?"

She doesn't stir, only continues snoring.

I gently pick her up and put her back in her bed. I pull the covers over her, kiss her on the forehead, and back out of the room.

I glance towards the open door to my bedroom.

No, thanks.

I head down the stairs and drop onto the couch, before grabbing the remote and turning on the television. Flipping through the channels, I come across a classic horror movie marathon. On the screen, Vincent Price is explaining the rules to a group of people who will get a staggering ten thousand dollars if they stay in the house for one night.

I should turn the channel, but I love this movie, and there's no way I'm going to sleep, anyway.

7

Two classic horror films and one early-morning sunrise later, I'm just drifting off to sleep when I'm jolted awake by the sound of Caitlyn coming down the stairs.

"—back and we can play later," she's saying as I blink my eyes open.

She freezes, surprised to find me on the couch, again.

"Hey, pumpkin," I say, rubbing my face.

"Hi …"

"You hungry?"

"Yep!"

She hurries off to the kitchen.

I can't keep doing this. In the past forty-eight hours, I think I've had a grand total of four hours of sleep, and today is going to be a long day.

I sit back on the couch and close my eyes. One moment. I want one quick moment to relax and not th—

"Dad, what's for breakfast?"

I sigh and get up to feed the little monster.

*

After breakfast, we set off into town.

Our first stop is the main square. We park on a side street and spend the next hour or so, strolling among the antique shops and occasional clothing boutique.

Caitlyn spots Murphy's, the old-fashioned soda shop on the main square, and asks if we could go in.

"How can you be hungry?" I ask. "We just ate breakfast."

"Because it's ice cream," she replies.

Her logic is airtight and I'm too exhausted to argue.

*

Murphy's has just opened and we are the only customers.

I'm hit by the memory of our last meal/milkshake here with Nicole. If Caitlyn remembers, she makes no sign. She's too preoccupied with petting the owner's black lab while we wait for our milkshakes. When they arrive—plain vanilla for me, peanut butter and chocolate for Caitlyn—we sit in a booth by the window and watch Kingsbrook come to life …

"—na race …? Dad? … Dad?"

I snort awake and sit up in the booth. I dozed off. It was only for a second. My head had drifted back, my eyes closed, and I was out. My milkshake sits undisturbed on the table in front of me, while Caitlyn's is almost halfway gone.

"I'm sorry, sweetheart. What did you say?"

"Do you wanna have a race?"

"A race? A race to where?"

"To see who can finish their milkshake first."

I'm still trying to get my senses in order. "I don't think that's a good—"

"And go!"

Caitlyn clamps her lips around the end of the straw and starts pulling it through. She closes her eyes tightly with the effort.

I leave my milkshake untouched and watch.

"You're going to get brain freeze," I warn her, but she's almost done.

The level of milkshake in her glass falls to the bottom.

She reaches the end and the remains of the milkshake slurp through the bottom of the straw.

Caitlyn gulps it down and opens her eyes. "I won!" she says, smiling triumphantly.

I know what's coming.

Wait for it … wait for it …

Caitlyn's eyes go wide. Then, she clenches them shut, and presses a hand to her forehead.

There it is.

"Brain freeze?" I ask.

"No," she grunts, squeezing her eyes closed even tighter. "I'm … I'm thinking really hard."

"Riiiiiight."

I watch in amusement as it passes. She finally relaxes, takes her hand from her forehead, and opens her eyes.

"There. I'm done," she says.

"You're done 'thinking hard'?"

"Yep."

"And what were you 'thinking hard' about?"

"Um …" Her eyes dart around as she searches for an answer. "The house."

"Really? And what about the house?"

She continues glancing around—and then she finds something. "We should get a pool!" she quickly says.

I raise an eyebrow at her and twist in my seat to look at the counter.

There's a guy sitting there on one of the stools, reading a paper. On the front page is a story about the measure to build a public swimming pool in Kingsbrook. I turn back to Caitlyn.

"A pool?"

She nods.

"A pool for swimming?"

"Yep."

"We have a place to swim. It's called a 'lake'," I smile.

Her face slowly drops and she looks down at her empty glass. "I'm sorry … I wasn't thinking about the house … I had brain freeze."

"No kidding." I laugh.

She's embarrassed but not mortified.

"Since you bring it up, what do you think of the house?" I ask. I realize that I haven't asked her how she's doing with everything, yet, and I can't help but feel a little guilty.

Now, she's really thinking.

"I like it," she finally says. "It's kind of big."

"It is, but we'll get used to it."

She shrugs in a way that says she's not convinced.

"Do you like your room?"

She nods, more certain of her answer. Then, she gets quiet. "Do you like your room?"

"Yeah. I guess so."

"Are you ever going to sleep in it?"

"I … Yeah …"

"… Okay."

She seems worried and I'm not sure where this is coming from. It might be from finding me on the couch the past two nights.

"Daddy had some bad dreams, that's all, and I wanted to sleep on the couch."

She runs her straw through the dregs of her milkshake.

"You shouldn't sleep in your room," she says.

"Oh? Why is that?"

"Because then, you won't have bad dreams."

I smile. "Bad dreams are nothing to be afraid of. They're just dreams."

"Okay," she sighs, as if to say *I tried to help*.

*

Stuffed with milkshakes, we wander a block off the main square and find ourselves among the stately houses. One maple-lined street is home to a row of bed and breakfasts with names like The Rosewood Inn and The Sleepy Hollow BnB, which doesn't make a whole lot of sense, seeing as the real Sleepy Hollow is hundreds of miles away in New York, but I'm sure it doesn't hurt the business.

We round a corner onto another street, and Caitlyn begins to make up story after story as we pass each house.

"The family that lives in that one, they're related to the Queen."

"Oh, yeah?"

"Yep. I read about them in a book. And that one" – she says, pointing to a white house with red trim – "a witch lives there. She puts spells on all the kids in town. And that one over there" – she continues before I can get a word in – "the man who lives there robs banks."

"Caitlyn."

"He does. He got rich by robbing banks with his gang."

"Caitlyn, stop." Stories of being related to royalty or magicians is one thing, but I don't want her making up stories about people committing crimes, no matter how far-fetched they are. "You know you shouldn't do that, right?"

She gets quiet and hangs her head.

"Okay."

At the end of the street there's another grand Victorian-styled house. The wooden sign in the front yard reads "Kingsbrook Historical Society" in gold-painted lettering.

"Want to check it out?" I ask Caitlyn.

She shrugs, which is enough for me, because I definitely want to go inside.

We walk up the path to the porch and I hold the door for her. We're greeted by a display that proudly proclaims, "Welcome to Kingsbrook!"

The paragraph and photos below the display briefly outline the town's history, from its beginnings as a trading outpost, to a lumber mill, to a resort town, to present day. Beyond the display, the first floor of the house has been converted into a mini-museum, with display cases and memorabilia. In the corner, an elderly man with a beak-like nose sits behind a desk.

"Hello." He smiles.

"Hi," I answer.

He moves around the desk. "Welcome to the Kingsbrook Historical Society. I'm Nathaniel Howard. I'm … Well, I'm pretty much the Kingsbrook Historical Society."

"I'm Daniel Price and this is my daughter, Caitlyn."

Mr. Howard's face lights up. "Oh! You're the new owners of the Nightingale House."

"Yes," I say, unable to hide my slight surprise.

He dismisses it with a wave of his hand. "I know just about everything that goes on in Kingsbrook. My family has lived here for generations. I know all the stories, and the Nightingale House is one of our prized jewels." He shakes my hand. "It's a pleasure to meet you."

He turns to Caitlyn. "And you, as well. Kingsbrook welcomes you both."

"Thanks. We're doing a little exploring today."

"Excellent! This is the place to start."

He leads us around the museum, giving a spiel he has to have given a hundred, if not a thousand, times before, but still takes immense pride in. He shows us maps and artifacts from when it was a trading outpost in the wild frontier of Maine. Then there are photos from when it was a lumber mill. I'm eating this up, but I can tell that Caitlyn is bored. Mr. Howard then comes to a display that showcases photos from when Kingsbrook became a summer getaway for the wealthy.

"I think you'll recognize this," he says with a knowing wink.

There are grainy black-and-white photos of the town square

with a parade marching through it. A description off to the side reads, "Fourth of July, 1900". There's photo after photo of the grand houses of the town, decked out in streamers and bunting, with parties on the lawns.

"People would open up their homes and show off a bit for the annual Fourth of July Celebration. They would have fireworks and picnics," he says, and points to the bottom of the display. "And the Nightingale House was no exception."

I crouch down to get a better look. "Huh. Check it out, Caitlyn."

Suddenly, she's very interested.

There it is—the Nightingale House.

It's more than a picnic. Splendidly dressed people sit at the tables that cover the lawn. The men wear top hats and tails. The women wear white, except for a brunette who is wearing some darker color that I can't discern, due to the photo being in black and white. Everyone else is looking at the camera, while she's looking at something else. There are streaks and blurs around the edges where children are playing. It's hard to believe that the regal house in the background is the same one Caitlyn and I woke up in this morning.

Mr. Howard taps the glass. "The couple sitting at the table front and center—that's Thomas Carrington and his wife, Abigail. They were the owners of the Nightingale House."

Thomas Carrington's expression is hidden behind a jet-black beard and mustache. Even seated, you can tell that he was tall with piercing eyes. Abigail is a beauty. She has flowing blonde hair, and although she's smiling, her face is careworn.

Caitlyn is staring at the photo with a grim expression.

"What do you think, Caitlyn?" I ask.

"Neat," she says, but her expression doesn't change.

Mr. Howard doesn't see her face, but he's thrilled that Caitlyn has described it as 'neat'. It's probably something he doesn't hear very often.

We make our way through the last few displays, but nothing

sparks our fascination like the photo of the Nightingale House in all its glory.

After completing the tour, we thank Mr. Howard as he sees us to the door and wishes us good luck on the rest of our exploration of Kingsbrook.

"What did you think?" I ask as Caitlyn and I stroll down the path, back to the sidewalk while holding hands.

"I don't like him. He's mean."

"Mr. Howard? Really? Why do you think he's mean?"

"Not him."

"Then ... who are you talking about, sweetheart?"

"... No one."

I want her to tell me. I feel like I need her to. I'm sure she's nervous about a new school and she might let her imagination run wild to deal with it, but I don't want her going into school and telling stories about someone being mean to her. Just like I don't want her telling stories about people robbing banks.

"Caitlyn, who are you talking about?"

She hesitates, and then answers, "Mr. Carrington."

"The man in the photo?"

"Yeah."

"Why do you say that?"

"Because he is."

Sure, I guess the guy looked like he may have been intimidating, and I suppose it's better if she's making up stories about people who are long gone, but I should still nip this in the bud before it gets out of hand.

"Well, we don't know that, okay? He might have been nice."

"No. He was mean."

"Caitlyn, you never met him and it's not fair to call someone mean or names if you don't know them."

"But I know him."

"Caitlyn, stop."

We take a few more steps towards the street.

"But you called that guy a 'jerk' and you've never met him."

"What guy?"

"The baseball guy. When you were putting together the TV thing. You called him a 'jerk' and you haven't met him."

"I don't remember saying anyone was— oh …"

She's talking about my little outburst at the Cubs' relief pitcher who blew a two-run lead while I was putting together the entertainment center. Had she not been there, I would have called him worse.

"Well, pumpkin, that's … that's different."

She stops and looks up at me. "How?"

"Because … I was talking about …" My argument fizzles out and she's waiting with those innocent, puzzled eyes.

I sigh. "You're right. I shouldn't do that."

She seems content with my answer and we resume walking back towards the sidewalk at the end of the path.

Now, I really hate that relief pitcher not only for blowing the save, but also for blowing my teaching moment.

8

Our next stop is Concord Elementary.

The school sits on the outskirts of town, nestled against the forest. It consists of a large brick building and a handful of smaller buildings that have been added as the town grew, and are connected by hallways. It gives the school the appearance of a living organism.

We find our way to the main office and a door marked 'Principal'. A stern woman in her fifties is sitting at a large desk, going over paperwork. She looks up as I rap on the door.

"Mr. Price, I presume," she says.

"That's me."

She walks around the desk and extends her hand. "I'm Principal Jean Craig."

Her handshake is like her demeanor: firm. "Nice to meet you."

"And you must be Caitlyn," she says, repeating the gesture.

"Hi," Caitlyn replies, also shaking her hand.

"We're very happy to have you here at Concord." She then addresses both of us. "How are you liking Kingsbrook?"

"So far, so good. We took a little tour this morning, didn't we, Caitlyn?"

Caitlyn nods.

"And the Nightingale House?" Principal Craig asks.

"We love it."

She slips momentarily into a wistful smile. "I love that Nightingale House. I grew up in Kingsbrook. Seems like everything has changed, except that house." Her stern demeanor quickly returns. "You're not planning on doing any renovations, are you?"

I laugh. "No."

"Good. Now, Caitlyn, let's go meet your teacher; Ms. Hancourt."

*

Principal Craig gives us a brief history of the school as she guides us down the hall.

"The school started with one building with six rooms, one grade in each room. Now, it's one grade per hall." We stop outside a door with a plastic plaque marked 'Hancourt'.

Principal Craig knocks. "Ms. Hancourt?"

"Come on in," a voice answers.

Principal Craig motions us to go inside.

Sunlight spills through the windows and across the desks. Books and papers are neatly stacked on shelves and cabinets around the room. The markerboard is a pristine white. At the markerboard is Ms. Hancourt. She's in her mid-thirties with cropped brown hair and plastic-rimmed glasses.

She approaches us with a broad smile. "Is this the Caitlyn Price I've heard so much about?"

Caitlyn seems delighted by the idea that she somehow has a reputation that has preceded her.

"I'm Ms. Hancourt."

"Hi," Caitlyn replies, warming to her instantly.

"Are you ready to start school in a few days?"

Caitlyn thinks for a moment, treating it as a serious question. "Not really. We haven't gone shopping. I don't have any papers or pencils, yet."

"We're going shopping right after this," I quickly say, feeling the need to defend myself for some reason.

Ms. Hancourt laughs. "Well, I can't wait to have you in my class."

I glance at Principal Craig, who takes the hint.

"Caitlyn," she says, leaning down to her. "Why don't you come with me, and I'll show you the rest of the school?"

Caitlyn looks at me and I confidently nod.

"Okay," she enthusiastically answers.

Principal Craig leads her out of the room. We can hear her asking Caitlyn about her favorite subjects as they walk down the hall.

I turn back to Ms. Hancourt. "Thank you for meeting with us, Ms. Hancourt. I really appreciate it."

"Of course, and please, call me Denise."

"I'm Daniel."

"Principal Craig told me what happened. I'm really sorry for your loss."

"Thank you."

"How is Caitlyn doing?"

"That's what I wanted to talk to you about, just so you know how she's ... uh ... 'coping'." I hate the sound of those words coming out of my mouth.

"It's all right. You two have been through a horribly traumatic experience."

Her tone sets me at ease and I realize that she understands more about child psychology than most, quite possibly more than the psychologist I sent Caitlyn to.

"So, how is she 'coping'?" she asks.

"Caitlyn's got an active imagination ... and sometimes, she uses it a bit too much."

Denise nods and patiently waits as I struggle to find the right words.

Flustered, I shake my head. "Sorry. This has been rough for

us, and I … I guess I wasn't ready to try to explain what's going on with her."

"I would say that I can only imagine what you're going through, but I can't."

Her answer stops me in my tracks. It's perfect, like she completely understands. Most people say something like, 'I know what you must be going through,' and give some advice or insight they have no right in giving, but not her.

"You said she had an active imagination. How so?"

"She makes stuff up about people … and things …" I finally drop my attempt at being delicate. "She lies, sometimes."

"I understand. Does she believe the stuff that she makes up?"

"No. She knows the difference, but you may have to call her on it."

"Are you okay with me doing that?" she asks, gently guiding me to tell her what she needs to know.

"Yes. I love her more than anything, but you have a job to do and it's not fair to the other kids. I just wanted you to know."

"Thank you."

The silence that follows is broken only by the cicadas outside the open windows.

"So," I finally ask, "is this the weirdest parent-teacher conference you've ever had?"

She laughs. "Not even close."

"You're kidding."

"Nope. I had a father offer me money to tell everyone in the class that his son was the smartest child I had ever seen. He wanted to boost his self-esteem."

We both laugh.

"I'm not that crazy," I assure her, but add, "Close, but not that crazy."

"And that's not necessarily a bad thing."

I can't tell you the weight that's lifting off my shoulders, the ease that she's putting me into, and I casually ask, "You have kids?"

She grows quiet. "No ... It's, uh, it's—"

I hold up a hand—it was a dumb question. "'No' is a perfectly acceptable answer, and I'm sorry. It's none of my business."

She nods, appearing somewhat relieved. Then, she reaches over and takes something from her desk.

"Well, here is my card. I give my contact info to every parent. If you have any questions about how Caitlyn is doing, feel free to call me."

I tuck it into my pocket. "Thank you. I really appreciate it. I'll only call if it's an emergency."

"Dad!"

Caitlyn bursts into the room, followed by Principal Craig.

"The playground is huge!" Caitlyn declares.

"She really liked that part of the tour," Principal Craig says.

"I'm sure she did."

*

After a trip to the store where we stocked up on food and copious amounts of school supplies, we're driving back to the Nightingale House.

"So, did you like the school?" I ask.

"Yep," Caitlyn absent-mindedly answers.

"Did you like Ms. Hancourt?"

"Uh-huh," she says, gazing out the window. "She's really pretty."

"Yes, she is," I reply and freeze.

It was a simple statement of fact, nothing more, but I have never spoken about another woman in front of Caitlyn and I'm worried she won't understand.

I glance sideways at her. She continues to stare out the window, watching the trees blur by.

Thankfully, my statement appears to have blurred by her, as

well, but the more I think about it, the more I realize that I wasn't just worried about how she would react. It's true that I've never spoken about another women in front of Caitlyn before, but this is also the first time that I've said that I found a woman attractive since Nicole died.

In the grand scheme of things, I know it's not a big deal. I wasn't ogling her or being a creep. She is attractive, but for a second, I'm overwhelmed with guilt; like there's a brick tied around my heart, pulling it down.

I take another glance at Caitlyn, who is still staring out the window. It's a bigger deal for me than it is for her. As I turn to look back at the road, my eyes brush past the rearview mirror to see Nicole staring at me from the backseat.

I gasp.

My hand slips on the wheel.

For a terrifying instant, we drift into the opposite lane. I grip the wheel and pull us back, but I almost pull too hard, sending us off the road. I'm able to get us back in our lane and avoid any disasters.

The whole episode is over in seconds, but my teeth are on edge and adrenalin is coursing through my veins. The moment I've got control of the car, I check the rearview mirror. The back seat is empty.

"Dad?"

I keep my gaze on the mirror for a beat longer and then look at her. She's more confused than scared.

"I'm sorry, sweetheart. I'm sorry. Daddy's hand slipped. It's okay."

She slowly turns back to the window.

That's it. I have to sleep tonight. Something like that can't happen again.

9

I may have overdone it on dinner.

A fully stocked kitchen after a few days of relying on pizza and Chinese food has filled me with zeal and I've gone all out— salads, steaks, and baked potatoes. Afterwards, Caitlyn and I hover just above a food coma as we play card games and talk about her first day of school tomorrow. I don't want to let on, but I'm worried about how it will go. Caitlyn, however, is taking it in her stride.

By the time I get her tucked into bed, I'm an absolute zombie. I kiss her goodnight, switch on her night-light, close the door, and head for my bedroom to brush my teeth and change. Stepping out of the bathroom, I stop and stare at the bed.

It looks inviting. So, why doesn't it feel inviting? Why am I dreading laying my head on the pillow? Why can't I feel comfortable in this room? The answer is that I'm letting my grief over Nicole play tricks on me. This afternoon was proof of that. It's just a bed. It's just a room. I'm going to have to get used to it, eventually … but not tonight, because I need sleep, and tomorrow is a huge day.

In addition to Caitlyn's first day of school, I've decided that it's time to get to work on the novel. It's time to try to get things as back-to-normal as possible. I couldn't get any sleep in this room the past two nights, and look what almost happened today on the road. So, tonight, I'm heading straight to the couch, which is where I would probably end up anyway.

I gather my pillow and a blanket from the bed and head off down the hall.

I set up shop on the couch, making my own little bed and turn on the television.

That same movie channel is having another classic horror movie marathon. On the screen, Lon Chaney is wrestling with a wolf that's biting him on the chest. Perfect. I've seen this film dozens of times and I'll be asleep in no time …

*

… or so I thought.

Two hours later, and I'm drifting in and out, nodding off for a couple minutes at a time, here and there. My brain is swirling with different fears and worries that won't let me sleep. I'm thinking about Caitlyn's first day of school tomorrow. What is that going to be like? I've done this before with Nicole and, I feel horrible about this, now, but last year, after we waved goodbye to Caitlyn as she got on the bus, Nicole and I went back inside and 'celebrated'. This is going to be a lot different.

And what about the book? I was excited when I made the decision to dive in tomorrow, but I'm having horrible anxiety about writing a sequel. My agent said that the second book is always the hardest. Everyone loved the first one. What if I can't pull it off again? I've already got the outline and had complete confidence in it when I lay down on the couch. Now, not so much.

And then there are the nightmares. What if I have another nightmare where Caitlyn gets hurt? I can't take seeing her broken body in the back seat of the car in that intersection or floating face down in the lake. I'd almost rather not get any sleep at all than see anything like that again.

And finally, there's this nebulous dread; this feeling that I shouldn't close my eyes, that I shouldn't turn my back on this house, not even for an instant …

This movie isn't really helping, either.

It's some haunted house movie starring George C. Scott. There's a woman holding a séance where she's scribbling on paper. A ghost takes control of her hand and writes messages on the paper and, for God's sake, what the hell am I doing? I need to sleep.

I grab the remote and jab the power button.

"I can't sleep …"

I search the darkness around me. It had to have come from the television as I was turning it off; one last snippet of dialogue before the signal was lost.

I pull the blanket up to my chin and settle my head onto the pillow …

Thump.

I let it go. I barely heard it; it was so faint. It has to be the plumbing or something—

Thump.

…

Thump.

With a grunt, I throw off the blanket and turn on the light.

Thump.

It's coming from the Writing Room. It's the same noise I heard yesterday when I was unpacking.

Thump.

I get up and walk through the darkness to the Writing Room.

Thump.

It came from the bookcase, just like yesterday. I snap the light on and stand there, waiting.

Nothing.

"Oh, come on," I whisper.

Thump.

There it is. I walk over and inspect every inch of the bookcase, waiting for the sound, again.

It has to be a rat that's gotten into the wall or into the frame of the bookcase.

Great. Stelowski not only forgot to mention the leaky pipes, now he forgot to tell me about the rats?

Thump.

Shit. I've been mentally berating Stelowski and not paying attention. I can't tell where in the bookcase it came from.

I creep over and sit at my desk, staring intently at the bookshelf.

"All right, you little bastard. Do that, again …"

June 10th, 1900

Three weeks have passed and the crowds that Father predicted still haven't materialized. Day after day, I stand behind the counter and watch the wealthy people of Kingsbrook go by like they're on parade. Father and Carol are constantly fighting. Before it was only about the pharmacy, but now, it's the smallest of things. A cracked teacup in Carol's china turned into a full-bore shouting match. The leaking kitchen tap caused them not to speak to one another for two days. When they are together at the pharmacy, it's toxic.

But everything is not entirely terrible. I have had the most fascinating day.

We received a telegram at the pharmacy this afternoon. It was delivered by a courier shortly after we opened. It was from Mr. Carrington! He placed an order for some powders and tonics, but couldn't be bothered to come into town, and wanted them delivered to the Nightingale House.

Father began hastily putting the order together.

I begged him to let me make the delivery. I was certain that Mr. Carrington had placed the order in the hopes that I would be the one to deliver it.

At first, Father said that was nonsense and that he would go.

I persisted and he asked why I was so eager. I told him that I'm stuck at the pharmacy all day, every day. I wanted to go out for a change. I told him I could take the bicycle and be there in twenty minutes. When he hesitated, I tried to appeal to his business sense. I told him that people know me as working at the pharmacy and that I could be a sort of advertisement. He's been trying to be the face of the pharmacy and it wasn't working, so I argued that he should let me try.

It worked!

I put everything in the basket of the bicycle. I also took some change from the register, and rode out to the Nightingale House. I have heard people in the pharmacy talk about the Nightingale House and Mr. Carrington. It sounds like Mr. Carrington is not well regarded. It can only be because they are jealous of him. How could they not be? He lives in one of the grandest houses in town and it's only his summer home. I've heard that he has homes in New York and Richmond. Not to mention the fact that he is the handsomest man in Kingsbrook.

As I passed beyond the limits of town and into the grassy fields on the way to Willow Lake, I wondered if Mrs. Carrington would be there. I really hoped that she wouldn't. I also became aware of the sweat that was running down my back in the summer heat—very unladylike.

All was forgotten, though, when I saw the Nightingale House. It really is beautiful. It looked like it was lording over the lake and surrounding hills.

I stopped in the street at the beginning of the stone path that led to the front door. I rested the bike against the bushes, gathered the powders and tonics from the basket, and carried them to the porch. I had to awkwardly shift them to my right hand to pull the chain. The bell rang from somewhere inside.

"Come in," a voice answered. His voice.

The interior of the house was gorgeous.

I made my way through the living room, which had high-backed chairs and a sofa arranged around the fireplace, and found him in the dining room, sitting at the table, gazing out at the lake. He looked at me and smiled. No. It wasn't a smile. It was that vicious little smirk he wore at my party.

"I see my little plan worked," he said.

I tried to hide my satisfaction at being proven right. He wanted to see me.

"I have the items you requested. Where would you like me to place them?"

"Over there is fine," he said with a wave to the dustbin.

I wasn't sure if he was serious, which he found amusing. He told me to put them on the table.

"How is the pharmacy business?" he asked.

I told him it was good and he scoffed, saying that his order probably doubled Father's business.

"Your home is lovely," I said.

"More so now that you're here."

So wicked!

I blushed and asked when Mrs. Carrington would return from Boston.

"In a few days. She'll be back for the Fourth of July Celebration and then she'll return to Boston. My mother-in-law's health isn't well."

"I'm sorry to hear that."

"I guess I'm stuck here, all by myself. So lonely."

I'm not versed in flirting or innuendo, but I felt I understood his meaning and found myself enjoying it.

"Would you like to see the house?" he asked.

"Very much so," I told him.

He guided me through the kitchen, the living room, and dining room, which was fine but then he led me to his office. His desk was in the middle of the room and there was a large bookcase with wooden panels on the side against the wall by the door.

"This is my little sanctuary," he said.

"It's lovely."

"Would you like to see a secret?"

I didn't know what he meant, but the gleam in his eyes said that he wanted to show me.

"All right."

He went around to the side of the bookcase and waved me over. He popped one of the wooden panels off the side to reveal a hidden compartment. Inside was a bottle of whiskey and the flask I had seen him drinking from at my party. He took it out and gently shook it at me. I could hear the liquid inside.

"Care for a drink?"

"No, thank you."

"Are you sure?"

"Yes, but don't let me stop you."

"Of course not." He smiled. He unscrewed the top and took a long sip.

It may have been none of my business, but my curiosity got the better of me.

"If I may ask, why do you hide your whiskey in there?"

"My wife doesn't approve of me keeping liquor in the house."

There was a trace of anger in his voice as he answered.

"Does she set the rules?" I asked, trying to be flirtatious.

"I'm afraid I may have pushed my luck in that regard once or twice," he said, returning the flask to the hidden compartment and replacing the panel. "Come. Let me show you the rest."

He led me out of the office and to the stairs. He made some pretense of not wanting me to lose my balance and offered his hand. I took it but when we reached the top, he didn't let go. We walked right past the two rooms at the top of the stairs and went to the door at the end of the hall.

"This," he said, "is my pride and joy."

Believe me when I tell you, it was the most beautiful room I have ever seen. The walls were paneled in rich wood. There was a settee, a writing desk, an ornate dresser, and a massive bed. The room even had a fireplace. On the mantle above, there was a framed picture.

"What do you think?" he asked, still holding my hand.

"Well, at least you have a fireplace for those cold nights."

He smiled that wicked smile and pressed my hand. "That's not the warmth I seek."

"Don't you have a wife for that?"

He pressed my hand tighter and drew me a little closer and repeated. "That's not the warmth I seek."

I understand that I had tried to be flirtatious earlier, but standing there in his bedroom, just the two of us, I felt that we may have gone too far.

I told him that it was a lovely house but then I began to feel like a fool for putting an end to our fun.

He appeared disappointed and led me back downstairs.

He showed me to the front door and we stood on the porch.

"If there's anything that you need, let us know and we'll bring it straight away," I said.

He took out his billfold and extracted a ten-dollar bill. He held it out to me.

I reached for the bill, but he pulled it back.

"On one condition," he said. "Whenever I make an order, I want you, and only you, to deliver it."

I was feeling flirtatious, again, and anxious to make up for my behavior upstairs.

"I think that can be arranged," I said, giving him my own wicked little smile. In that moment, I remembered, and brushed my hair from my shoulders to reveal the silver butterfly necklace I had purchased with the money he gave me before. I could tell that all was forgiven when he extended his hand.

"Thank you for your business, Mr. Carrington," I said, taking the money.

"Please, call me Thomas."

"Well, thank you, Thomas."

I deposited the money in my pocket and held out my hand to shake his. You'll never believe what he did.

He gently took my hand and raised it to his lips. "My pleasure," he said and then he kissed the back of my hand! All the while, he held me with his striking blue eyes.

I felt like my face would burst from smiling as I walked down the path to the bicycle and he went back inside. I stole a look back towards the house as I mounted the seat and saw him watching me from the window of the study.

Father was thrilled at the prospect of more business from Mr.

Carrington, but I didn't tell him about the money. Why should I? He was clear that it was for me. I may have to pay another visit to the jewelers.

It's been a long, wonderful day.

Good night.

10

'Will someone please turn off that beeping?' I mentally plead as I slowly come into consciousness.

I try to move, but every joint in my body objects. I groan and lift my chin off my chest. My head weighs a ton.

Please, make the beeping stop.

I open my eyes. The bookcase fills my field of view.

Oh no.

I fell asleep in my office chair, waiting for that stupid sound. My back is in agony and there's a wonderful spot of drool on my shirt. The beeping is coming from the living room. It's the alarm on my phone.

Please, don't tell me I've overslept! Not on Caitlyn's first day of school. I'm going to have to drive her in, which will look great after meeting her teacher and her principal, yesterday.

I drag myself out of the chair and into the living room. I snatch my phone off the end table.

Thank God. I've only overslept by twenty minutes. It's not the end of the world, but I need to wake up Caitlyn and get her ready.

I climb the stairs, trying to rub out the drool stain on my shirt.

As I stand outside her door, instead of her customary snoring, I hear her quietly talking.

"… Okay, now it's my turn … What's it like in there …? How cold …? Okay, your turn … No … No, I told you. I don't know Rebecca …"

I'm tempted to sit here and listen because I want to know what she's up to, but we need to get moving. I knock on the door and push it open.

"Caitlyn?"

She's sitting at the vanity, in front of the mirror. She turns to me with startled eyes, like I've caught her red-handed, but I have no idea what she's guilty of.

"Hey." I look around the room. "Who you talking to?"

She continues to stare.

"You okay?" I ask through a stifled yawn.

"Yes."

"Great. Let's go. First day of school. I'm making pancakes."

She shoots up, and runs past me into the hall. Her footsteps make a rapid-fire drumroll down the stairs.

There are dirty clothes hanging off the back of the chair of the vanity she just vacated.

"Caitlyn?" I call in exasperation, but she's gone.

I walk over and collect the clothes from the chair. In the mirror, I can see the slightly open closet door on the other side of the room, directly behind me.

"Come on, Caitlyn," I groan. "The basket is right in there."

I carry the clothes halfway across the room and stop.

Hold on.

I turn, walk back to the vanity, and stand in front of the mirror.

I can still see the open closet door. I shouldn't be able to, because I'm standing right in front of the mirror. There's no reflection of me. It's like I'm not here.

A ringing begins to build in my ears. My head starts to hurt and my eyes strain. The ringing grows deafening. Every other sound fades until all I hear is the high-pitched tone. I'm not there. In the mirror, the door to the closet begins to slowly swing open—

"Dad?"

I turn around. Caitlyn is standing in the doorway. The door to the closet is only slightly open, as before. The ringing has stopped.

"Am I getting pancakes or not?" she asks.

I look back at the mirror. There I am, my mouth open, holding the dirty clothes in my arms. I step to the side so that I can see the closet in the reflection. The door is only slightly open and there's Caitlyn in the doorway, waiting for pancakes.

God, I'm tired. I look like I'm nursing a once-in-a-lifetime hangover.

"Sure," I say, holding up the dirty clothes. "Just as soon as you figure out where these go."

"Sorry, sorry, sorry," she says. She sheepishly takes the clothes from my arms, opens the door to the closet, and deposits them in the laundry basket.

"There. Now, can I have pancakes?"

"I don't know. I think you've earned oatmeal."

"I said I was sorry."

"Oatmeal with raisins."

Caitlyn rolls her eyes and makes mock puking sounds as she goes out into the hall and down the stairs.

I start to follow, but can't help taking one more look in the vanity mirror from across the room.

My reflection is still there, wearing that stupid, puzzled stare.

*

Two helpings of pancakes later, I wave goodbye as the yellow bus rumbles away with Caitlyn onboard.

I was right to be worried last night. This is all hitting me harder than I thought it would. Between the lack of sleep, my mind seeing Nicole, and having to send Caitlyn off for her first day of school by myself, there's no more denying that I'm not coping very well. It wasn't supposed to be like this, but this is how it is. I can't let Caitlyn see it. She's going to have enough to worry about. I want her focusing on school and making new friends—not on her father, who is slightly losing it.

I'll be fine.

The most important thing I can do now is try to establish a routine. It's time to get to something normal. It's time to write.

I go to the kitchen, pour myself another cup of coffee, and then, filled with equal parts excitement and anxiety, I head to the Writing Room.

Seconds later, I'm sitting at my desk, surrounded by the works of authors who have inspired me. There's a beautiful view of Willow Lake outside the window and the endless possibilities of a blank page lie before me. My particular method is to write everything out longhand in notebooks. It makes editing a lot easier. I already know the plot. I know all the twists and turns that are going to keep the reader up late into the night. I'm about to begin. I crack my knuckles and take a breath. This is a moment to relish.

"Here we go …"

I sit there, gaping at the blank page …

… and I can't write a damn word.

I use every trick in the book to get the juices flowing. I try starting in the middle of the chapter. That doesn't work. I try stream of consciousness writing. Nothing gets me in the groove.

Eventually, I try to force it. For an hour, I clunk along like a car on square wheels. After another hour, I stop to read what I've written … What is this garbage? It's all over the place. I kept mistakenly calling one of the main characters 'Rebecca', even though her name is Kristen. The prose is disjointed and confusing. It's five pages of absolute drivel.

I curse and roll my neck, releasing a series of loud cracks. I really needed that sleep I never got last night. I get up, walk around, jump up and down, shake out my hands, sit back down, and try again. After another half an hour, I stop, go over what I've written … and drop the notebook on the desk.

"Okay. I guess it's not happening today."

I push myself away from the desk. I hate giving up like this, but I've got to take it easy on myself. It's been months since I've tried to write. Of course, I'm rusty. These are new surroundings, a new book, and no Nicole. I'll try again tomorrow.

This means that my day has now become regrettably open. If I'm not going to write, the only way to feel better is to take advantage of this beautiful morning.

*

Accompanied by my cup of coffee, I step barefoot off the deck onto the cool grass and walk down to the pier.

The wooden slats have been warmed by the sun. The surface of the pond is a sheet of murky glass.

I can't have many more days like this. I need to crank out the book. No one knows that more than me, but for now, I'm going to stand here and sip my coffee.

As I stare out at the lake, standing at the end of the pier, my hand distractedly reaches inside the neck of my shirt and pulls out Nicole's ring.

This day should have been hers. It was taken from her. It was taken from us. At the funeral, one of her friend's husbands said that her death was part of God's plan. If Caitlyn hadn't been there, I would have hit him. Instead, I told him, 'Well then, I guess God's an asshole.' Thankfully, Caitlyn didn't hear that. Before Nicole's death, I believed that there was a God, some sort of benevolent hand, watching over the world, guiding things, intervening with small miracles here and there but afterwards? No way. There's no justification for what happened. None.

85

As I run my finger around the edges of Nicole's ring, my eyes fall on the water below me off the end of the pier.

My finger stops.

What is that?

It … It has to be some kind of weed that's floating to the surface.

I peer closer.

It's not possible, and I know I'm really tired, but my first thought is, *That looks like hair.*

The tendrils continue to slowly rise.

It has to be a weed, right? But I swear to God, it looks like a blond hair is rising up out of the depth and any second, I'll see a head …

Okay. I need to know what this is.

I lie down on my stomach and reach off the pier towards whatever is rising from the darkness below. I grunt as I strain. It's only inches from my outstretched fingers.

I'm about to touch it when suddenly, it sinks, as if violently pulled back under by some unseen hand.

I'm so startled that I quickly pull my hand back and stand up to get away from it. There's a light pressure on the back of my neck and a faint *snap*. I take deep breaths and instinctively put my hand onto my chest. I can feel my heart racing—wait … I can feel my heart. What I can't feel is Nicole's ring.

"No …"

I look down. Nicole's ring and the chain are gone.

"No!"

Through my panic, I know what had to have happened.

As I was lying on the pier, the ring was dangling over the water. At some point, it must have slid between the wooden slats. When I stood, the ring couldn't fit. The chain snapped, and now, Nicole's ring is at the bottom of the lake.

Staring down at the cloudy water, I drop to my knees, bury my face in my hands, and begin weeping, uncontrollably.

11

"Do you sell magnets?"

The guy behind the help desk at the hardware store looks up from the car magazine he's reading. "Sure. What kind of magnets are you looking for?"

"Well ... um ... the magnetic kind?"

"What are they for? You need them for some cabinets or doors? You mounting something? We've got neodymium disks, pull magnets, magnetic tape."

"I'm trying to fish a ring off the bottom of a lake."

"A ring?"

"Yeah."

He sucks air through his teeth and shakes his head. "Magnet ain't gonna do it for you."

"What?"

"Gold and silver aren't magnetic. They don't stick to magnets."

"Why not?"

"Because they don't."

"You're kidding."

"Sorry."

"Shit."

"How deep is the lake?"

"It's deep."

He puts down his magazine. "All right. Let's see what we can do for ya."

*

I grunt and begin pulling the rope.

It's a lot deeper off the end of the pier than I thought. It has to be close to forty feet. I keep pulling. The rope piles up on the wooden slats next to my feet. There's resistance on the other end.

I've lost count of the number of attempts I've made. My clothes are soaked in water and sweat. The butchered head of the rake appears at the surface, covered in weeds. I cut off the wooden handle so it would sink. I haul it up onto the pier and begin sifting through the stinking, slimy tendrils. There are some flecks of mud, but most of it has come off on the rise to the surface. After I inspect each handful, I toss the weeds into the water off the side of the pier. Once I go through all the weeds I've pulled up, I hold up the head of the rake and inspect the teeth, praying that by some miracle, I've managed to snag Nicole's ring.

Just like every previous attempt, there's no ring.

I had hope when I first started. The guy at the hardware store helped me come up with it. I'm pretty sure he could tell I had been crying and felt bad for me. It also was apparent that he didn't have much else to do.

I came home and found the spot on the pier where I figured I was lying down when I lost Nicole's ring. Then, I dropped the rake into the water, let it sink to the bottom and pulled it back up. The first couple of times, it came up totally empty. I realized that I needed to literally rake the bottom. I tried again, but this time, after letting it sink to the bottom, I took a few steps down the pier, and pulled it towards me. I was rewarded by a slight resistance, and I could feel the weeds being pulled out of the mud below. The rake came up with a big clump of vegetation. I happily sat on the pier and sifted through it. It came up empty, but I believed that with everything I snagged, there was actually a chance I could hook Nicole's ring. That kept me going for the first couple of tries, but soon, I wasn't even pulling up weeds anymore, meaning I had raked the spot clean.

I try moving around. I throw the rake out further off the end of the pier. Maybe the tide carried the ring further out. Wait. Does a lake have tides? I'm willing to try anything, but at this point, it's starting to feel like I've tried everything.

The discarded weeds form a layer over the water below me. I'm starting to snag them, again, as I pull the rake up. My optimism is disappearing. It's being replaced by aching arms, a stiff back, and cold, chapped hands, but I keep telling myself, "Okay, this will be my last throw."

I think I said that thirty throws ago.

My arms, legs, and back are screaming in agony. I'm coming up empty almost every time. I'm not even getting any weeds. I even try to rake the bottom directly under the pier. I'll throw it on one side, carefully lie down on my stomach, and pass the rope to myself under the pier. I'm rewarded with nothing but more weeds.

My mind has gone numb. I'm not putting any thought into where I should throw the rake head. It's mechanical.

I set my feet, wind up, and am about to make another toss when the pier starts to shake.

All my weight is going forward off the edge. I'm staring straight down into the water.

"Shit, shit, shit, shit, shit!" I stutter.

I'm about to fall, but at the last second I pinwheel my arms backwards, stopping my momentum.

"Whoa! Easy tiger!" a voice says behind me.

I'm able to steady myself and shuffle backwards. Another inch, and I would have been swimming.

I look back to see Mildred, halfway down the pier, frozen in place, holding a cup of coffee in her hand.

I lean over and put my hands on my knees to catch my breath. "Mildred! Good lord, you almost sent me in."

"I'm sorry! I'm sorry, Daniel!"

She's got that panicked expression on her face and printed on the side of her mug are the words 'SASSY BITCH'. I can't help it. She's such a comical picture, I start laughing until I'm shaking and have to sit down. She's laughing, too. Her whole body starts to tremble, and coffee begins sloshing out of her cup, which brings more laughter. She can't control herself and gives up, dumping the coffee into the lake.

"Cold anyway," she says, "but I do hate to waste the whiskey."

I'm laughing so hard, my aching muscles can't take it. She comes to the end of the pier and sits next to me. We laugh until we're out of breath and it feels like I've done a million sit-ups.

"Okay," she says, wiping her eyes. "I have to ask, what are you doing out here? I've been watching you for hours. You weedin'?"

"No," I reply, still out of breath. "I lost ... I, um, I wear my wife's wedding ring on a chain around my neck. And I came out here and—" The wave of grief that slams into me is unbearable. Seconds ago, I was laughing harder than I have in months. Now, my throat is closing. "—the chain broke ... and Nicole's ring ... it ..."

All her merriment evaporates in an instant. Her mouth hangs open and she even chokes up. "Oh, Daniel ..."

"It's gone," I say, managing little more than a whimper. "I lost it ... It's gone ... I'm losing her, again ..."

It's taking everything I have to hold back the sobs but there's no stopping my tears.

Mildred puts a comforting hand on my back.

For a while, we do nothing but sit and stare out at the water. Occasionally, a breeze will pass and gentle waves will lap against the support poles of the pier. Mildred remains silent the whole time, calmly rubbing my back with her hand. It's exactly what I need. Eventually, I'm able to get myself under control.

"Thank you, Mildred," I sigh.

"You want me to bring you some whiskey?"

"Nah. I appreciate it, but I'm good."

"Suit yourself." She stands and looks at the weeds that are starting to wash up on the shore. "Your beach is a mess. You should probably get a rake to clean it up."

I stare at the butchered rake head in my hand.

She jokingly nudges me with her knee. "Don't worry, you can borrow mine."

She walks back down the pier and heads towards her house.

I'm gonna sit out here for a little while longer.

*

After a few minutes, I'm back at it.

I feel like if I stop, then I'm giving up on Nicole.

I toss the rake out from the pier and it sinks into the water. The rope gradually slides off the pier after it. It takes almost a minute for it to stop as the rake reaches the bottom. There's no way Nicole's ring is that far out, but I don't care.

I start slowly pulling it in. There are brief moments of resistance as it rips the few remaining weeds out of the mud. I keep pulling, careful not to go too fast, so that it stays in the mud. It finally arrives at the bottom off the edge of the pier. I keep pulling. There's almost no resistance as it begins to rise.

I'm already scouting where to throw it next. Just one more time. I wonder if there's some way that I can get it und—

The rope stops.

I pull but it doesn't budge.

Slowly, it begins sinking back into the water, like there's a massive weight on the other end.

I tighten my grip and p—

Shit!

The rope yanks me down.

I strain and with all I've got, but the rope starts to slide from my hand, straight down into the water. I further tighten my grip and kneel down, bracing myself on the pier, but I'm still being pulled towards the water. My hand is inches above the layer of discarded weeds, floating on the surface. I have to lie down on the pier but it's no use. Still clutching the rope, my hand is pulled below surface up to my elbow.

The rope stops. There's still tension, but I can't see past the layer of weeds.

Something touches my wrist.

I let go.

The rope rapidly slides off the pier, into the water. I sit back, stunned, watching the rope go. Whatever is on the other end of the rope reaches the bottom. There's about three feet of slack, floating on the surface among the weeds, next to the pier.

What the hell was that?

It wasn't a fish. It was dead weight like a stone or a log, but whatever touched my wrist has to have been a fish. I've been making a nice little habitat for them with all these weeds.

"What are you doing?"

I turn towards the shore behind me.

Caitlyn's standing at the base of the pier, bookbag slung across her back.

"Oh. Hey, pumpkin." I get to my feet. I must be quite the sight. "I was, uh … just …" I have to tell her the truth. "Well, sweetheart, I lost Mom's ring. The chain broke and it fell in the water and I was trying to see if I could get it back."

I don't know what she's going to say. I was inconsolable when it happened a few hours ago. I'm worried how it might affect her.

She surveys the floating weeds that have washed up on shore and surround the pier. "Do you want me to help?"

"No. That's okay, pumpkin. Thank you. I might try again tomorrow."

"Okay."

I clap my hands. "All right! Let's go inside. I'm gonna take a shower, make us dinner, and I want to hear all about how your first day went."

She shrugs and begins walking back to the house.

"You can be happier about that, you know?" I call after her.

She waves her hands and sarcastically drawls, "Yeahhhhh."

I'm not mad. That was objectively funny.

I look down at the end of the rope, floating in the water. I'm tempted to leave it there, but there's that one in a million chance that Nicole's ring is on the other end of it, or whatever cinderblock I snagged.

I … I almost don't want to …

But the thought of Nicole's ring wins out.

I drop down on the pier and reach out. I hesitate for a split second, then quickly snap up the end of the rope. My fingers briefly break the surface, but I hurriedly pull them back. I stand up and pull.

There's no resistance.

Whatever it was must have fallen off.

The rake head quickly rises out of the water, and dangles from the end of the rope.

No cinderblock. No weeds. No ring.

Damnit.

*

After a quick shower, I change my clothes, and get started on dinner. I'm taking it a little bit easier than yesterday with some chicken and veggies. Caitlyn sits at the alcove, scribbling in one of her new notebooks.

"How was today?" I ask while sautéing some vegetables.

"It was okay," she says in a manner that suggests it was not.

I stop tossing the vegetables. "What happened, sweetheart?"

"Nothing."

"No. Not nothing. Come on. Tell me."

She fidgets and puts down her pencil.

"Caitlyn?"

"A boy was making fun of me at recess."

"A boy was making fun of you?"

"Yeah. Peter Sanders."

"What happened?"

She fidgets again.

I turn off the burner and go and sit across from her in the alcove.

"Sweetheart?"

"He was making fun of someone and I told him to stop."

"That's good, Caitlyn. That's what you should do. Did he stop?"

She's trying not to look me in the eye.

"... No."

"Did you tell Ms. Hancourt?"

"... No."

"Do you want me to talk to Ms. Hancourt?"

She quickly shakes her head.

"Are you sure?"

She nods.

"Okay, but you tell me if you want me to talk to her, okay?"

She nods again, but I can tell she's not going to do that.

It's probably because I'm a little bit raw after these last few days, but this pisses me off. Screw this Peter Sanders kid.

"And if he still doesn't stop, maybe you show him who's boss. You know, rough him up a little bit."

She looks at me with her jaw dropped, which I've earned. Even I can't tell if I'm joking, but she would never do that. Caitlyn is far too nice and caring, but I want her to know I've got her back, and I'm sure I've said the right thing because her shock melts into a smile.

"Okay, besides the smelly Peter Sanders, how was the rest of school? You have any homework?"

"Yep."

"All right, dinner's going to be ready in a few minutes. Let's get started."

*

We knock out her homework as we eat dinner. Her assignments are light. After all, it was only the first day of school. Most of it is orientation stuff.

Then, it's some boardgames and a movie on the couch.

This is exactly what I needed to get my mind off Nicole's ring. I still have the best thing we ever did, which is this little munchkin sitting next to me.

The prince and the princess begin waltzing around the castle, the music crescendos, and the credits roll, ending the movie.

"Okay, Caitlyn," I say. "Eight o'clock. Time for bed."

Without much of a fuss, she hops off the couch and heads upstairs.

While she gets ready for bed, I turn on the light in the Writing Room and fire up the computer for some background writing music. I'm going to try to get some writing done to make up for this afternoon, but first, I head upstairs to tuck Caitlyn into bed.

I enter the room just as she's crawling under the covers.

I go over and kiss her on the forehead.

"Good night, pumpkin."

"Good night, Dad."

"Know what?"

"What?"

"I'm really proud of you for standing up to that Peter Sanders."

She smiles, unsure of how to respond.

I kiss her forehead again, go to the door, and remember to hit the night-light.

"Get some sleep. Love you."

"Love you too, Dad."

She snuggles deeper into the covers.

I close the door and head back downstairs into the Writing Room, when I sit in my chair and grab the pen.

"All right. Let's try this again."

*

I don't get far.

It's not bad. My main character is trying to find out who sent the hitman after him. This stuff should be riveting, but I can't get into it. Thoughts of Nicole's ring elbow their way back into my mind.

Maybe I'll try again with the rake tomorrow.

No. I've got to accept it. It's gone. I've got to stop thinking about it. This is what I need to focus on.

But maybe one more throw with the rake. Just one.

No. Move on.

I keep going back and forth until I have to put my pen down. I need to concentrate. I've got to reset my brain and focus on this hitman. I stand up, jump around a little bit, shake out my hands, and take some deep breaths. The clock on the computer monitor says that it's 11:30 p.m. Damn. I want to finish this chapter before going to bed and at this rate, the sun will be up before that happens.

My muscles ache from a night in the office chair and pulling the rake through the mud. My throat is parched. Some aspirin and a glass of water is what I need to get this chapter going.

I pause the music on the computer and step out of the Writing Room.

The darkness combined with the silence is a bit too eerie, but that's quickly remedied by turning on the table lamps in the living room as well as the light in the dining room on my way to the kitchen.

I pour myself a glass of water and shake two pills out of the bottle from the cabinet. It's a cloudy night and I can barely see past the deck into the yard through the window.

Final decision made: no more fishing for Nicole's ring.

It's gone and I have to face it. Also, I'm not sure my body and sleep-deprived brain can handle another day of that.

I pop the aspirin in my mouth and wash it down with a gulp of water. I down the rest of the glass, load it into the dishwasher, and leave the kitchen.

As I cross the dining room, there's the sound of giggling from the Writing Room.

"Caitlyn?"

Silence.

I shake my head. I'm hearing things.

I walk into the Writing Room and plop back down in my chair.

"All right. Here we go for real this t—"

I stare down at the desk.

There's a silver butterfly necklace with two tiny blue stones on a silver chain with a broken clasp, sitting on the notebook. It's clearly been left for me to find.

I look towards the door.

"Caitlyn?"

She must have come down the stairs while I was in the kitchen, left it, and went back upstairs. I guess I really did hear her giggle. I've never seen this necklace before, but I'm sure I don't know every bit of jewelry Caitlyn has.

Necklace in hand, I walk upstairs and open Caitlyn's door.

She's asleep, or at least pretending to be. What is she doing? I

97

walk over to her bed and whisper. "You lost this, pumpkin. I'm going to leave it right here." I place the necklace on the nightstand, next to her medallion.

I wait for her to open her eyes but she doesn't. She must have fallen right back asleep or she's doing an amazing job of faking it.

We'll talk about it in the morning. Right now, I need to get this chapter done.

As quietly as possible, I go back downstairs into the Writing Room, and plop into the chair. I go to grab my pen, but stop.

Sitting on the notebook is a silver butterfly necklace with two tiny blue stones on a silver chain with a broken clasp.

12

The toast jumps from the slots in the toaster as I flip the bacon in the skillet. The eggs are already on the plates, waiting for Caitlyn to join me.

I can't get the necklace out of my head.

Did I just imagine that I took it up to Caitlyn's room and actually left it there in the Writing Room? Am I really *that* tired? It's possible, I guess. That's the only thing I can come up with, or, at best, I went upstairs to Caitlyn's room and forgot to bring the necklace with me, but that adds to a whole other problem that I can't ignore; I really might be starting to lose it. The lack of sleep, the visions. I'm not only seeing things that aren't there, I'm hallucinating actions that I'm not really taking. This can't be simple, run-of-the-mill processing of grief, and if it keeps up, I'm going to have to talk to someone. I know there's no shame in it. Under the circumstances, it's understandable, but it just adds another level of difficulty to everything. I suppose I can try to keep it a secret from Caitlyn and go to therapy sessions while she's at school, but I don't want to sneak around or lie to her when I want her to be honest. Merely thinking about it is giving me a headache and I'm not there, yet. I'm simply allowing myself that option if this keeps up.

Last night, I slept on the couch, again. I got some sleep but only three or four hours. That chapter that I wanted to finish before going to bed? Yeah, that didn't happen. Not even close. Instead, I crashed on the couch, lights on, thinking about the necklace.

Caitlyn walks into the kitchen, dressed and ready for school.

"G'morning, pumpkin. How'd you sleep?"

"Good," she replies, sliding into the alcove.

"I've got scrambled eggs, bacon, and toast. You want juice or milk?"

"Juice, please."

"You got it."

I pour her a cup from the fridge and set it on the table.

"Thank you."

"You're welcome."

I bring our plates over from the counter by the stove and sit across from her.

"Listen," I say, scraping some butter across a wedge of toast. "That necklace you left on my computer? I really appreciate it, but why did you leave it there for me to find?"

She bites off the end of a strip of bacon. "I didn't leave it there. It was my friend. She said you were sad about losing Mom's ring. She said you could have the necklace and wear it like Mom's ring."

She's making things up, again, but how can I be upset? She's trying to do a nice thing. I have no problem letting this one slide.

"Well, you can tell your friend that's very sweet, but I'll be okay," I say with a knowing nod. "She can have the necklace back."

Caitlyn just munches her bacon and takes a sip of juice.

I take a bite of my toast. "So, what's going to happen on your second day of school?"

"I don't know."

"You gonna learn how to be a rocket scientist?"

"Dad, I told you I want to work with animals."

"Rocket animals?"

"What are 'rocket animals'?"

"I don't know. I guess today, you have to learn how to build them."

"They don't teach you how to make rocket animals in second grade."

"Einstein made rocket animals when he was in second grade."

"Who's 'Einstein'?"

I'm clearly failing as a parent.

"Are you gonna make some friends?" I tentatively ask. I want to nudge her in the direction of making some real friends as opposed to the imaginary ones.

"I don't know." She shrugs with a little more uncertainty than I'd like.

"You should try," I say, attempting to be encouraging without being pushy. "It's exciting, getting to meet all these new kids. A lot of them probably like the same things you do."

"Maybe," she replies, looking down at her glass of juice. "What if Peter Sanders makes fun of me, again?"

"Hey, pumpkin, look at me."

She does.

"You don't worry about what Peter Sanders says, okay? He's just a bully. Bullies try to make other people feel bad and do you know why?"

"No."

"Because they feel bad about themselves. You are amazing, Caitlyn Nicole Price. Peter Sanders ain't got nothing on you."

She smiles.

"And, if you work hard this week and we get your homework done right when you get home, we'll go swimming in the pool this weekend."

"The pool?"

"Yeah," I say with a nod towards the window.

"You mean the lake?"

"I thought you said it was a swimming pool."

"I didn't say that!"

"I'mmmmm pretty sure you did."

"No, I didn't!" she laughs.

"Oh, no. You called it a puddle."

"Dad!"

"Okay, okay, okay. Fine. Let's finish up breakfast. The bus is on its way."

*

I close the front door as the bus pulls away.

After talking and joking with Caitlyn over breakfast, this morning is a lot easier than yesterday.

Before getting to writing, I grab the necklace off my notebook in the Writing Room. Finding it there when I thought I had taken it upstairs last night had really messed with my head, so I decided to have nothing more to do with it.

I carry the necklace up the stairs and into Caitlyn's room.

The place is a mess, again. All it took was one day for some dirty clothes to find their way back to the vanity. I pick them up, taking a second to check my reflection in the mirror, and then toss the clothes into the closet.

Holding the necklace in my hand, I scan the room.

I don't even know where Caitlyn keeps her jewelry. I've never seen a jewelry box or anything of the sort. There's not one on the vanity, window seat, or in the closet.

Finally, I set it on the nightstand, next to the medallion, which is where I thought I put it last night. That being done, I step over the stuffed animals and toys that litter the floor as I make my way to the door ...

Know what?

Instead of leaving, I turn around, begin picking up the items

102

on the floor, and putting them away. A few minutes later, her room is neat and organized.

I know it's her mess, and she should be the one to clean it up, but she was looking out for me by giving me the necklace.

It was a really sweet thing to do and I'll look out for her, too.

June 12th, 1900

The pharmacy has become a perfect balance of anticipation and despair.

On one hand, I'm forced to endure this endless boredom, working behind the counter. The throngs of customers still haven't arrived. It's gotten to the point that Father has been forced to make a decision. He had promised Carol that we would never sell alcohol at the pharmacy, but he had to go back on his word. Carol was furious. Father tried to argue that we would only market it as a medicinal remedy and not for recreation. When Carol continued to argue with him about how expensive it would be, he said that we would buy cheaper alcohol and repackage it. I know all of this because their voices easily carried through the curtain that separates the storeroom from the store. They only stopped when a potential customer opened the door, was startled by their voices, and promptly turned and left. Finally, Father said that we didn't have a choice if the pharmacy was to survive. After that, Carol left without saying a word.

The only joy I get from the pharmacy is the anticipation I feel at the possibility that Mr. Carrin—Thomas will place another order, giving me an excuse to go to the Nightingale House to see him, or that he may drop by the store.

Throughout the day, I constantly watch the window, hoping my wishes will be answered.

Instead, almost every day, I have to see Patricia Fleming and her herd of friends take their lordly stroll across the green. I have to watch as they stop and speak to the nobility of Kingsbrook. I can imagine her put-upon tone and her laughing as she spreads what I'm sure is unfounded gossip about the person she spoke to only moments ago.

Why should someone so horrid be blessed with such a leisurely life while I'm stuck here, in this Hell?

I often dream of what it would be like to have wealth, stature, and peace … to have Thomas. He is all those things wrapped into such a striking package. That's exactly what he is to me—everything that I want.

I find myself constantly fiddling with the necklace, wishing it was a magical amulet that could summon him at my will.

But I guess I shall have to wait.

It's all I can do, besides dream of Thomas and the Nightingale House …

13

"Come on, Dad!" Caitlyn cries as she races towards the water's edge.

"I'm coming," I call after her. I'm really dragging.

It's Sunday. At least, I think it's Sunday. The days are starting to blur.

I'm honoring my promise to Caitlyn that we would go swimming today, but I made that promise before I had endured endless sleepless nights, and before I spent this morning clearing the weeds from my search for Nicole's ring, but Caitlyn held up her end of the bargain with her homework throughout the week.

She runs into the water and falls down with a laugh.

I gingerly dip my foot in the water and pull it back.

"It's freezing!"

"No, it's not!" Caitlyn says, slapping her arms on the surface.

"It's ice-cold, you polar bear!"

"You promised!"

"Ugh. Fine."

I'm not joking. It feels like it's subzero. I hesitantly ease myself forward, hissing as the water creeps up my legs and let out an audible gasp as I submerge my … waist. The sand below my feet is coarse, but gradually becomes a soft mud as I advance.

I continue my theatrics of adjusting to the water as Caitlyn slowly swims up behind me.

"Come on, Dad! You just gotta go under real quick and it'll be over. It won't be cold."

"Yes, it will!"

"No, it won't," she says, creeping closer.

I point a finger at her. "You stay away from me."

She giggles and swims, like a shark approaching its prey.

"Stay away!"

"Daaaaaad …"

"Nooooooooo!" I pretend like I'm going to run for the shore, but I go really, really slowly. "Leave me alone!"

Caitlyn swims up behind me and launches onto my shoulders.

I cry out as I allow her to push my head under the water.

OH MY GOD! IT'S SO COLD!

But Caitlyn's right. The shock is brief. I can hear her muffled laughter through water.

I bob back to the surface. She's still hanging on my shoulders. I can stand on the bottom but she can't.

"You're mean," I tell her.

"I was helping you."

"Yeah. Some help you are," I say, wiping my eyes and nose.

Caitlyn spends the next hour or so jumping off the pier. She doesn't go all the way to the end. The pier goes out about sixty feet, so it'd be a bit of a swim back every time. She could do it. I have no doubt of that. Our apartment back in Portsmouth was terrible but the one bright spot was that it had a swimming pool. Caitlyn spent almost every day of her summers splashing around. Whenever Nicole and I wanted some alone time, we'd encourage her to go swimming so she'd be tired and go to bed early. So, Caitlyn is a fantastic swimmer, but until she's used to swimming in the lake, I don't want her jumping off the end of the pier, where it's really deep. However, she seems perfectly content to jump from the side.

Eventually, she gets bored of it and swims up to my side. I know what's coming.

"Throw me, Dad!" she screams as she leaps up at me.

I catch her under the arms and hurl her away into deeper water. Her arms flail and she laughingly screams as she flies through the air and splashes down.

This was our favorite game when I would join her in the pool in Portsmouth.

Before she resurfaces, I duck down and swim a few strokes underwater. She's going to try to find me. This is how our little game works. I hold my breath for as long as I can and then burst upwards. She tries to catch up to me as I go back under and swim away slowly so that she can catch up. When I resurface, she's right next to me. She leaps up, I grab her arms, and throw her, again.

We would play this every day in the summer at the apartment pool, and I can tell you that every year, it gets more and more exhausting. I'm getting older and she's getting bigger. Which is why I wouldn't miss this for anything, no matter how tired I might be, because one day, I won't be able to do it.

And Caitlyn's loving this.

At the apartment pool, she could see where I was going, but the darkened water of the lake makes it a little more of a challenge.

We keep playing. She screams with delight every time I throw her, but soon, I can't throw her as far. I'm so tired that I stop going underwater in between throws. She swims back, laughing and crying out, "Throw me, Dad!"

I do.

Again, and again, and again.

While my enthusiasm is quickly draining, Caitlyn is showing no signs of slowing down.

"Throw me!"

I grunt as I hurl her away.

SPLASH!

Her head bobs out of the water and she comes paddling back.

"Again!"

"Okay."

I catch her under her arms and throw her across the water. She resurfaces and swims back.

"Again!"

I do, but I'm so tired. Her legs aren't even clearing the surface when I throw her. She splashes down, pops back up, laughs, and comes back.

"Again!" she cries as she leaps at me.

I can't anymore. It's not that I don't want to, I just can't—but I don't want to disappoint her. I try to throw her, but it's more like a shove. Thankfully, she doesn't seem to care. She loves it.

"Okay. That's enough," I say, breathlessly.

"No! Again!" she cries.

I oblige. I try to make it the grand finale and launch her as hard as I can.

It's better than my previous attempt, but that's it. I'm done. I can't do this anymore. I need to sit down.

She resurfaces, more thrilled than ever.

She hastily bobs her way back to me, laughing.

"Again!" she cries, and leaps at me.

I hate her. I hate my daughter.

Enraged, I dodge to the side. As she falls past me, I put my hand on the back of her head and hold her underwater.

She knows. She knows and she's going to tell, and it will ruin everything!

Suddenly, it's night. The Nightingale House looks different, somehow. The yard is different. Mildred's house is gone. I can feel my daughter grab at my wrist as she struggles.

"Let him go."

Nicole.

She's standing right next to me, not the broken Nicole from

my nightmare—no, it's the Nicole I knew. But her eyes are filled with rage.

"Let. Him. Go," she says.

I blink.

It's daytime.

I'm in the lake. My hand is still on the back of Caitlyn's head, holding her underwater as she struggles.

I quickly pull it away.

Caitlyn bursts out of the water, hacking and coughing.

"Caitlyn! Oh my God! I'm so sorry!"

She shakes her head, coughs again, and smiles. She leaps up at me and playfully screams. She hangs on my shoulders and tries to push me underwater. She thinks it's a game.

I can't. I can't do this. What just happened? What did I just do?

"Sweetheart, stop. Please, stop. Stop!"

Caitlyn falls off my shoulders and back into the water.

I start walking back towards the shore.

"Dad, where are you going?" she asks, disappointed.

"Dad's tired," I say. "I'm going to sit down for a minute. You keep playing."

My legs are going to give out. I go to the porch, grab a towel and a chair, and bring them down onto the lawn to be closer to keep an eye on Caitlyn.

What was that? Am I really so tired that I would be angry at Caitlyn for wanting to play with me?

My trembling is not from the cold water. I wrap the towel around my shoulders. Caitlyn continues to laugh and play.

It was so vivid.

I can get irritable when I haven't slept but that was something I've never experienced: hatred. Hatred for my own daughter. I can still feel the sensation of Caitlyn struggling against my grip. The rage in Nicole's eyes. She never looked at me like that. I don't even know where I would remember that from. It was a nightmare. Maybe I fell asleep on my feet. Is that what happened? Is that even a thing?

I feel like I'm going to be sick.

I need sleep. I can't do another restless night, chasing the sound of dripping water, and having vivid nightmares. That reminds me that I need to look for that drip before it gets dark, but for right now, the sun is starting to warm me. My nerves are calming.

"Dad, are you getting back in?"

"Not right now, pumpkin. I'm going to sit here and watch for a bit, okay?"

She pouts but then dives under the water.

I know I shouldn't while Caitlyn is swimming, but maybe just a quick nap. A short shut-eye to get my wits back. I'm not sure I can even help it. My eyelids droop. My breathing slips into a rhythm. My head lists to the right and I catch a glimpse of Mildred stepping off her porch and walking in my direction.

"Damnit," I whisper.

"How we doin'?" she cheerily asks once she's within earshot.

Caitlyn waves. "Hi, Mildred!"

"Hi, sweetie!"

She turns to me and stops. Her smile vanishes.

"Jesus," she says, quietly. "You look like shit."

"I haven't been sleeping well."

"It shows." She plops herself onto the grass beside my chair. "Everything okay?"

"Yeah ... well ... not really. Problems writing."

She shrugs. "It's probably gonna take some time. New house. New town."

"Having problems with the house, too ... Mildred, the couple that lived here before us—"

"The Thompsons?"

"Yeah. Did they have any problems with the house? Leaking pipes? Drafts? Anything?"

She thinks for a moment. "They had raccoons under the porch

in the summer of '97. Other than that, they lived in that house for thirty years and loved every minute of it. Nothing like what you're talking about and I'm sure they would have told me. We were close."

"Then why now?" I groan, more to myself.

Caitlyn shrieks with laughter from the water.

Mildred looks at her and then back at me and has a thought. "Caitlyn?" she calls.

"Yes, Mildred?"

"Tuesday night, we are having a sleepover at my house. Just you and me. We're going to watch movies, eat cookies, and play games."

Caitlyn stops splashing. "Really?"

I sit up. "Mildred, you don't have to do that—"

"Listen," she says, lowering her voice. "You *really* look like shit. Literally, you look like a spent turd in a chair. Let me take her off your hands for one night. You can have the house to yourself. Get some sleep or, better yet, go out. Whatever you need to do."

After a brief consideration, I have to admit that it sounds like a great idea.

"You sure?" I ask.

Mildred nods and turns back to Caitlyn, who is still waiting for an answer.

"You bet your cutie little booty. Tuesday night, we're having a Girls' Night."

Caitlyn excitedly splashes. "Okay!"

"Thank you, Mildred," I say. "That's incredibly kind."

She waves me off. "It'll be fun. I would offer to take her tonight or Monday, but I may have a gentleman caller."

*

That night, I'm tucking Caitlyn into bed by the soft glow of the night-light.

112

"Are you excited to stay over at Mildred's on Tuesday?"

She nods, exhausted from playing in the lake.

I kneel beside the bed and stroke her hair. Her little medallion rests on the nightstand.

"Are you liking school?"

She nods, again. "I really like Ms. Hancourt."

"Good. Are you making friends?"

"I made one friend."

This is the first mention of a new friend since we moved.

"Really? Is she in your class?"

"No, but she follows me to school sometimes."

"Oh … Does she live in town?"

"No. She lives here."

"Here? What do you mean?"

"In our house. She's the one I told you about. She's happy we're here, because she hasn't had anyone to play with in a long time."

My heart sinks. It's back. Since that night with the necklace, she hasn't mentioned her imaginary friend. I thought it was over. Now, she's retreating into make-believe, again.

"This is your imaginary friend?"

"She's real. She stays in my closet."

I glance over at the closed closet doors. "Is she in there right now?"

She glances over my shoulder and an odd smile plays on her lips.

"No."

"Oh … Then, where is she?"

"She's behind you."

It's the certainty with which she said it that's causing the goosebumps to race across my skin. I know that it's the power of her suggestion, but it suddenly feels like there *is* someone standing behind me—and I can't turn around. It would only encourage her behavior.

"Okay," I say, quietly. "That's enough for tonight." I kiss her forehead. "Get some sleep."

I lean back and her eyes are already closed.

I stand, motionless. Finally, unable to resist, I turn around.

A man is staring at me.

I catch my scream mid-throat. It's my own reflection, staring at me from the mirror of Caitlyn's vanity.

I look back at Caitlyn. Her eyes are closed but she's lightly smiling. I can't tell if she's asleep. As I walk across the floor, I can't shake the feeling that there's someone else in the room. Fighting the urge to look back, I step into the hallway and close her door.

14

The next morning, after another night of troubled sleep on the couch, Caitlyn and I are discussing her upcoming sleepover while I make waffles for breakfast. She's excited, but something is gnawing at my chest. It finally hits me as the bus rumbles away with Caitlyn on board; tomorrow night will be the first night that Caitlyn and I have spent apart since Nicole's death. Granted, she's only going to be next door, but the idea of us not sleeping under the same roof casts a shadow over my afternoon. I spend another day, staring at the blank page, unable to write. I even stupidly get emotional over the idea that one day, Caitlyn will move out, and I'll be alone. Yes, I'm perfectly aware that she's eight. I'm attributing my heightened emotions to my lack of sleep.

So, throughout the course of the day, I decide that tonight, Caitlyn and I are going to have some fun.

*

I'm waiting to pounce when she comes in through the door after school.

"Do you have any homework?" I ask.

"A little," she answers, apprehensively.

"Let's do it. Let's get it done, right now."

"Why?"

"Because you and I are hitting the town."

We rifle through her reading and math assignments. I try not to help her too much, but I want our evening underway and make my math hints entirely too obvious.

Once we finish, we head out to the car.

"What do you feel like for dinner? Anything you want."

"Anything?"

"Anything."

"Can we have waffles?" she asks. "I know we had them for breakfast, but I like waffles."

"Excellent choice."

We find an IHOP just outside of Kingsbrook and feast on Belgian waffles, swimming in syrup and piled high with whipped cream. After that, we go roller skating, which is painful on such a full stomach, but she holds my hand as we skate around the rink, so it's worth it. I'm treating it like I won't see her for months, rather than a simple twenty-four-hour period where she'll be next door.

By the time we make it back to the house, I'm wiped out, but Caitlyn is wired.

"Okay. That is a wrap. Go get ready for bed," I tell her.

"I'm still awake."

"How? How is that possible? Because I'm beat."

"That's because you're old," she laughs.

"Hardy har har, Little Missy. Get ready for bed. You need a good night's sleep for Mildred's tomorrow."

"Ugh …" She rolls her eyes and heads upstairs.

I sort through the mail as water begins to run through the pipes in the wall, on its way to the upstairs bathroom. There's some junk mail for Nicole. It's irritating to get the odd mailer from a magazine or credit card company addressed to her. It's an unwelcome reminder that she's gone.

The water shuts off and a moment later, I hear a rhythmic thumping coming from her room.

"Caitlyn?"

I climb the stairs and find her jumping on her bed.

"Hey! Knock it off! We talked about this," I admonish, but not too harshly.

"You said I could do anything I wanted tonight," she says, in between leaps.

"Except break the bed, young lady."

She lands with a giggle in a sitting position.

"So, 'anything I want' doesn't mean 'anything I want'?" she asks.

Great. She's beginning to grasp the concept of technicalities.

"Fine. One more thing, but I have to approve it, and then you have to go to sleep."

She scrunches up her face in thought and it's like a lightbulb turns on over her head.

"I want to play hide-and-seek like at Sarah's birthday party!" she proclaims.

I nod. "All right."

She flies from the bed and down the stairs.

"Just one round," I say, following her. "Then you have to go to bed."

She stops in the middle of the living room and gives me a thumbs-up.

"Do you want to turn the lights off like at Sarah's party?" I ask.

She hesitates and grows worried.

"It's okay," I say. "We can leave the lights on."

She frowns. "Then it'll be too bright."

The evening is suddenly in danger of ending on a downer.

"I've got it!" I proclaim and head towards the kitchen.

There's a bag of tea candles in the pantry that Nicole and I purchased forever ago at IKEA. I bring them into the living room and hold them up. Caitlyn approves. We spend the next twenty minutes or so placing lit candles in every room, hallway, and even on the stairs. The only room we ignore is the basement. Then, we turn off the lights.

The effect is breathtaking. This is the lighting the house was built for. Every room is filled with a soft, flickering glow and dancing shadows.

"All right," I say, once we return to the living room. "You want to hide first, or should I?"

"I want to hide first."

"Okay. I'm going to go into the bathroom and count to fifty. You better hide good."

She eagerly nods, but stands rooted to the spot, not wanting to give away the direction she's going to run.

"Here I go." I slowly begin stepping backwards towards the bathroom. "One ... two ..."

"Dad! You can't start counting until you're in the bathroom!"

"Three ..."

"Dad!"

I finally back into the bathroom and slowly close the door as I continue loudly counting. "Four ..."

The door clicks shut.

Her footsteps hurtle across the living room and up the stairs. I feel bad that the house won't let her conceal where she's going and continue counting. Her footsteps run down the upstairs hall and suddenly stop right above me. Then, in between the numbers I'm calling out, I can hear her talking but it's too muffled to understand. Her tone sounds like she's quietly pleading with someone. I wait, straining to hear ...

She stops talking.

What is she waiting for?

Oh, shit. I've stopped counting.

"Thirty-nine ..." I call out.

Immediately, her footsteps resume down the hall, and as best as I can tell, stop in the upstairs bathroom.

I continue counting, speeding it up to reach the end.

"Forty-eight … forty-nine … fifty!" I open the door and step out. "Ready or not, here I come!"

I begin 'stalking' through the rooms on the first floor, pretending to be a giant ogre who is genuinely mystified as to where she could be.

"Where is Caitlyn?" I say, in a deep, gravelly voice as I roam the living room and poke my head into the Writing Room. "Where is she?"

I turn and begin stomping up the stairs. "Fee, Fi, Fo, Fum …"

I stand at the top and stare down the hallway.

"Caitlyn …? Oh, Caitlyn?"

A candle is on the nightstand in her room, giving it an otherworldly glow. The pile of stuffed animals on the window seat watches me as I prowl around the room. "Where is that stinker?" I say, loud enough for it to carry down the hall to the bathroom where I know she's hiding. I stomp over to her closet. "Is she in HERE?!" I dramatically throw open the door. Of course, she's not. "Hmmm …"

I leave the closet open and stomp out into the hall. "I think I smell her …" I start walking towards the bathroom. "I smell her in the room where all stinky girls go and hide …"

I reach the bathroom door and grasp the handle.

There's a sound behind me.

Startled, I turn just in time to the see the hem of Caitlyn's nightgown as she disappears into her room. Then, there's the sound of her closet doors closing.

"You, little lady, are quite the scamp," I laugh.

She had been hiding in the guestroom and tried to sneak into her room after I searched it.

I triumphantly walk back down the hall, into her room, and over to the now-closed closet doors. "That was really clever to try to hide in your room after I searched it." I grasp the knob. "But now … I'VE GOT YOU!"

I throw open the closet doors.

The clothes hang from the rack and the basket is on the floor … but Caitlyn's not here.

"Caitlyn?"

I can't wrap my head around this. I kneel down and push the clothes basket aside. I turn on the closet light. It's empty. "Caitlyn?"

"Dad?"

I jump and pull myself out of the closet. Caitlyn is standing in the doorway, looking disappointed and hurt.

"How did—? Where were you?" I ask.

"I was hiding in the bathroom. In the shower."

I look from her to the empty closet and back. "But … you ran across the hall … I saw you."

I realize her hurt and disappointment aren't directed at me. Caitlyn looks around the room.

"Katherine, I told you not to play," she says.

I glance around, trying to figure out who she's talking to.

"Sweetheart … who's Katherine?"

Her eyes find me. The candlelight flickers across her face. For the first time in my life, I'm afraid of my daughter. It's like she knows something I don't and she's trying to protect me from it.

"I don't want to play anymore," she mumbles and goes downstairs, leaving me alone in her room.

June 15th, 1900

Today, my wish was granted! Well, not all of it, but I finally go to see him!

I won't bore you with more of my miserable situation, the pharmacy's woes, or Father and Carol's constant arguing.

This entry is going to be about nothing but him!

The decorations in the square for the Fourth of July Celebration have started. They've begun constructing the games and concession stalls that will fill the green.

I'll admit that I don't think much of Kingsbrook, but the speed of the construction and the scale of the decorations are impressive. The view out of the pharmacy window is filled with men building the stalls and women hanging the bunting from every lamppost and the gazebo. At least it is something new to watch from behind the counter at the pharmacy, which is where I spend most of my time.

Father was in the storeroom, executing his plan to save the pharmacy with cheap liquor. He purchased it from a man in Portland. I asked him 'who?' and he would only answer, 'an associate'. It arrived in a wooden box. The bottles were big, bulky, and unlabeled. Father also received a shipment of smaller, sample-sized bottles. He had already made a sign advertising it as one of the finest cognacs from Paris. So, as I was saying, he was in the storeroom, transferring the cheap alcohol into the smaller bottles, when I spotted a group of official-looking men walking across the square, led by the Mayor.

There was Thomas. He stood out from the rest of the group with his blue eyes and tall frame.

"Father, I'm stepping out," I said.

"Where are you going?" he asked from behind the curtain.

"Out. Only for a moment."

I didn't wait for an answer. There was no one in the store, so he didn't have to worry about any theft taking place.

I ran around the counter, out the door, and into the warm afternoon.

The air was filled with the sounds of hammers and saws.

I had no plan. I only wanted to see him and for him to see me.

I could barely make out what the Mayor's voice was saying above the din of construction. He was explaining the parade route through the square and the order of the festivities. The group of men surrounding him were nodding, chatting, and laughing among themselves.

I wanted to get Thomas's attention without anyone else noticing but it was impossible. I couldn't wave like a child, making a scene, and embarrass him in front of everybody.

Finally, the Mayor made a sweeping gesture around the square, saying something about a marching band. Everyone in the group followed his gesture with their eyes. To my satisfaction, everyone continued following the Mayor's gesture except for Thomas, who stopped when he saw me.

Our eyes met. His lips curled into a smile and he nodded in my direction. It was our own little moment amid the crowd.

I know it wasn't much, but it was everything that I had been hoping for. That one look, that one nod, erased days of misery and boredom.

So, of course, it had to be slightly spoiled.

Among the group being led around by the Mayor was his daughter, Patricia Fleming.

My focus had been on Thomas and I hadn't seen her. She had been lost in the crowd, but as they moved on, she stopped and was staring at me. She had only been a few feet away from Thomas and it was clear from her expression that she had seen the whole thing. She nodded at me in that condescending politeness that she has perfected.

So be it. Let her be jealous all she wants that I'm the center of Thomas's attention.

I didn't return her acknowledgment. Instead, I turned and walked back into the pharmacy, feeling lighter than air.

The rest of the day was spent watching an endless loop of the memory of his smile and that nod.

At one point, Father came out of the storeroom and asked me why I was humming. I wasn't even aware that I was doing it.

I guess that is what it's like when the sun smiles at you.

15

It's cereal and toast for breakfast this morning. I don't have the energy for anything else.

Last night, I tried to get Caitlyn to talk to me more about 'Katherine', but she refused. She said that she was 'mad at her'. I eventually gave up. Caitlyn went to bed and I went around the house, collecting the spent tea candles. As I walked through every room, I caught myself taking furtive glances around corners and behind doors, almost expecting to find Caitlyn's imaginary friend hiding there.

I made no pretense of almost sleeping in my room. It was going to be another couch night. I watched a Chicago Cubs game I had DVR'd and tried to make sense of it all. In the end, I nodded off somewhere around two in the morning, after having convinced myself that my fatigue and grief were causing me to see and hear things and Caitlyn had used it to reinforce her imaginary friend, who now had a name. That has to stop but I can't do it, right now. I don't want to upset her and then send her to Mildred's. I'll wait until after the sleepover. Two more days won't hurt.

I avoid the conversation when she comes down for breakfast and she doesn't seem to want to talk about last night, either. Instead, we talk about the sleepover.

"After you get on the bus, I'm going to take your stuff over to Mildred's," I tell her, pointing to the pillow and Disney Princess duffel bag she's brought down from her room. "When you get dropped off later today, you can just go to her house. She'll be waiting for you."

"Okay," she replies through a mouth full of Corn Pops.

"If you need anything, you tell Mildred, and she'll call me."

"Dad, I know. You already told me."

"And you be good for Mildred. It's a really nice thing she's—"

"Daaaaaad."

"Caitlyn, this is a big deal. It's the first night we've spent apart since—" I catch myself but it's too late. "It's a big deal, sweetheart."

She nods, lost in thought.

"I love you, kidd-o."

"I love you too, Dad."

*

I step onto Mildred's porch and knock on the door.

She answers with a cup of coffee in her hand and warm smile on her face. "Come on in."

"Just dropping off Caitlyn's things."

The aroma of fresh coffee and the faint trace of her clove cigarettes hang pleasantly in her kitchen as I walk through the door.

"You can set that stuff anywhere. The guestroom is all made up."

"I can't thank you enough for doing this, Mildred. She's really excited."

Mildred laughs. "So am I."

"If anything happens, if you need anything, just call me. I should be home all night."

"Oh God, I hope not. Go out. Have an adventure. Bring home a companion."

It's my turn to laugh. "What about you? How was your night? Did you have a 'gentleman caller'?"

She slyly smiles over the rim of her coffee mug.

"A lady never tells."

*

For three hours, I've been cranking out page after page in the Writing Room. It's not my best, but it's better than what I've been writing, and now, I can no longer ignore the fact that I'm starving. I close my notebook, go to the kitchen, and make myself a sandwich.

I carry it to the alcove, sit at the table, and stare out at the lake as I contently chew and mentally begin outlining the next chapter. Maybe I could get it in before calling it a day. That would be some serious progre—

... drip ... drip ...

I stop.

... drip ... drip ...

"Damnit," I whisper and stand.

... drip ... drip ...

I have to find that damn leak. It's here, in the kitchen. At least, one of them is, because I've heard them all over the house. I scan everywhere and inspect every inch of the ceiling, walls, and take everything out of the cabinets, but there's not a sign of water anywhere, even under the sink.

"Enough," I say out loud.

It's time to call the plumber.

I sit at my computer in the Writing Room and pull up Yelp on the computer. I begin scanning the entries for local plumbers and comparing the reviews. I dial the number of the one with the highest rating.

"So, you're hearing the dripping but you haven't seen any signs of water damage?" a man with a heavy New England accent asks after I complete my rambling description of the problem.

126

"Yeah. I've searched everywhere."

"Hmm … That could be a problem. To find it, we may have to rip up some of the walls."

"Fantastic." I suddenly feel a migraine coming on.

"Do you know when they've done any remodels?"

"I can find out." I have Stelowski's phone number here on my desk, somewhere. "You think they may have done a shoddy job?"

"It's possible. More likely that they haven't changed all the plumbing in the place. Who knows how many patch jobs they've done? Might be something as old as the house."

This is getting more expensive by the moment.

"Shouldn't be too hard find out about the remodels. You said the house was old?" he asked.

"Yeah."

"If it's historic, you can sometimes find some of that stuff online."

"Give me a second," I say and began typing.

"Oh, you don't have to look, now—"

"Hold on. Let me see."

I'm on a mission. If there's more damage happening in the walls every moment that I can't see, I want to take care of it, now.

I enter 'Nightingale House' into the search bar.

There are hundreds of hits, mostly real estate listings, and some photos.

"This could take some time," I sigh in defeat. "I'm not even sure what I'd be looking for."

"No worries. It'll be in the public records, which I think Kingsbrook has online. What we can do is run a scope through the walls, along the pipes, and see where it's coming from …"

He continues laying out his plan while I continue scrolling. This is going to be an ordeal. He's asking something about how attached I am to the hardwood floors. I try to find older articles, hoping to get lucky. There's a society piece from the *Kingsbrook Herald* that's dated 1900, announcing the arrival of the Carringtons at the Nightingale House for the summer holidays. I recognize the names from our tour of the Kingsbrook Historical Society.

I distractedly click on the link.

The page loads.

Suddenly, I'm not breathing.

"Mr. Price?" the plumber asks. "You still there?"

"Yeah … yes … sorry. I'm going to have to call you back." I hang up the phone before he has a chance to answer.

A photo accompanies the article on the screen—a photo of the Carrington family. The caption below reads:

*Thomas and Abigail Carrington and their daughter,
Katherine.*

June 17th, 1900

Every morning, I've been waking and getting to the pharmacy early, hoping that it will be the day that Thomas places another order, and today, just like my wish to see him, I was finally rewarded!

When I went out to the kitchen for breakfast, I found Father sleeping on the sofa in the parlor. I tried to be quiet but he awoke. He made some excuse about staying up too late and accidentally falling asleep on the sofa, as if I don't know what's going on with him and Carol. They hardly ever talk anymore, and I think Father has started drinking.

Working at the pharmacy has become somewhat of an escape for me. I can't stand to be around either Father or Carol. It isn't much of an escape, but at least I'm away from the house. I'm incredibly lonely but there's always the hope of a letter from Thomas.

This morning, I opened the pharmacy a full hour before our posted time. There wasn't much to do, so I took one of the local newspapers and read for a while. Father arrived at the normal hour. He tried to sound upbeat, as he always does, but the bags under his eyes proved too heavy. Father went to the back to do the book-keeping. I dusted the shelves and bottles, just as I had done yesterday while keeping an eye on the front door. I couldn't help myself, and multiple times, I went out to the street to see if the courier was approaching.

Finally, at eleven o'clock, the courier arrived. Father appeared from the storeroom at the sound of the bell and the courier handed him the letter. Father cut open the envelope with the penknife he keeps in his desk in the storeroom and glanced over the note.

I asked if it was from Mr. Carrington, although I knew full well that it was.

Father nodded.

"It's smaller than last week's order," he said with a frown and began assembling the items on the list. To my surprise, they were more feminine in nature—perfume, hair conditioner, cosmetics, etc.

I was confused at first and then had a wonderful thought. He was clearly buying them as a present for me! (I could not have been more mistaken, as what follows will tell.)

I placed the items in the bicycle basket and pedaled to the Nightingale House.

This time, I took care that I was presentable after the ride, making sure no hair was out of place and smoothed out my clothes. I pulled the chain next to the door and heard footsteps. I was prepared to meet him with my own wicked little smile.

The door opened and it was his wife.

She regarded me as if I was a stray cat.

"May I help you?"

I stammered like a fool but finally said, "I have a delivery from the pharmacy."

Thankfully, Thomas hurried in from the living room to save me. "Ah, here it is."

I can't be sure, but I thought I saw Mrs. Carrington recoil from him as he approached.

"I meant to tell you. I ordered some supplies from the pharmacy in case you had forgotten anything in Boston." He took the items from my arms and gave me a glance that told me to play along. "This is the girl from the pharmacy."

Mrs. Carrington said it was nice to meet me. Thomas pointed out that we had met before at my birthday party, which caused her to be embarrassed and worried.

"You bought me that lovely journal," I offered, trying to be helpful.

"Of course, of course," she said, shaking her head. "Forgive me. These past few days have been a whirlwind."

I told her I was sorry to hear about her mother. "I hope she's feeling better."

"Thank you, she is feeling a little better … but … how did you know about my mother's health?"

Thomas came to my rescue, again. "I dropped by the pharmacy to pick up a few things while you were away and we had a brief conversation. She thanked me for the journal. I told her the gift was your idea, which led to her asking about you."

I thought the excuse was perfectly clever.

There was the sound of the back door in the kitchen banging open and small frantic footsteps approaching. Through the dining room burst a young girl with long, straight blonde hair and wearing a very pretty dress. She was laughing but stopped when she almost crashed into Thomas. His look of annoyance caused her to shrink backwards. She shrank even further when she saw that there was a stranger in the room. She drifted towards Mrs. Carrington and clung to her leg. Then, a man entered from the kitchen, out of breath. I recognized him from the party as the driver of the Carringtons' carriage.

"I'm sorry, sir," he said. "We were playing tag and I told her to stay outside, but she didn't listen."

"She seldom does," Thomas grumbled.

Mrs. Carrington introduced the man as their valet, Theodore Whitlock. She then turned her attention to the little girl, hiding behind her hip. "And this little one is our daughter, Katherine."

"Hello, Katherine," I said, but she said nothing.

"You'll have to forgive her. She's painfully shy," Mrs. Carrington said.

I nodded.

She glanced at her husband, then at me. "I can't remember; have we invited you to the Fourth of July Celebration?"

"Yes, ma'am."

"Good. We shall see you then." She looked at her daughter. "Say goodbye, Katherine."

"Bye," the girl whispered.

"It was very nice to meet you, Katherine," I replied.

"I'll show you out," Thomas said, and escorted me to the door.

We walked down the path to the street, where the bicycle was resting against the bushes.

"She was supposed to be gone for a few more days," he quietly said. "I only received the telegram yesterday that she was arriving this morning."

I asked him why he didn't tell her that I had made a delivery to the house before.

"My wife can be suspicious, sometimes."

"I'm sorry to hear that."

"It's understandable around such a beauty as yourself."

Can you believe he would say those words while only a few yards from his home and wife? I can and I relished it.

"You'll forgive me if I don't kiss your hand as before but there might be eyes watching us."

I told him that I understood.

"If I had my way, I'd kiss more of you," he said.

I fought to keep from smiling but lost.

"There also won't be a delivery next week. I'm worried she'll grow more suspicious, but I do expect to see you at the Fourth of July Celebration."

"You may count on it," I said.

His eyes gleamed with approval.

"Until then," he said and walked back towards the house.

My eyes followed and I was certain for a split second, I saw Mrs. Carrington watching us from an upstairs window. The curtain fluttered and she was gone.

I know it's dangerous. I know it's wrong, but I don't care. It's harmless fun. Besides, I have no friends, the pharmacy is failing, and Father and Carol rarely speak. Those beautiful eyes and thrilling conversations are the only good things I have in this town.

I will now begin counting the hours, minutes, and seconds until the Fourth of July.

Good night.

16

Portland Beacon, *September 29th, 1900*

GIRL MISSING

*Police are searching for Katherine Carrington, the eight-year-old
daughter of Thomas and Abigail Carrington. She disappeared from
the platform at the Portland Train Station on the night of the 28th,
sometime around 9:30 p.m.*

*According to a statement by Thomas Carrington and the
family's valet, Theodore Whitlock, the girl wandered off from
the platform while they were securing luggage. After several
minutes of searching, Mr. Carrington reported his daughter
missing to the station superintendent, Frank Buckland, who
contacted the police.*

Under the article is the same photo of the Carringtons from the
Kingsbrook Herald. I quickly return to the search page, desperate
to find out more, but there's just one more article that only states
that she was still missing. After that, the stories stop.

I do a search for Thomas Carrington. There are some short

biographies that mention he was the son of a lumber tycoon, and the articles about the disappearance of his daughter, but nothing else until I come across one more mention in the *Kingsbrook Herald*, dated October 2nd, 1900.

Thomas Carrington, son of Adolphus Carrington, was found dead of a sudden illness early yesterday morning, in the bedroom of his home, the Nightingale House, on Willow Lake.

I stare slack-jawed at the screen. The faces of the Carringtons stare back, especially Katherine with her wide eyes.

The silence of the house becomes unbearable.

I'm rethinking everything that I've dismissed over the last two weeks; the noises, the visions, the girl I saw last night in the hall.

What if …? What if …?

I look up, half expecting to see someone in the room with me. It's empty but I don't feel alone. The shadows have grown long from the setting sun.

Okay. That's it. I'm out.

I shut off the computer and walk out of the Writing Room. I go to the kitchen, grab my keys, wallet, and phone, and leave through the back door.

I need to think right now and I damn well can't do that in this house.

*

The streetlamps are just beginning to blink on as I park the car in the main square.

My first instinct was to race over to Mildred's and ask Caitlyn about Katherine, but I couldn't do that in front of Mildred without having to explain. I could have taken Caitlyn home and asked her, but that would have ruined the evening and I would eventually have to explain it to Mildred, anyway. I should wait until morning to talk to Caitlyn, but I can't help myself.

134

I pull out my phone and dial.

"Hello?"

"Hey, Mildred. It's Daniel. I just want to make sure Caitlyn's doing okay."

"Yep. She's fine. We're eating pizza and watching movies."

"Great. Can I talk to her real quick?"

"Sure."

The phone changes hands.

"Hi, Dad."

"Hey, pumpkin. How was school?"

"Fine."

"Just 'fine'?"

"Yes," she answers, confidently.

"Did ... did, uh ... did your friend, Katherine, follow you to school today?"

I can hear her fidgeting.

"Caitlyn, did Katherine come to school with you today?"

There's a long pause.

"Dad?"

"Yeah?"

"I don't want to talk about that. I'm still mad at her."

"Okay." I desperately need to know, but I don't want to upset her while she's at Mildred's.

"Can I go back to watching movies with Mildred, now?"

"Of course, sweetheart. Can you put Mildred back on?"

"Okay."

"Good night, pumpkin. I love you."

"Love you too, Dad."

The phone changes hands again.

"Everything okay?" Mildred asks.

"Yeah. I just wanted to hear her voice."

"Don't worry. I'll take good care of her."

"Thank you, Mildred."

"And, Daniel?"

"Yeah?"

"Please, try to have some fun tonight."

*

Sitting in a booth at Murphy's, I stare into my root beer float and listen to the loud laughter from the group of kids in the next booth.

My phone call accomplished nothing. I still need answers but Caitlyn isn't going to give them. Maybe Mildred could talk to her. No. I can't ask her to do that. I don't know who else to talk to. Caitlyn said that Katherine sometimes follows her to school. I need to know if she talks about Katherine at school or acts like Katherine is there, but there's no one that I can—

Wait. There is somebody I can ask.

I take out my wallet and find the card with Denise Hancourt's contact info.

'You promised you would only call if it was an emergency,' I remind myself.

'This is an emergency.'

'You're going to have to explain that you think your daughter is talking to a dead girl. Do you want her teacher to think you're insane?'

'You're having an argument with yourself. So, I'd say we're past that.'

I dial before I can change my mind.

"Hello?"

"Ms. Hancourt?"

"Yes."

"Hi … umm. Hi. This is Daniel Price, Caitlyn's daughter. I mean, her— I'm Caitlyn's dad." I wince in a manner that has to be audible through the phone.

"Oh. Hi. How are you?"

"Good. Uh, good … How are you?" I have not thought this through, at all.

"I'm good. Everything all right?"

"Well … Look, I'm sorry for calling you outside of office hours, but I'm a little worried about Caitlyn and I wanted to talk to you to see—"

The group of kids in the next booth erupts in laughter over something on one of their phones.

"—if she was acting strangely."

"I'm sorry. I didn't catch that."

"Sorry. It's a little loud in here."

"Where are you?"

"That ice-cream shop on the square."

"Murphy's?" she asks.

"Yeah."

"I love that place. I live right around the corner."

"Oh." My mind quickly comes up with a plan to buy myself some more time to figure out what to say. "Care to join me?"

There's a pause and then a light laugh.

"Sure."

*

Minutes later, she walks through the door and spots me.

I hastily stand as she approaches.

"Thank you so much for coming to talk to me, Ms. Hancourt."

"Of course. And please, it's 'Denise'. We talked about that."

"Right, right, right."

We sit in the booth.

"Actually, I should be thanking you," she says, casually removing her jacket and tossing it onto the seat beside her. "I had to get out of my place. Grading, paperwork, filling out forms. The first couple weeks of the year are always a mess. I really needed a break."

One of the high school kids working behind the counter waves to Denise.

"The usual, Ms. Hancourt?"

She nods and smiles. "You bet." She notices my expression. "I told you; I love this place."

"To the point that you're a regular?"

"Guilty. So, what's up?"

"I wanted to know how Caitlyn was doing."

"As far as I can tell, she's doing fine."

"Is she … Is she making friends?"

"She keeps to herself, but that's not surprising for a kid in a new school, and after what happened … I think she's handling it well."

The high school kid steps out from behind the counter with a foamy cappuccino and sets it down in front of Denise.

"Thank you," she says, reaching for her purse.

I hastily get out my wallet. "No, no, no. I got this."

"Daniel, you really don't have to."

"What's the total?" I ask.

"Four seventy-five," the kid replies.

I hand him a ten. "Keep it."

"Thanks." The kid smiles and heads back to the counter.

Denise raises an eyebrow as she brings the cup to her lips. "Are all best-selling authors such big spenders?"

"Only until their first flop."

She snorts, sending puffs of foam in every direction. She tries to cover her mouth but it's too late. The joke, compounded with the foam on the tip of her nose and glasses, causes us to burst into laughter.

Once we get ourselves under control, she relaxes. "Okay. Now that the ice is sufficiently broken, what's on your mind? You're worried that Caitlyn's not making any friends?"

"It's, uh, it's slightly crazier than that."

She leans forward, elbows on the table.

"Intriguing. Go on."

I proceed with my plan, which is to tell her everything, starting

138

from the day we moved in, to Caitlyn's 'friend', to our visit to the Kingsbrook Historical Society, to our game of hide-and-seek, to my discovery this afternoon of Katherine Carrington's disappearance.

"—and that's when I called you."

She's been listening in rapt attention, her mouth hanging open. For a moment, I wonder if she believes the crazy theory that has been building in the shadows of my psyche; that my daughter might be talking to a ghost. Then, her lips curl into a smile.

"That is … amazing," she says.

"But?"

"Well, I mean, Daniel, there's a perfectly logical explanation for all of this."

"That's what I thought, too, but I'm having a hard time finding it. How could she have just happened to pick the name of a girl that lived in that house, who disappeared over a hundred years ago for her imaginary friend?"

Denise ponders it over a sip of her cappuccino.

"She could have seen something at the historical society. Maybe she saw Katherine's name in a photo or an article."

"But she's had the imaginary friend since right after we moved in, and that was days before we went to the historical society."

"Yeah, but she didn't use the name 'Katherine' until last night, right?"

"Yes … I guess I hadn't thought of that."

"So, she had the imaginary friend, which isn't unusual at all, and then decided it was Katherine after seeing something at the historical society, or maybe she saw something about it online, like you did."

My anxiety is quickly evolving into embarrassment. As it grows, I look down at the table to avoid making eye contact with her.

"Doesn't that sound more likely than your daughter talking to and you seeing a ghost?"

She's being nice and I'm an idiot. Here is a grown adult telling me that there are no monsters under the bed.

I shake my head. "I am so sorry that I called you out here."

"No! No! It's okay."

"You have to think that I'm crazy."

"Not at all! Daniel, raising her on your own, after what happened, a new town, you said you're not sleeping, and if you'll excuse me for saying, but you look it. Something like this was bound to happen."

"I appreciate you letting me off easy, but I've wasted your time."

"Knock it off. This is so much more fascinating than the other calls I got from parents today. And, I got my usual," she says, lifting her cup and taking a sip. "Plus, it's a hell of a story. Are you going to write about it?" She asked it in a joking-but-not-really-joking tone.

I shake my head. "Not my genre. I'm more of a political thriller type of guy."

"I know. I read *In the Shadows of Justice*."

"Really?"

"Oh, yeah. It's not every day a best-selling author moves to your town."

"Did you like it?"

"I did. When am I getting a sequel?"

"I need a good night's sleep first."

"Best-selling author …" she muses. "What's that like?"

I'm dying to tell her. This has turned into one of the first conversations in a while with someone that's not about Nicole's death and it's taking my mind off the house. It's taken a pleasant turn and I'm in no rush to have it end.

I glance out the window, across the square.

"You know what? I haven't eaten anything since early this afternoon and I'm starving. As a way of saying thank you and for putting my mind at ease, can I buy you dinner?"

17

After an initial hesitation, she agrees to my offer. We walk across the square to La Piazza, Kingsbrook's fanciest, and only, Italian restaurant. I'm a meat and potatoes man. I've been learning to cook because I want to make sure Caitlyn eats well. I'm still a novice, but Denise is an outright foodie, which was the product of a semester studying in Tuscany.

"That's sounds terrible," I say with mock sympathy.

"Yes. Vineyards and cafés. It was truly awful."

"And this was towards your degree in …?"

"Political Science."

"Riiiiight."

"I've always wanted to be a writer," she says over her glass of wine. "They say everyone has at least one good book in them."

"Well, I hope that's not true or I'm out of a job."

She picked out a bottle of wine, insisting that we split it, but I reminded her that I haven't had my first flop, yet.

She chuckles but then grows quiet. "Listen, I really do appreciate you buying me dinner, but I need to be clear that … I don't want to seem ungrateful … but …"

"No. Please, I completely understand. I wanted to know what was going on with Caitlyn. That's all. And after the day— no, weeks that I've had, I needed to get out for a night. This is my way of saying thanks for helping me with Caitlyn … and for reminding me that there are no such things as ghosts."

She laughs.

I glance around the restaurant and to my horror, I hear myself blurt out, "You know, I think this may be the first time I've been to a restaurant with another adult since my wife—" I stop myself mid-sentence.

It's like a lead ball just crashed onto the table in the middle of the conversation.

"I'm sorry," I say, shaking my head. "I was thinking out loud."

"Nothing to be sorry about," she says, reassuringly. "Again, I can't imagine what you and Caitlyn have been through. To lose someone you love like that; it's not fair."

There it is, again, like before in her classroom. Her answer is perfect, as though she truly understands.

"No, it's not," I reply.

There's a silence that's not uncomfortable. Then, she seamlessly shifts gears.

"So, *In the Shadows of Justice* …"

"Yeah …?"

"I have a question."

"Fire away."

She takes the bottle of wine and refills our glasses. "You know about your little plot hole, right?"

I cast my eyes to the ceiling. "The guy's car?"

"The guy's car! How did he get back to the car? He left it at the house!"

She's right about the plot hole. It's something my editor and I missed, but the internet definitely did not. However, that's not what I'm thinking about. It's her handling of Nicole. She handled it in a way that only someone who had experienced a similar tragedy would. There's something there in her past. I know it.

For the moment, I file it away, and we delve into the details of *In the Shadows of Justice*.

*

We spend the main course breaking down the novel, discussing character arcs and fun stuff like who we would cast in the main roles, should the big-screen adaptation ever come to fruition. Denise knows her stuff and could absolutely be an author. We order another bottle of wine and take our time.

After the main course, the waiter clears our plates and asks us if we'd like any dessert.

I'm all in, but Denise gives me a pleading look.

"I'm worried that this is getting a little expensive."

I lean in over the table. "If you don't let us get tiramisu, I'm never speaking to you, again."

Without missing a beat, she throws her hands up in feigned disgust. "Fine." She looks at the waiter. "He's such a jerk."

"Yes, ma'am," the waiter says and walks away.

"And two espressos, please," she calls after him.

The tiramisu arrives in dainty teacups and perfectly pairs with the espressos.

We've been talking for hours about anything and everything. We're clicking on every cylinder.

Finally, it reaches the point where we're the last two diners in the restaurant, and the chairs are being placed on the tables.

Our poor waiter has had enough, and respectfully drops the check.

I happily pluck it from the table.

"Are you sure?" Denise asks.

"More than you know. This is exactly what I needed."

She smiles. "Me too. Thank you, Daniel."

*

143

She accepts my offer to walk her home, and even though she lives just around the corner, we decide to take the long way.

We stroll through Kingsbrook, admiring the old houses, and talking of this and that—her job, other genres that I might want to try, her travels, where we grew up, etc.

Eventually, the conversation slows, and I can't contain my curiosity any longer.

"Can I ask you something?"

"Sure."

"Well, it's a little personal and if you don't want to answer, I completely understand."

"Ooooh. This sounds interesting."

"Well, I've formed a theory and I might be way off-base."

"A theory about me?"

"Well, it's more of a general theory, but … yes."

"I know so much about you. It only seems fair. Ask away."

"Okay. Here goes … I sort of feel like anyone who has been through the kind of loss I've been through, they can recognize it in other people. I could be totally wrong, but I'm pretty sure I see it in you."

She stops and stares at me.

Oh no. I may have just stepped way over a line, but her expression softens.

She scoffs. "Is it that obvious?"

"I'm a writer. I'm very observant," I reply in an attempt at humor.

She sadly smiles and we resume our slow stroll.

After a thoughtful silence, she takes a breath.

"It was back in Boston. I was married to a man I loved and he loved me. We wanted to start a family and we had a son—Toby. When he was seven, he started getting really weak. We took him in for tests. He had something called aplastic anemia. His, uh, his bone marrow wouldn't … We lost him … and it wasn't quick. It took a year … a year of helplessly watching him suffer … After that, our marriage disintegrated. We were scared to have another child because we worried what would happen. We couldn't move on. We were stuck in that horrible place ... We couldn't be together anymore, even though we still loved each other ... I'm sure we still do, but I haven't spoken to him in years ... I don't even know where he is ..." She shakes her head. "I think that's why I became a second-grade teacher. Being around children the same age as Toby when he ... left, it's like I get to experience that part of him, you know?"

We continue walking in silence.

"It's not fair," I say.

She sadly smiles. "No. No, it's not."

"Thank you for telling me."

"Not too many people know that story, so consider yourself lucky."

In that moment, I feel closer to her than I've felt to anyone in a while.

She stares down at the sidewalk, lost in her own tormented world; a world of what could have been, what should have been but will never be. I know that world, well.

"Man, how great is tiramisu, though?" I dramatically sigh.

She laughs and lightly nudges me with her elbow.

*

"This is me."

We stop in front of a large, Victorian home that has been separated into units.

"Daniel, I had an absolutely amazing time. Thank you."

"Denise, this was a perfect evening, and if you ever need a break from grading and paperwork, let me know. We'll do this again, and you can tell me all about the novel *you're* writing."

"Deal," she laughs. Then, she grows somber. "Listen, I know tonight was nothing but harmless, and we're adults, but let's keep it to ourselves, okay? It's not technically against the rules for a teacher to see the parent of a student socially, but Principal Craig really, *really* frowns on it and I'm still relatively new to Concord. If it got around, it could make things kind of difficult for me at work."

"Our secret. My lips are sealed. Scout's honor."

She smiles.

"Good night, Daniel."

"Good night, Denise."

We hug.

"Thank you, again," she says next to my ear.

"Thank you."

She turns and walks up the path to the door. I wait on the sidewalk as she gets out her key and opens the door. She looks back at me and gives me a slight wave.

I wave back.

Once she closes the door, I begin walking back to the main square, calmer and more content than I've been in months.

*

The smile hasn't left my face by the time I pull into the driveway of the Nightingale House.

I walk through the front door and flip on the light, filling the living room with a warm glow. With a flourish, I toss my jacket onto the couch. I've got the place to myself, and I'm going to enjoy it for a while before I go to bed.

I stride into the kitchen and grab a beer from the fridge … and then make it two. I take my beers out into the living room and plop down onto the couch. Firing up the television, I find the Cubs game that I DVR'd this afternoon. I kick off my shoes, prop my feet up on the coffee table, crack open a beer, and settle in.

Look, I know this may not seem like the height of cutting loose to you, but for me, it's kind of a big deal. For the next few hours, with the place to myself, I get to belch as loud as I want. I can swear at the television as loud as I please (and it's the Cubs, so it will happen frequently), and best of all, I can fast-forward through the commercials and the pitching changes. This is the most 'at home' I've felt since we moved in.

I'm halfway through my second beer, sitting forward on the couch as the Cardinals mount a rally in the top of the ninth. Bases loaded, one out, and the Cubs are clinging to a one-run lead. The Cardinals batter slaps one on the ground towards the hole between short and third. I curse because it's going into the outfield, but at the last moment, the shortstop snags it, pivots, and throws to second. The second baseman bare hands it, drags his foot across the base, and fires to first. The ball pops into the first baseman's glove a fraction of a second before the runner reaches the bag. Double play. Game over. Cubs win.

I jump off the couch and yell in triumph, because I clearly had something to do with this victory, even though the game was played earlier this afternoon.

This has officially been a good day.

I finish my beer and head upstairs to my room, pausing outside Caitlyn's door.

It feels strange for her room to be so dark. I can't tell you why, maybe it's the slight buzz I have going from the beer, but I quickly step inside, reach down, and flip on the night-light before walking down the hall to my own room.

I change into some pajama pants and a tee-shirt. While scrubbing my face and brushing my teeth in the bathroom, I start making plans for tomorrow. Let's shoot for three chapters. It's an ambitious goal but in my current mood, I'm confident that I can get it done.

I hit the light, step out of the bathroom, and climb into bed, taking up my customary side.

The moon is visible through the window. The silvery light cuts sharp angles across the fireplace.

It's unbelievably quiet.

How long should I wait before asking Denise to grab dinner again? Not romantically. That's not what I'm looking for. It was just such a great night, and it's been a while since one of those and I wouldn't mind doing it again in the not-too-distant future.

I sigh, roll onto my side, and see Nicole.

She's there, in the bed, lying next to me. Her body is shattered. Blood runs down her face and seeps into the bed. Her open, lifeless eyes stare blankly ahead.

I tumble out of the bed, onto the floor, and back away until my back slams into the wall. I reach up and hit the light switch.

The bed is empty.

I remain on the floor with my back against the wall. My hands and legs are violently trembling.

It's grief. I know it's just grief. It's some part of my sleep-starved brain laying a guilt trip on me for spending an evening with another woman and not thinking about Nicole.

I press my hands against the side of my head and wait for my body to stop shaking.

Finally, I stand up and grab my pillow from the bed.

It's going to be another night on the couch … and maybe another beer.

July 4th, 1900

My hands are shaking so hard, it's difficult to write.

Because Father insisted on being open during the Fourth of July Celebration, one of us had to work. Carol left yesterday to visit her sister in Philadelphia. At least, that's what Father told me. So, one of us was going to have to work and one was going to the picnic. He wanted to go so that he could talk up the pharmacy. I argued that I had been offered the invitation and it would be rude if he attended without me. It took some convincing but Father finally allowed me to attend the Carrington's Fourth of July Celebration, but only after I promised to mention the pharmacy to everyone at the picnic. It was a lie, but I don't care.

I spent far too long in front of my mirror. I tried on three different outfits and settled on a green summer dress. I also wore the butterfly necklace.

The day could not have been more perfect. There was red, white, and blue bunting on every house and ribbons on the trees in the square. The parade wouldn't start for another two hours, but people had already begun to stake their claims on the sidewalks to watch. The main square was beautiful. There were games and concession stands.

I ventured close enough to the pharmacy to peer inside. Father was behind the counter, reading a newspaper. There were no customers, of course. I felt a pang of guilt at how miserable he looked, but it's only fair for all the time I've wasted behind that counter.

It got warmer and I ducked into the only other establishment that was open, besides the pharmacy, which was the soda shop. I purchased a chocolate malt with some of the leftover money Mr. Carrington gave me, and enjoyed it in a booth, next to the window.

When it was time for the parade, I left the shop and settled into a corner of the square, nabbing a spot right next to the street. As one of Kingsbrook's most esteemed citizens, Thomas was going to be in the parade, and I wanted him to see me. As people all around me sipped lemonade, ate popcorn, and chatted, I began to grow restless.

Finally, there was the distant sound of the marching band. It appeared down at the end of the street. The parade was led by a drum major in full uniform, carrying a baton. He was followed in perfect step by the band playing 'Stars and Stripes, Forever'. Next there were the floats, pulled by teams of horses, from the different social societies of Kingsbrook: the Order of the Elks Lodge, Sons of Union Veterans, Women of Main, and the fire brigade.

Then came the most illustrious residents of Kingsbrook, riding in open-topped carriages and dressed in their finest. There was the Mayor, his wife, and of course, his daughter, the gossip Patricia. She saw me and waved, as if I was part of the peasantry. I waved back, while touching the necklace with my other hand, hoping that she remembered Thomas's instructions she heard while eavesdropping— that I should buy something pretty for myself. To my satisfaction, she stopped waving and glared at me for a moment before the carriage carried her away.

Some of the other residents I recognized from my birthday party, such as Mr. Abernathy, who owns the bank, or Mr. Patterson, who owns the grocer's.

At last, I was rewarded.

There he was, resplendent in his coat tails and top hat with those blue eyes, mustache, and beard. Even though he was sitting, he still seemed to tower above his wife and daughter. As they drew nearer, my heart swelled. I couldn't wait for him to see me. They came even with my spot. I waved and smiled. He saw me. He looked right at me … and nothing. He took no notice of me. He recognized me, surely, but showed no pleasure in it. I was just a face in the crowd. Someone to ignore.

The parade filled the square and stopped. The Mayor got out of his carriage and mounted the steps to the gazebo. He gave some remarks, thanking everyone for their hard work, and declared it the best Fourth of July Celebration Kingsbrook had ever seen. Someone nearby mumbled that he gave the same speech every year. All the while, I couldn't take my eyes off Thomas. He didn't so much as glance at me. After his speech, the Mayor got back in his carriage. The band started up, and the parade marched out of the square.

I couldn't understand it. Had I done something wrong? I wasn't expecting anything grand. Just a small acknowledgment that he was happy to see me. One of our shared, knowing glances. He had no problems with sly winks or smiles before. Why was he ignoring me now? Then, I was furious with myself. I was behaving like a child. What could I really expect of him? His wife and daughter were there. I would see him at the picnic, where I was sure he would pay me at least some attention or maybe contrive a way for us to be alone.

My only means of transportation to the picnic was the pharmacy bicycle, which was in the alley behind the store. To avoid Father, I went around the block to the back of the pharmacy, rather than the front door. I took the bicycle and quietly rode away.

I didn't know how fashionable it would be to arrive on a bicycle, so I took the long way out of town, avoiding the main route, which was sure to be an endless train of guests heading to the picnic. I made it to Willow Lake without being seen, but as there was only one road leading to the Nightingale House, it could no longer be avoided. As I suspected, there was a steady stream of fancy carriages. Even at a distance, I could see the white tables and chairs arranged on the lawn. I did my best to keep my head up as I pedaled alongside the carriages, but it was so humiliating. There were some polite 'hellos' and I caught one or two derisive chuckles.

But the worst was just beginning.

To my horror, I saw that Thomas and Mrs. Carrington were out front, greeting the guests as they arrived. I almost turned and rode away but it was too late. The road wasn't wide enough to turn and if I tried to brake, I would be thrown.

With as much dignity as I could muster, I brought the bike to a stop, rested it against the bushes, and walked to the gate.

Mrs. Carrington smiled at me as if it was all perfectly normal. Thomas looked bored.

"Thank you so much for coming, Ms. Harker," Mrs. Carrington said.

I thanked her for inviting me. As much as I didn't like seeing her there, I was grateful to her for making me feel welcome.

I turned to Thomas. With my back to his wife, I tried to give him a coy smile. "It's good to see you again, Mr. Carrington."

He shook my hand with a cordial grip. "Please enjoy yourself at our home."

He released my hand and went on to the next guest.

That was it. No playful pressing of his finger to my palm. No wink. No vicious smile.

I was no one.

I joined the growing mass of people on the lawn and wished that Father had come instead of me. I tried to be social and make polite conversation while feeling totally out of place. Even my green dress went against the standard white that everyone was wearing. For most of the afternoon, I tried to hide on the outlying fringes of the gathering and avoid speaking to anyone.

As the afternoon wore on, so grew my appetite. I was finally forced to join the crowd as the food emerged from the house. It was carried by waiters who deposited the dishes on long, cloth-covered tables. The valet, Mr. Whitlock, oversaw the proceedings. I found a spot at a table a few yards away from the head table, where Thomas sat with his wife. I noticed the coldness between them. It was the same as I had seen the other day when I made the delivery. They were polite to the guests and each other, but he and his wife clearly didn't have the connection that he and I shared.

In the corner of the lawn, a photographer was setting up a camera.

After the food had been set on the serving tables, Mr. Whitlock conferred with the photographer, who nodded. Mr. Whitlock held up his hand to the crowd.

"Ladies and gentlemen, before dinner, we'd like to take a photograph to commemorate this occasion. The exposure will take twenty seconds. So, if you could please remain very still. Ready?" he asked the photographer who nodded from behind the camera. Mr. Whitlock turned back to us. "Here we go. One, two, three …"

The photographer pulled the shutter open and shouted, "Very still, now!"

The children, including the Carringtons' daughter, continued to run around the edges of the lawn, but their parents were too afraid to move to stop them. They instead hissed at them to settle down.

I couldn't help staring at him. He was such a striking figure. Powerful. A man who got exactly what he wanted.

The photographer snapped the shutter close. "That should do it. Thank you, everyone!"

Mr. Whitlock held up his hands, again. "Thank you, everyone! And now, dinner is served!"

I ate but couldn't taste the food. I was wrapped up in my own misery. I wanted to leave but it would have been a spectacle to get up during dinner, go to the bicycle, and ride away. I was trapped.

It was then that I formulated a plan.

After dinner, everyone would go to the backyard to watch the fireworks. I would follow, but then slip away while everyone was watching the display. I no longer cared about seeing him, since he clearly didn't care about seeing me.

The sun set and cake was served. People relaxed into their chairs, stuffed with food. Conversations slowed as daylight waned. Mr. Whitlock announced that the fireworks would begin shortly and that everyone should go to the backyard.

The Carringtons went first. Once they disappeared around the side of the house, everyone slowly rose to their feet. I stalled for as long as I could and stayed towards the back. Mr. Whitlock waited for everyone to clear the front yard and I noticed that he did not seem happy to see me. I could stall no longer and began following the crowd.

The backyard was beautiful. Lighted torches had been placed around the perimeter, giving it a soft glow. Rows of chairs had been arranged on the grass, with the lake spreading out before them. People were settling in, pleasantly chatting. In the water, there were two floating platforms, where the silhouettes of two men were at work. The cooks and waiters that had been hired for the celebration were coming out of the house to watch the fireworks. The men on the platform gave a signal and Mr. Whitlock began extinguishing the torches, making it darker. I tried to spot Thomas, but everyone had their backs to me and the darkness made it difficult to identify anyone.

The last torch was extinguished and everyone held their breath. Suddenly, a rocket shot upwards from one of the platforms and burst into a red, flowering ball. The crowd gasped and clapped with delight. More fireworks went up, eliciting more cheers.

This was my chance.

A few of the waiters who had been working in the front yard were rushing around the side of the house. I wished to avoid them, so I quietly made my way through the open back door and slipped into the house, unnoticed. I went through the dining room and living room. The concussion from the fireworks shook the walls. I was almost to the front door when suddenly, I was grabbed and pulled into the study. I was shoved up against the wall and lips pressed against mine. I was shocked, then terrified, and then I saw his eyes as he pulled away. He delighted in my expression and kissed me, again. This time, I returned his kiss. It was the most amazing thing I've ever experienced. His hands passed over my dress and under. He pulled away, once more.

"I thought you were ignoring me," I said, breathlessly.

"I had to. My wife is suspicious."

We kissed again.

"Why is she suspicious?"

154

He smiled. "History."

I wasn't sure what he meant but stopped caring when he kissed me again.

"After the celebration," he said, "she'll be going back to Boston. Then, we can—"

"Father?" a small voice asked.

He forcefully shoved me against the wall so that I was hidden behind the door. He was pressing so hard, I couldn't breathe. Through the crack of the open door and the doorframe, I could see his daughter, standing in the living room, looking into the study.

"What the hell are you doing?" he growled.

She cast her eyes down to the floor. "The fireworks scared me and Mother told me to go inside and wait until they are over."

"Then go up to your room."

She hesitated, because going to the foot of the stairs would bring her closer to him, but she relented and went up the stairs.

His hand, which was pressed against my chest, gradually relaxed.

"Did she see us?" I asked.

"She better not have."

It was the first time I had seen him truly angry and I was a little fearful for myself.

"You should go. I'll send for you when they're gone."

I wanted to set his mind at ease and put my hand on his cheek. "Do you promise?"

He smiled. "We leave a key under the table on the porch. I'll place an order and you can use the key to let yourself in." He pulled me closer. "But I warn you; only use the key if you're ready," he said, and kissed me, again.

"For what?" I asked.

He chuckled. "I need to get back to the guests."

He kissed me one last time before going back through the living room and towards the kitchen to rejoin the party.

I went out the front door, past the empty tables and chairs, and grabbed the bike from the bushes.

I was shaking the whole ride back to town. When I arrived at the house, the light in the parlor was on. I found Father sitting in the chair by the fireplace. There was a half-full decanter on the table beside him and a glass in his hand.

"Angel! How was the picnic?" His words were slurred and the air stank of liquor.

I've never seen him like that.

I told him it was fine and that I had talked up the pharmacy. I asked him how business had been. He said it was fine, making liars of us both.

"I'm going to bed," I told him.

"Good night," he drunkenly mumbled.

I dressed for bed, but there is no way I can sleep. My heart is still pounding. My stomach is turning. I thought I was tired but I'm not, so I decided to pour out these words. But now, it's really late and I'm going to try to sleep and dream of what is to come.

Good night.

18

I groan and stretch out, pressing my feet against the opposite armrest.

It was another night on the couch, but if I'm being honest, it may have been the best night of sleep I've had in this house.

Of course, the image of Nicole had been disturbing, but I think my body decided that I was getting sleep, no matter what.

I feel good. Not great, but better than I've felt in a while and I keep playing last night over in my mind, conveniently leaving out the part about going to bed upstairs.

I get up and make myself a full English breakfast and brew a strong cup of coffee. For our honeymoon, Nicole and I took a trip through the UK and stayed at nothing but B&Bs and now, I love an English breakfast. I sit at the alcove and enjoy my breakfast while I stare out the window at the lake.

For the first time, I feel at peace here. The house holds no menace or sense of dread, like before. It's just a house. My house.

After breakfast, I go upstairs, strip down, and jump in the shower. I even catch myself whistling, which is weird for me. My thoughts turn to the novel. I can't wait to hole myself up in the Writing Room and get to work.

But first things first.

I towel off, pull on a pair of jeans and a sweater, and head over to Mildred's.

*

I tramp across the dew-covered grass towards her house, step onto the porch, and knock on the door.

A breeze kicks up off the lake. I turn my head.

Nicole is standing there near the water. The concern in her face, the worry …

"Good morning, Mr. Author."

Mildred has opened the door, wearing a wide grin.

I glance back to the lake. Nicole is gone.

"Hi, Mildred."

"Come on in."

"How'd it go?" I ask, stepping into the kitchen.

"It was great. We played games. We watched a movie."

"Which one?" I ask, gathering Caitlyn's things from the floor by the table.

"*The Wizard of Oz*. We both knew the words to every song."

"That's my girl."

"So," she says, casually taking a sip of coffee. "What did you get up to last night?"

"Nothing. I just had a quiet night at the house."

Her eyes widen and she points an accusatory finger. "Liar!"

"What?"

"Liar! Liar, liar, liar! The lights were off at your house almost all night. You went out!"

"No, I … Look … It wasn't … It was nothing."

My stammering causes her eyes to widen further.

"Something happened."

"No. Nothing happened," I reply.

"It did! Something had to have happened. Why else would you lie about being home?"

My face is burning. "Look, Mildred. I had a great night and I don't want to—"

Her hand flies to her mouth. "Oh my God ... Oh my God! You had sex!"

"Mildred!"

"You did! You got laid!"

"No, Mildred. I did not have sex."

"Then you at least had a date."

"It wasn't a date."

"Ohhhh. I see ... but you were with a woman."

"Okay. Yes, Sherlock. I had dinner with a woman."

"And it went well?" she asks like a prosecutor cornering a witness.

"Yes. We had an amazing dinner," I concede, hoping it will shut her up.

I'm so wrong.

"You. Had. A. Date!" she cries out triumphantly. She puts her coffee cup on the counter, and proceeds to do an aged victory dance.

"Mildred, please stop."

She goes to the cabinet and pulls out another mug. "Put those down," she says, pointing at Caitlyn's things. She fills the mug with coffee, carries it to the kitchen table, sits in a chair, and pats the seat next to her. "Sit down and tell me everything."

"Mildred, I don't think—"

She pats the chair, again, and repeats with a little more insistence, "*Everything*."

There's no escape.

"Fine." I sit in the chair and take the coffee. "But you have to promise not to tell Caitlyn because it could cause a lot of problems at her school."

She blinks. "Caitlyn? Why would I tell Caitlyn? What does this have to do with her school? What problems?"

Oh, Goddamnit.

I try to hide my face by looking at the table. "Well … you know, I don't know how she would react if she knew I had dinner with … umm … another woman."

She's not buying a word of it. "Daniel?"

I reluctantly raise my eyes to meet her stare.

"What does this have to do with Caitlyn?"

I sigh. "It was her teacher."

I'm worried Mildred's jaw is going to crash through the table.

"But, Mildred, please. I'm serious. It wasn't a date. It was a very pleasant dinner and Caitlyn can never know, because it could get her teacher in a lot of trouble at school."

She ditches the teasing. "You don't have to tell me everything. Just what you want to."

I recount the evening, except the part about my lunatic detour into the supernatural. I tell her how we connected and about Denise's son, which I know there's no danger she'll repeat to anyone.

Once I'm done, Mildred sits back with her coffee.

"You going to see her, again?"

"I hope so. I wouldn't mind us having dinner from time to time."

"Think it might grow into something more serious?"

"No. Just friends."

"You sure? You don't think it might grow into something a little more 'naked'?"

"Mildred!"

"I'm kidding! I'm kidding!" She laughs.

I sip my coffee and wait for her to settle down.

She wipes her eyes and catches her breath. "Daniel, I'm so glad. I can't tell you how much better you look."

"I feel a lot better."

"Good." She shrugs. "And I'm just saying that if nudity should happen—"

"Mildred, stop."

She smiles.

*

I've been at it for hours and I'm cranking out page after page in the Writing Room. After a few more jokes at my expense over at Mildred's, I came home and set to work in my notebook. It took me about an hour to hit my stride, but now, I'm on fire. The characters are emerging out of the fog of my mind and coming to life. The dialogue is cracking. I'm turning some nice phrases in my descriptions. I haven't felt like this since the accident. I'm completely immersed in a world of my own creation.

Jake Solomon is prowling the streets of Washington D.C., late at night, on the trail of the hitman who nearly killed him. Only a jump from a rooftop spared him from the assassin's bullet. Now, with the help of an intrepid reporter who Jake doesn't entirely trust, he has the hitman cornered, but he thinks the reporter might be working with him to get Jake to—

Thunk.

I'm so caught up in my writing, it takes a repetition of the noise to register.

… thunk.

There it is, again, in the bookcase.

I'm tempted to let the rat or whatever critter is living in there to have its day. I don't want to leave my characters in the lurch.

… thunk.

With an exasperated sigh, I drop my pen, swivel my chair, get up, step around the desk, and over to the bookcase.

I stay absolutely still.

One minute passes … then two …

Come on, Mickey. If we're going to do this, let's do—

… thunk.

There. At least, I think it was there, on the side of the bookcase.

I carefully crouch down and hold my ear to the cold wood. There's that 'ocean' sound you always hear when you press your ear against something; a low, distorted rumble.

Another minute goes by ... then another.

There are no sounds of scratching or scurrying from inside. Waiting ... waiting ...

Then, I hear something—not scratching or scurrying from inside the bookcase, but a voice. A whisper right next to my ear.

"Rebecca's here ..."

I fall backwards, away from the bookcase.

My heart is pounding. My chest is heaving. I stare at the spot. On the desk, my phone begins to ring.

I pick myself off the floor and work my way to the desk, keeping my eyes on the bookcase.

I check the caller ID and hit 'answer'.

"Denise?" I ask.

"Mr. Price?"

I'm still focused on the bookcase.

"Mr. Price, are you there?"

There's an edge to her tone and apparently, we're on a last name basis, again.

"Yes," I answer, eyes still on the bookcase. "Is everything all right?"

"Everything is fine, but there's been an incident with Caitlyn."

I instantly forget the bookcase. "Is she okay?"

"She's fine, but could you come to the school, please?"

19

The twenty-minute drive to Concord Elementary feels like hours.

Denise, who is now Ms. Hancourt, again, didn't go into details. All she would say over the phone was that Caitlyn was fine, but that she was in a bit of trouble. I asked what kind of trouble and she only reiterated that I should come in.

Kids are playing on the playground as I make my way from the parking lot to the main entrance.

I try to mask my panic from the staff as I walk into the main office and up to the desk.

The secretary looks up from her computer. "May I help you?"

"Uh, yes. I was asked to come in. My daughter, Cai—"

"Mr. Price?"

Principal Craig is standing in the doorway to her office.

"Come with me, please."

*

"Apparently, there was some sort of incident on the playground during recess," she says, leading me down the hall to Ms. Hancourt's classroom.

"What kind of incident?"

163

"Caitlyn shoved a boy."

"She *shoved* a boy?" In my entire life, no sentence has made less sense.

"Yes, but that's not why we asked you to come in."

"Then why did you—?"

We stop outside the door to the classroom.

"I'll let Ms. Hancourt explain."

She gestures for me to go in.

Caitlyn is sitting at a desk with her eyes down.

Denise stands off to the side with her arms folded, her expression just as confused as mine.

I quickly go to Caitlyn and take her face in my hands. "Sweetheart, are you okay?"

She meekly nods.

"What happened?"

Caitlyn hesitates.

Principal Craig chimes in. "During recess, she shoved a boy named Peter Sanders and knocked him down."

Oh no. I thought there was no way she would do it. I still can't believe it.

"You saw her do this?" I ask.

"Some of the other kids say that they saw Caitlyn sort of shove him, and Peter says she did it," Denise says in a softer tone than Principal Craig.

"Where is he now?"

"He's with the nurse. He was pretty shaken up."

I turn back to Caitlyn.

"Sweetheart?"

She brings her eyes up just enough to look at me.

"What happened?"

She sniffs. "I was talking to her," she says, barely above a whisper. "Peter was making fun of me for talking to her. He wouldn't stop … She got mad."

"Who, sweetheart? Who got mad?"

Caitlyn's eyes slide back down to the desk.

"Caitlyn says she didn't do it," Denise says, quietly. "She said … She said Katherine shoved Peter."

My heart sinks. I don't have a problem with Caitlyn standing up for herself or anyone else, but if she's blaming her imaginary friend, then this is a new step, the one the psychologist had warned me about. Caitlyn insisted that her lie is real and it's my fault. I suggested that she show Peter Sanders 'who was the boss' and I didn't call her on it when she insisted that her imaginary friend gave me the necklace, even if she was trying to be nice.

"Who's Katherine?" Principal Craig asks.

"It's her imaginary friend," I sigh.

Caitlyn's head snaps up. The hurt and betrayal on her face are more than I can bear and I look away towards Principal Craig.

"Since we moved, she's had an imaginary friend named 'Katherine', but the thing with this Peter kid, I may have—"

"Mr. Price, that's not why we called you here."

"Then, what is?"

Principal Craig points to the whiteboard behind me. "That."

I turn and freeze.

Scrawled across the board in the uneven hand of a child are the words "Hancourt is stupid", "I hate you", "stupid stupid stupid" and finally:

"We wanted you to see before we erased it," Principal Craig says after a long silence.

"I … I can't believe it."

165

"That's why we wanted you to see it," Principal Craig replies and nods to Denise, who picks up an eraser and begins wiping away the writing.

Stunned, I turn to my daughter. "Caitlyn?"

"I didn't do it," she weakly pleads.

"Caitlyn, don't lie to me. Not now."

Her face springs up, again, and the words come out in a frightened torrent. "It was Katherine! I told her not to, but she wouldn't listen! She didn't like that Peter was making fun of me for talking to her, so she pushed him."

"Caitlyn—"

"Then she got mad at Ms. Hancourt for saying that I was in trouble. I told her not to write that, but she said that's what her dad called Rebecca—"

"Caitlyn—"

"—and that Ms. Hancourt was going to ruin everything between you and Mom, because last night you and Ms. Hancourt—"

"Caitlyn, stop it!" I yell.

Denise stares at me in shock.

A tense silence fills the room.

I desperately try to convey with a glance to Denise that I haven't told Caitlyn anything about last night, but her thoughts are clear; She believes that I did, and now, Principal Craig will know.

I can already see the suspicion growing behind Principal Craig's eyes as she looks from Denise to me.

I have to get both Caitlyn and myself out of here.

I look at Denise and Principal Craig. "I'm going to take her home for today."

"We think that would be best," Principal Craig replies through tightened lips.

I hold out my hand. "Come on, sweetheart. Let's go home."

Keeping her eyes to the floor, Caitlyn slides out of her chair, takes my hand, and we begin walking towards the door. We pass into the hall, followed by Principal Craig and Denise. Children begin entering from the doors leading to the playground. Their voices echo off the walls and their shoes squeak across the floor.

We arrive back at the main entrance. I turn back to Denise and Principal Craig.

"I'm really sorry about this."

Principal Craig nods, somewhat sympathetically. "It'll be fine. We know that this is a rough time. Thank you for coming in." She looks down at Caitlyn. "We'll see you tomorrow, okay, Caitlyn?"

Caitlyn doesn't respond.

"Caitlyn?" I ask.

"It's okay," Principal Craig says with a consoling smile. "Again, thank you for coming in."

She turns and begins walking back towards her office. As she walks away, she says over her shoulder, "Ms. Hancourt, if you can come see me in my office, please?" and continues walking.

I face Denise.

"I didn't say anything to Caitlyn. I swear to God."

Her wounded expression doesn't change. "You'll let me know if there's anything else you need, Mr. Price?"

"Sure … I'm sorry."

I don't know what to say. What else can I say?

"Thank you for coming in," she replies.

She shakes her head and begins walking towards the office.

20

"Caitlyn, please tell me what happened."

"I did," she says, staring out the car window.

"No. You have to tell me what really happened. It's okay that you stood up for yourself if he was picking on you, but you can't blame your imaginary friend, okay? Caitlyn?"

That's the extent of our conversation on the drive back to the Nightingale House.

*

As soon as I open the front door, she makes a beeline for the stairs and up to her room.

"Caitlyn, please come back here."

She doesn't stop. She goes into her room and slams the door.

I should go up there and demand that she opens the door and speaks to me. Instead, I sit at the dining-room table and stare out over the lake for an hour. The rejuvenation I felt this morning is gone. I'm back to being tired, frustrated, and now embarrassed over what happened with Denise. How am I going to fix that one? I can't, right now. That's a problem for later. I need to figure out how to talk to Caitlyn. I need to be comforting but firm, understanding but strict.

What I really need is some backup. I need Nicole.

We used to say that there should be a questionnaire or some kind of test to prove that you could raise a child before you had one, but joked that we'd fail it. I really wish I had taken that test, right now. I really wish Nicole was here.

Well, Nicole's not here. I'm on my own. The first thing that is going to happen is that Caitlyn is going to have to admit the truth and take responsibility. I'll sort out the rest later.

"Caitlyn, can you come down here, please?" I call towards the stairs.

To my surprise, Caitlyn pokes her head around the entrance to the living room.

"Pumpkin, how long have you been standing there?"

She shrugs.

I motion to the chair across the table. "Please, sit down."

She cautiously enters the room, pulls out the chair, and eases herself onto it.

"Am I in trouble?" she asks.

"A little. You're going to tell Ms. Hancourt that you're sorry and I want to know where you heard that word, but right now, I want to know what's going on. Tell me what happened with the boy you shoved."

"I didn't push him! It was Katherine!"

"Okay, okay, okay. Just tell me what happened."

She glances towards the living room. Her eyes lock onto something. I try to follow her gaze to see what she's looking at, but the room is empty.

"Caitlyn?"

She squirms in her seat. "At recess, Katherine wanted me to draw a picture of us, so I did, and I was showing it to her and then Peter asked what we were doing."

"What was the picture?"

169

"... It was me and Katherine. He asked who Katherine was, and I said I was the only one who could see her. He said that was dumb and started making fun of it. Katherine got mad and pushed him. Peter started crying because Katherine pushed him so hard. Ms. Hancourt came over and Peter said I pushed him, but I didn't! It was only because he was standing so close to me and it looked like I pushed him, but it was Katherine!"

I had hoped that talking to her alone would get her to admit that she was making it up. Instead, she's insisting that her lie is real and it's my fault. There were multiple times I could have checked this behavior and I didn't. She's coping with Nicole's death in a way I'm not able to handle.

"Okay. Listen, Caitlyn, you can't—"

"Ms. Hancourt told me to go inside and wait for her, so I did, but Katherine was really mad at her. When we got in the classroom, Katherine started writing on the board—"·

"Sweetheart, you have to—"

"And I told her to stop, but she wouldn't. I kept trying to erase it, but Katherine kept writing. She wrote that word. She said that's what her dad called the other girl, and that's what Ms. Hancourt was, and when Ms. Hancourt came in the room, Katherine dropped the marker, and I was standing there, so it looked like I was writing it!"

I'm getting sick to my stomach and my hands are starting to tremble.

"Caitlyn—"

"I tried to tell Ms. Hancourt, but she wouldn't believe me!"

I start rubbing my eyes. This is a disaster.

"Caitlyn, please stop."

"It's true! It was Katherine!"

I take my hands away and glare at her. "You have to stop lying, Caitlyn. Katherine is not real."

Her eyes dart towards the living room.

"Caitlyn, look at me."

170

She does.

I lower my voice. "Stop … lying … to me."

I've never spoken to her like that, almost menacing, but I don't care.

"… She is real," Caitlyn says, quietly.

The trembling in my hands grows. Bile is churning in my throat. For the first time in our lives, the thought of spanking Caitlyn crosses my mind.

"Caitlyn …"

"She's in this house. Sometimes she comes out to play with me because she hasn't had anyone to play with in a long time. Other times, she stays in my closet."

"What are you talking about?! Caitlyn, where do you get this stuff? Why would there be someone staying in your closet?"

"She's hiding from her dad … He's in the house, too."

I have to press her. I feel like I have to keep her going until I can point out how ridiculous this is, then she'll break and have to admit she's making all of this up.

"Okay. She's hiding from her dad in your closet. Where's her dad?"

"I … In your room," she says, staring at the table.

"Why does she have to hide from her dad?"

"Because he's mean. He's the reason she's here … She drowned in the lake … Now, she's in the house … He won't let her leave."

"'Won't let her leave'? Caitlyn, what do you mean? You said she followed you to school, so she can leave the house."

"No, not the house … He won't let her *leave*."

"Caitlyn, I still don't understand. Why won't he let her leave?"

"Because if she leaves, he has to leave."

"Sweetheart, what does that even mean?"

She doesn't answer.

I'm going to be sick and I'm struggling to keep a lid on my frustration.

"Caitlyn, sweetheart, what does that—?"

"Sometimes Katherine can hear Mom."

"… What did you just say?"

"Katherine can hear Mom … She's here, too."

This has gone too far. The lid is off.

"Caitlyn, that's enough."

She continues to keep her eyes on the table as she speaks. "Mom tries to talk to Katherine, but her dad won't let her."

"Caitlyn …"

"Katherine says that Mom is worried about us."

"Caitlyn Nicole Price, stop it, now."

"Mom wants us to leave, but Katherine needs us to stay."

"Stop it!"

"Katherine says she's sorry, but she needs our help and Mom can't get—"

I slam my fist down on the table. "GODDAMNIT, CAITLYN! STOP IT! JUST STOP IT! DON'T YOU FUCKING DARE BRING YOUR MOTHER INTO THIS!"

Caitlyn looks up at me in horror. Her eyes fill with fearful tears that spill out and run down her cheeks.

I can't believe I said that to her, but I'm still boiling and my hand is throbbing.

"Go to your room."

She sniffs. "Daddy … I'm sorry …"

"Go to your room, now."

After a long silence, her chair scrapes across the floor as she gets up from the table. She walks out of the dining room. Her footsteps quicken as she reaches the stairs, as do her choked sobs. A moment later, her bedroom door closes.

The image of her looking at me like I was a monster causes all the rage and frustration to drain out of me, to be replaced with a feeling of regret I've ever known.

I lean back, sigh, and hang my head.

What did I just do?

I've blown it.

I wanted her to open up to me. I should have listened and tried to have been understanding. Instead, I yelled and cursed at her. I had hurt her. I had hurt our daughter. If Nicole was here, I don't know what she would say.

I can't let this fester. I have to tell her I'm sorry. I slowly go upstairs and stop outside her door. I can hear her crying inside.

"Caitlyn, can I come in?"

The sniffling stops. There are footsteps. Then, there's the sound of something sliding across the floor. She's blocked the door.

I should tell her to open the door, but after what I've done, if she wants to be alone, I'm going to have to respect that.

"Okay … Caitlyn, I'm sorry. I should never have said that … I'm so sorry … I love you, sweetheart."

Her footsteps retreat into her room, and from what I can tell, back to her bed. The stifled crying resumes.

*

I've been sitting at the dining-room table for hours, going back and forth between wondering what to do, berating myself, and feeling sorry for myself.

I go upstairs to see if Caitlyn wants anything to eat, but when I reach her door, I can hear her snoring. It might be better to let her sleep and try to apologize again in the morning, so I head back downstairs to the kitchen.

I'm about to open the fridge when I spot Mildred's bottle of scotch sitting on top of it. In frustration, I grab it, hold it in my hands, and pull out the stopper.

Fuck it.

I steady myself, take a deep breath, raise the bottle to my lips, and drink. The liquid burns like gasoline as it travels down and pools in my stomach. When I can't take it anymore, I stop, and wait for the effects. I was a little tipsy with Denise last night (my God, was that only last night?) but I haven't been drunk since

Nicole and I enjoyed our last date night while Caitlyn was at her grandparents'. Drinking was something I avoided after her death, but right now, I don't care.

I failed Caitlyn and I failed Nicole.

After another gigantic swig from the bottle, I'm seized by a fit of coughing as it ignites my throat. Once it passes, I put the bottle back on the fridge. I've drunk more than half of what had been left in a matter of minutes.

This is going to be bad.

I go to the sink and pour myself a glass of water. I down it in one gulp, trying to put out the fire in my gut, and grip the side of the sink.

After a few minutes, I'm already getting slightly dizzy and lightheaded. On my empty stomach, the effects of the scotch are almost immediate. My fingers are growing less and less responsive.

I lean against the counter, no longer feeling happy or sad. I just don't feel, which is what I want, but this was a mistake. The effects are still coming, and it's going to get worse. I need to get to bed, right now.

Grabbing a glass of water, I head upstairs.

I steal a moment outside Caitlyn's door to listen to her rhythmic snoring.

"I'm so sorry," I whisper, before glancing down the hall.

The door to my bedroom is open. I'm pretty sure that I closed it. I always keep it closed.

I go down the hall and step inside.

For the first time, the room feels warm and inviting, but not in a 'cozy' way. It's as though I've somehow won its approval, like it finally wants me in here. I stare at the big, warm, welcoming bed. My balance starts to go. I teeter for a few seconds, take a deep breath ... and blow it through my lips like a horse.

I turn around and close the door behind me.

I go downstairs, shuffle over to the couch, collapse in a heap, and pass out.

July 20th, 1900

Two weeks and no word from Thomas. I'm more confused than ever. I know he must be waiting for his wife to depart for Boston, but I need to see him. I need to talk to him. I shouldn't doubt his affection for me. I don't but—

It's that Patricia Fleming's fault.

This afternoon, I was working at the pharmacy. Father stayed home. He said he was not feeling well, and after all the whiskey he drank last night, I don't doubt it. I was happy to work alone at the pharmacy. It gets me out of the house. There's been no word from Carol. Father said that she is still at her sister's in Philadelphia, but I'm beginning to doubt that. He is constantly in a foul mood. I almost miss his foolish optimism.

So, as I said, I have no problem working at the pharmacy on my own. It gives me some time to myself and to keep an eye out for the courier. My heart leaps at every shadow that passes in front of the store window, only to fall when it's not someone carrying an order from Thomas.

The pharmacy is in trouble. We've only done a fraction of the sales that Father was so certain the summer crowd would bring. There's the odd straggler who wanders in out of curiosity or the vacationer who has forgotten something in New York. When they see the prices of our exotic toothpowders from India, they leave and go to the grocers.

And that was how today started—with me behind the counter, reading a book, and waiting.

Around one o'clock, the bell rang, announcing a customer, or I hoped, the courier, or anyone besides the person who actually walked in the door: Patricia Fleming, the town gossip.

"Good afternoon," she said, in her overly polite tone.

"Good afternoon," I returned.

She made a half-hearted pretense of 'shopping', and eventually made her way to the counter.

175

"How's business?" she asked, taking in the empty store.

I had been trying to ignore her with my book, but knowing it was hopeless, I closed the book and addressed her. "We're thinking of having a sale. People seem to find our products slightly too expensive."

"Couldn't hurt," she said, unfazed.

She eyed my necklace.

"That's something pretty," she said. "A present from someone?"

"That's not your business," was all I could think to say.

Instead of backing down, she seemed to enjoy my rebukes. "No. You're right. It's yours ..." She pretended to admire a display of lip balm on the counter. "And how is your business with Mr. Carrington?"

I couldn't hide my surprise, which is what she wanted to see. I wanted her to leave.

"Did you come in specifically to pry into my life?" I asked.

"No. My friends and I take a walk every afternoon through the square. I thought I'd stop in to see if there was any business between you and Mr. Carrington, and there clearly is."

"Congratulations, and now you can leave."

She shook her head as though she pitied me. She went to leave but turned back.

"Do you know about Mr. Carrington?"

"He prefers me to call him 'Thomas'."

Her smile was that of a snake. I felt I had said the wrong thing, and quickly added, "And I know how you like to gossip."

"This isn't gossip. I'm willing to tell you to help you, but if you'd rather not hear it ..."

I should have said no right away and asked her to leave again, but I couldn't. Instead, I remained silent, which she took as her cue to tell me her sordid little story.

"I'm sure you've heard that he has an affinity for women and likes to drink?"

I didn't answer.

"Well, two years ago, he became particularly friendly with the *nanny they hired to look after their daughter. The daughter saw them together and told Mrs. Carrington. It nearly ended their marriage, which would be scandal enough, but they rely on income from her family, since his family cut him off. So, Mr. Carringt—"* She caught herself and gave a condescending smile. *"I'm sorry, I mean 'Thomas', would be ruined. She said that she would cut him off unless he stopped drinking. It's also why they hired a valet. She wouldn't trust him with another nanny in the house."*

I stared at her with her infuriating smile.

"I don't believe you," I said.

She acted as though she was offended. "I'm only giving you advice that could help you, but suit yourself. I know he can be quite charming, but like you said, it's your business. Not mine."

With that, she left.

I spent the rest of the day turning her words over in my head, and catching myself fiddling with the necklace.

Eventually, after another slow day, I closed the pharmacy and returned home.

The door to Father's room was closed and I could hear him sleeping inside.

I retreated into my own room and proceeded to write these words.

I'm now more desperate than ever to talk to Thomas. I know it's nothing more than gossip; cruel gossip spread by a jealous girl that was only meant to put doubt in my head.

I hope the courier comes tomorrow. I want to see him. I want him to kiss me again, and reassure me that Patricia Fleming is nothing more than the horrid liar I know her to be.

Good night.

21

The tiles of the downstairs bathroom are nice and cool on my back.

It's six-thirty in the morning and about an hour since my last dry heave. I've been downing Advil to stop the hammers in my head. My mouth tastes like asphalt, and I only got about three hours of restless, drunken sleep. The worst is over, but this is the kind of hangover that costs you an entire day.

I have to get up. Caitlyn will be awake soon and I need to make breakf-uuuuuck. Let's not think about food.

I pull myself off the floor, go upstairs, take an ice-cold shower, and pull on some clothes. The shock to my system makes me feel semi-human.

I walk down the hall and gently knock on Caitlyn's door.

"Caitlyn?"

There's no answer, so I slowly open the door.

"Caitlyn, I want to talk—"

She's not in her room.

"Caitlyn?"

"I'm down here," she responds from the kitchen.

I find her sitting in the kitchen alcove with a bowl of Fruit Loops in front of her that she's not eating; she's only pushing her spoon around in the now-discolored milk.

"Hey."

She continues stirring.

"You want me to make you anything? Toast? Waffles?"

She shakes her head.

"Caitlyn, listen, I'm really sorry for what I said."

"It's okay," she says in a flat, unconvincing tone.

"No, sweetheart, it's not. Not at all. I'm having a really hard time right now, and I know you are, too. I was a jerk last night and I'm sorry. You don't have to pretend that your imaginary friend talks to Mom. If you want to talk to me about Mom, you can. I want you to."

Without a word, she gets up and walks out of the kitchen, mumbling something about getting ready for school. She goes through the living room and up the stairs.

"You need to apologize to Ms. Hancourt toda—" I call after her but her door shuts.

I make some coffee and wait for her to come back down, but as the minutes wear on, I realize she's running out the clock until the bus arrives.

Sure enough, her footsteps hit the stairs just as the bus pulls up at the end of the driveway. I get up and walk through the living room but only catch a glimpse of her back as she opens the front door.

"Have a good day, pumpkin. I love—"

The door closes behind her.

The house is silent.

"Damnit," I whisper and head for the Writing Room.

*

For two hours, I try to get the words out, but I'm distracted. I'll scratch out a few lines and then I'll see Caitlyn's wounded expression flash through my mind. I'll wait for it to pass, scratch out a few more lines, and it happens again, and I'll remember the horrible things I said to her.

Finally, I curse and hurl my pen against the wall. It's going to be another non-productive day.

I can't write, but I need to do something active. I don't want to sit on the couch and wallow in the misery of this hangover or the memory of last night. The only solution I can come up with is to get some housework done.

To make the best use of my time, I'll get some laundry going while I clean.

I collect the dirty clothes from my room and then head to Caitlyn's room.

I open the closet and grab the clothes basket. I'm about to close the door but instead, I stare at the empty space under the hanging clothes, imagining a little girl hiding there, smiling up at me.

"So, this is where you hang out, huh?" My frustration suddenly spills out. "You know what? I'd really appreciate it if you left my daughter alone and not get her into trouble at school. And while you're at it, leave my wife out of it. It's bad enough Caitlyn thinks you're real, but telling her that you speak to her dead mother? What sort of friend does that? And I don't give a damn if you're sorry."

Silence.

I'm standing here, berating an empty closet, like an idiot.

Basket in hand, I close the closet door, and began walking to the—

Clink.

I stop.

It came from inside the closet, like a coin dropping onto the floor.

I turn back and wait.

Nothing.

Putting the basket down, I go back and slowly open the closet door.

There, sitting on the floor of the closet in a small puddle of water and flecked in mud, like it's just been pulled from the bottom of the lake, is Nicole's wedding ring.

July 28th, 1900

I'm lying in bed.

I don't know what to write … or even if I should write.

It had been weeks since I'd heard from him. Days of sitting and waiting. Carol hasn't returned. I asked Father about her and he said that she sent a telegram that said she was staying in Philadelphia for a few more days. I think he's lying. There was no telegram. He doesn't know where she is or when she's coming back. He's quieter and continues to drink.

Mr. Carrington's promise that he would send for me when Mrs. Carrington was gone was the only thing sustaining me.

So, this morning, I nearly sprang over the counter when the courier arrived. I tore open the letter. Mr. Carrington had made good on his promise.

I went about putting the items on the very short list together. I was about to head through the storeroom to the bicycle in the alley, when Father called out to remind me to have Mr. Carrington pay his account. In fact, he insisted upon it. I guess it has come to that. Father needed him to pay his account, now, no matter how small the balance. I took some change from the drawer.

When I arrived at the Nightingale House, I did my best to make myself presentable and walked to the porch. I checked under the pot on the table and found the key he told me about. My hands were shaking and I felt short of breath. There were so many things I wanted to ask him. I opened the door and went inside. I called out his name but there was no answer. I walked to the dining room, thinking that I might see him through the window, out by the lake. There was a note on the table. It read: They're all in Boston. Join me upstairs.

I placed the items on the table and walked up the stairs. The bedroom door at the end of the hall was open.

I nervously pushed it open and found him waiting by the fireplace. Without a word, he moved to kiss me, but I stepped back. He asked what was wrong and I told him what Patricia Fleming had said. He grew upset and said that Patricia Fleming was telling salacious stories. It had all been a misunderstanding that was in the past. He also told me that Patricia Fleming was just jealous of me, because he had turned down her advances some time ago.

I asked him what his feelings were towards me.

He told me how beautiful I was. How much he cared for me and how empty he felt without me.

The w

22

I've been sitting here at the dining room for hours, staring at Nicole's ring, when Caitlyn arrives home from school.

Caitlyn stops when she sees the ring on the table in front of me. She doesn't look surprised or scared, as if she knew what she was going to find when she walked through the door.

"How was school?" I mechanically ask. It's an absurd question. It's a reflex; some part of me is desperately trying to deny what's happening, because that would make it real.

"Katherine wanted to show you she was sorry."

This isn't happening. This isn't real.

"... I'm going to go to my room," she says.

She waits for a response I can't formulate and goes upstairs.

*

The sun goes down, and I'm still at this table.

I'm trying to rationalize this. Maybe Caitlyn found it on the shore and put it in her pocket. That has to be what happened. She's trying to reinforce the existence of her imaginary friend. That's all. Everything else can be attributed to my lack of sleep, the stress, what had happened with Denise, what's happening with Caitlyn … right?

I can't deal with this. I can't deal with what's right in front of me but I can't ignore it. This is what it must feel like to have a psychotic break.

I need to let my mind escape, to run away from what is on this table. It feels like the air is pressing in on me. I keep expecting to see black fog building near the floor.

I have to focus on something else. I need normalcy. I have to do something else before I lose my fucking mind.

Something clicks.

It's like the decision is made for me. It makes no sense, but it makes perfect sense.

I'll escape into a world of my own making.

I'll write.

I stand up and walk almost unconsciously to the Writing Room.

I sit at my desk, open up my notebook, and begin frantically writing.

It's the most ridiculous nonsense I've ever written, but for some reason, I keep telling myself it's good, even though somewhere deep down, I know this makes no sense. I'm writing a scene where my main character is chasing a girl down to the shore of a lake. I'm going into vivid detail, describing his rage and hatred of this girl. I have no idea who this girl is. She hasn't been a character anywhere before. I'm so focused that I can see it in my head. I'm the main character, angrily chasing the girl to the water's edge. I catch her by the hair and yank her backwards. She cries out. I shove her head under the water to quiet her screams. She struggles but she knows, she knows what happened, and she was going to tell, and no one could ever kno—

"I can't sleep …"

I snap out of it. I've forgotten all about the ring. I've also forgotten about dinner.

"I'm sorry, pumpkin," I say, looking up. "Did you want me to—?"

The doorway is empty.

"Caitlyn?"

The house is still.

I hold my breath in the silence.

… drip … drip …

It came from the living room.

I don't want to get up. I don't want to see. I want to close the door and wait for the sun to rise, but that would mean Caitlyn is out there with it, and I know whatever it is, it won't leave us alone.

I step out of the Writing Room and look up the stairs. The only light is the dimmed glow coming from under Caitlyn's door.

… drip … drip …

It's in the dining room.

I quietly walk across the living room, into the dining room, and stop by the table. I search again for the source of the dripping water. I press my ear to the wall. Maybe it's inside—

Clack.

I nearly cry out.

It came from the kitchen.

There's a faint, rusty groan of a door opening.

I step into the kitchen and turn on the light.

The basement door is open.

I take out my phone and pull up the flashlight app. My hands are shaking so bad, I almost drop it. I point the light down into the darkness of the basement. Particles of dust drift in and out of the beam. I begin descending the stairs at an agonizing pace. I keep the light pointed to my left, to illuminate the basement as I continue down. Finally, I arrive at the landing at the bottom of the stairs.

The old wooden shelves sit against the stone walls. The single bulb hangs from the ceiling. I walk to the center of the room and pull the chain.

The bulb snaps on.

The shelves and carboard boxes sit undisturbed, collecting dust.

Everything is as it should be.

I release the air I've trapped in my chest and turn off the flashlight app.

Rational thought returns. I'll call the plumber tomorrow.

I pull the chain again, plunging the basement into shadow, and begin walking back to the stairs.

"I can't sleep …"

I stumble across the landing as I turn around.

A girl is standing in the middle of the room.

Her head is turned towards the floor. Her wet hair falls about her face, obscuring it from view. Her soaked nightgown clings to her frail body. Drops of water fall from the hem to the floor.

… drip … drip …

I scramble back against the wall and try to bring the light back up on my phone, but the image of the girl begins to fade.

As it fades, a soft whisper emanates from the shadows.

"I can't sleep …"

August 2nd, 1900

I'm sorry that my last entry ended so abruptly.

I haven't written for days. I couldn't bring myself to describe what happened.

I didn't want to write but I feel I have to. Something's changed. He has changed. He changed that day, right there in the room. Of course, I was awkward and he was strong and forceful ... I asked if he loved me. He wouldn't answer. He only smiled. When I asked again, he grew annoyed and changed the subject, saying I should get back to the pharmacy before my father became suspicious.

After we dressed, we went downstairs to the front porch. I was still trying to make sense of it all. Then, I stupidly remembered Father's request that he pay his account. Mr. Carrington found that terribly funny and laughed. When I asked him why it was funny, he said that of course, he would pay. He went back inside and returned with a ten-dollar note. I told him I didn't have enough change. He laughed even harder and told me to keep it.

I felt stupid and ashamed. I asked when I would see him again, and he said, "When I need more deliveries."

I became upset, which stopped his laughter, and made him more irritated. He told me to have a safe journey, went back inside, and closed the door.

I wept the whole way back to town. I'm not even sure why. I told myself that I was overreacting, but this time felt different.

I didn't go to the pharmacy. I went home and took a bath. I took care to keep my hair from getting wet because Father would have noticed. Afterwards, I went to the pharmacy and found Father reading a newspaper.

"There you are," he said. "I was beginning to worry."

I told him that it was such a lovely day that I had taken a longer route back.

He asked about my bloodshot eyes and I told him that a bug had flown into my eye while I was riding to town. I gave him the ten-dollar bill and told him Mr. Carrington had paid his account. It made him happy.

I felt myself growing upset and asked if I could have the rest of the day off. He said I could.

I went home and didn't leave my room for two days. I told Father I wasn't feeling well, which wasn't a total lie.

More days passed.

I felt more distant from Father than I ever have, not that we've ever been particularly close.

One afternoon, I made the mistake of asking when Carol might return. I thought that she might be someone to talk to, but Father spat back, "I don't know and frankly, I do not care."

He's spending less and less time at the pharmacy, and more time at home, drinking, leaving me to run the store. He's also warned me not to include our home address on any correspondence about the pharmacy. I can only assume it's because of debt collectors.

There's been no further word from Thomas, no orders or stops to the pharmacy.

And today, I had the most unwelcome visitor of all.

A group of young women were walking past the store window and one of them looked in. It was Patricia Fleming.

We locked eyes.

I could see her tell her friends to go on without her and she came in through the door.

"Good afternoon," she said.

I was in no mood to play her little game, so I simply glared at her.

"Is that any way to treat a customer?" she asked.

"If you're not making a purchase, I must ask you to leave."

"All right, all right," she said, in a way that indicated I was no fun. "I only wanted to know how your 'business' was with 'Thomas'."

"It's fine," I replied. "And there's no point in lying about him to me. He told me what happened."

She appeared shocked and angry.

"Told you what happened?"

I nodded.

"And what exactly did he say 'happened'?"

"That you tried to become overly familiar with him and that he turned you away."

Her shock and anger melted into a smile. "Oh. That's what he told you?"

"Yes."

"And you believed him?"

"Of course," I answered, defiantly.

She began to laugh. "I can assure you it was quite the opposite. It was at their last Fourth of July Celebration. The handsome lecher tried to corner me in his office. I laughed in his face and told him I wasn't his nanny. It's only out of respect for his wife that I haven't told anyone."

I could feel my stomach sinking into the floor. I didn't want to believe it.

"You're lying," I said.

"Believe what you like. It appears you already have."

"Why would Thomas lie to me?" I asked, trying to fight back tears.

"Yes," she said, mockingly. "Why would he lie?"

She knew as plainly as if I had told her.

I was stunned, mortified, but deep down, I knew she was right. I had suspected it as soon as I left the Nightingale House.

She shook her head in pity.

"Well, I'll leave you to your work and your little 'bliss'," she said with a nod to the necklace.

She turned and walked out of the pharmacy.

Thankfully, there were no other customers, because I spent the rest of the day weeping in the storeroom.

I'm such a fool. Such an idiot.

After closing the pharmacy, I came home and locked myself in my room.

I never want to leave.

23

I watch through the windshield of the parked car as the sun begins to rise above the hills surrounding Kingsbrook. Caitlyn is sleeping across the back seat.

Once I regained my senses in the basement, I ran upstairs to Caitlyn's room to find her sitting up in her bed.

"Get your things," I said. "We're going for a drive."

In the five minutes it took to pack up some of her things, the house remained still. I stayed by Caitlyn's side the entire time. When she was done, I picked up her duffel bag, took her hand, and led her out into the hall and down the stairs. I didn't bother turning off the lights. I wasn't going to let the shadows anywhere near us.

Caitlyn didn't say a word. She was resigned to my decision and didn't protest but stopped at the door.

"Wait! I forgot my medallion! It's by my bed." She went to go back upstairs but I gently, but firmly, grabbed her wrist, and led her out the door.

"We're not going back into this house for a while, okay?"

"But I—"

"Go to the car, please."

It was more of a command than a request.

He shoulders sagged, but she obeyed.

Ironically, she had reminded me of Nicole's ring, which was still sitting on the dining-room table. I almost went in to grab it. I started to go through the door, but was stopped by what sounded like a little girl crying at the top of the stairs.

I turned around, walked out, and shut the door behind me.

*

It was late, and I could have gotten us a hotel, but for some reason, I felt safer being on the move in the car. It had followed Caitlyn to school. I worried that it might find us if we stopped, so I kept driving.

As we aimlessly drove around Kingsbrook, I tried to get her to talk.

"Caitlyn, you have to tell me what happened to Katherine."

"I told you, and you didn't believe me."

"I know, pumpkin, and I'm sorry, but I need to know, right now."

"I don't want to talk about it," she mumbled.

"Caitlyn, please."

She looked at the back seat. "Can I lie down?"

I couldn't put her through any more. Not tonight. "Okay."

She clumsily climbed to the back seat and lay down. She was out in no time.

I continued driving around Kingsbrook. I drove through the town square, past La Piazza, where only forty-eight hours ago, Denise and I had had a wonderful dinner. God, only forty-eight hours ago?

At last, I decided that I had to pull over. I wasn't tired but I worried that I wouldn't know I was tired until I smashed the car into a tree.

I found an overlook in the surrounding hills, parked, and now I'm watching the sun come up. Most of the buildings and homes in Kingsbrook are silent shadows, but some of the lights in the windows are starting to come to life.

To the sound of Caitlyn's snoring, I try to think of what comes next.

One thing is certain; she is never going back in that house. Ever.

*

The sun finally clears the cedars, oaks, and pines.

I know what I'm going to do. I've just been waiting to call until I was certain that she would be up.

She answers on the third ring.

"Daniel!" Mildred sings into the other end of the phone. "You're up early. Want to grab some coffee on the porch? I've got a new blend from that shop on the square—"

"Mildred, I need your help."

*

An hour later, we pull into Mildred's driveway. Caitlyn stares at the Nightingale House and gives me a look of panic. I reassuringly shake my head.

Mildred's waiting on her porch. She forces a smile as we walk up.

"Hi, sweetie," she says, gently stroking Caitlyn's hair.

"Hi, Mildred," Caitlyn yawns.

"Let me take your things."

Caitlyn hands off her duffel bag and Mildred carries it inside. I crouch down to Caitlyn. "It's only for a little bit, okay?"

She nods.

"I want you to be really nice for Mildred and if you need anything, you call me."

She nods again and rubs her eyes.

I hug her tightly. "I love you, pumpkin."

She hugs me and whispers in my ear. "Don't go back in there."

Mildred steps back onto the porch.

"Everything's ready for you, Caitlyn."

Caitlyn lets go of me and goes inside.

With Caitlyn gone, Mildred's demeanor goes from warm and welcoming to concerned.

"I called the school and told them Caitlyn's sick and won't be in today."

"Daniel, what's going on?"

"There's … It's something with the house. I need a few days to sort it out."

"What? Like a gas leak or something?"

"… Yeah."

She cocks her head in disapproval at me.

"You know, for an author, you're a terrible liar."

"It's only for a few days."

"She can stay here as long as she needs … and so can you."

"Thanks. I may take you up on that."

"But you're not going to, are you?"

"We'll see."

She throws up her hands in disgust. "Fine. You do what you have to. Don't worry about Caitlyn. I'm going to make that girl some pancakes." She turns to go inside but stops. "Be careful, Daniel."

"I will."

She shakes her head one last time and goes inside.

24

I should go. I know I should simply take Caitlyn and go someplace else. We'll stay at a motel until we find a new home. I'll sell the Nightingale House and never set foot in it again.

But I can't do that.

I can't just leave because of what Caitlyn said—that sometimes, Katherine can hear Nicole.

She also said that Katherine can't leave because of her dad.

I've seen Nicole in there and I chalked it up to grief and fatigue, but now?

What if Nicole's in there? What if we leave and Nicole is trapped? Caitlyn said that Thomas Carrington won't let Katherine leave. What about Nicole?

I can't leave without knowing. It'll forever be on my mind if we walk away now. Caitlyn is never going back in there. That's done, but I have to know.

But how? How do you do that?

There's two ways that I've heard of … and they're not from the most reputable of sources.

*

The plastic bag containing my purchases hangs from my hand as I walk into the Nightingale House.

It's mid-afternoon and, ironically, the house feels warm and welcoming. Golden sunlight streams through the windows and birds are singing outside. It's just as beautiful as it was the day Nicole and I visited for the first time, but I know better.

I'm not sure where I should go. Stuff's been happening all over the house, but I don't want to go in the basement, Caitlyn's room, or mine for that matter. This probably isn't going to work, but if it does, whatever is here can make the trip down the stairs, or up from the basement to talk to me.

I sit on the couch and withdraw the first of my purchases from the bag: a Ouija board. The receipt comes out with it. It feels ridiculous to remove the thin plastic wrapping. I also feel stupid looking at the toy company logo on the box. I take off the lid and set it off to the side, along with the instructions. Who doesn't know how this works? I place the board on the coffee table in front of me and remove the plastic heart with the clear plastic hole. I quickly consult the instructions and discover it's called a 'planchette'. I place it on the board and lightly rest my fingertips on its edge. I've heard you're not supposed to do this alone, but I'm not asking anyone else to do this with me.

Deep breath. Here we go.

"Ummm … hello?"

I wait, my fingertips barely touching the planchette.

There's no movement.

"Is anyone here?"

The plastic heart remains motionless.

I can't believe I'm about to ask this …

"Nicole, are you here?"

I almost want it to move. I want it to slide over to the word 'NO' on the board and spell out 'NICOLE IS NOT HERE'. Then, I'll head out the door and never look back.

Instead, the planchette stays right in the middle of the board.

Thank God Caitlyn's not here to see this.

"Katherine? Are you here?"

I wait … My arms are getting tired.

I keep trying to come up with different versions of the same question over and over, again.

"Will someone speak to me?"

"Is there something you're trying to tell me?"

"Who is here in this house?"

"What is it that you want?"

The only time the planchette moves is when I'm startled by the sound of the motor in the fridge kicking on in the kitchen.

*

An hour later, and the planchette still hasn't moved under my fingers. How shocking that something I learned from the movies is wrong. I finally take my fingers off the planchette and put it and the board back into the box. When I walked into this house, I was terrified. Now, I'm tired and bored.

Time for Plan B.

From the bag, I take out the large sketchpad and pencil. I rip out a couple pages and stack them on top of the pad in my lap.

I'm going to try that 'spirit writing' thing I saw in that George C. Scott movie.

Am I going to have more luck than with the Ouija board? Of course not, but I feel like this is more my style. When I'm writing some of my best stuff, I feel like I'm in a trance and the writing is coming from somewhere else. It sounds strange, I know, but I'm willing to give it a shot.

I take the pencil in my right hand and touch it to the paper. I start making scribbles and long loops. There's no pattern, no rhyme or reason to it. I try to let my mind wander. Wait, or should I concentrate? No. I think it's wander. Just relax. I close my eyes and allow my hand to roam across the large sheet of paper. I don't know how long I'm supposed to allow this to go on. From time to time, I'll catch myself intentionally drawing loops and then have to tell myself not to plan or attempt to force anything. The pencil continues to hiss across the paper.

I finally open my eyes.

The paper is covered in scribbles, swirls, and loops. The side of my hand is coated in graphite. Tossing the paper aside, I start again on a clean sheet. Deep breaths. I let my hand flow. Closing my eyes might be a bad idea. I can't tell if I'm becoming ultra-zen-like or if I'm falling asleep.

Without opening my eyes, I swipe the second scribbled-covered sheet of paper from the top and start on the next one. The sound of the pencil moving across the paper and the flowing movement is hypnotic. I try visualizing the room while keeping my eyes closed.

I twitch.

Not because some spirit has seized hold of me, but because for a brief second, I did fall asleep. Can't do that again. The last thing I want is to fall asleep on this couch in this house, alone.

I open my eyes just a bit, but I can't open them more than that, even though I'm trying really hard. This feels weird and my eyes refuse to open further. The pencil is still moving but it's miles away. It suddenly feels like I'm locked inside my own body, that I'm being shut out from my own senses.

I'm panicked *but I'm not.*

The room is different.

It's the living room of the Nightingale House but there are lamps mounted to the wall. The couch is firmer. It's not a couch. It's a chair with a straight, high back. All the furniture is different. This isn't my living room.

It is my living room.

It's my living room. My chair. My house.

I can see the paper in my lap, gleaming, white, pristine. The pencil is in my hand. The point is so sharp.

A thought fills my mind with a pleasant warmth.

What fun it would be to shove the pencil through my eye.

It's the answer to all of this—my daughter, this man in my house and his child. It will all go away.

I lift the pencil from the page. It's incredibly heavy because part of me doesn't want to do it, is fighting against me, but it would solve everything, for both of us. He would never find her. His child would be taken away and he would be out of his misery. It would all be over. Just a quick press, puncturing the eyeball, through the socket, and into the brain.

I turn the pencil and grip it so that the sharpened end is pointed at my face.

Why am I struggling? It's perfectly natural.

I slowly pull the pencil towards me. It's as though my arm is trying not to stop me. I know he is fighting but I keep on pulling it towards me. The point inches closer to my eye.

I try to calm the voice that is screaming in my head to stop. It sounds like me, but it isn't.

The point of the pencil is so close, I can't focus on it. All this voice has to do is give up. This is what it wants. I know this is what it wants. That's why he has that box upstairs in his dresser, just as I did.

Closer … closer …

Just let go. Let go and you can be in this house forever.

I smile as the tip of the pencil touches my eyeball.

One last speck of pressure should do it.

The woman is there, standing before me, filled with a white-hot light. Her eyes are brimming with rage.

"Stop it," she says.

No. Only one more inch. One more.

"Let him go!"

Almost … almost …

"Let him go, now!"

She flies at us.

I sit back and gasp.

I feel repulsive, like I'm covered in filth. I'm pouring sweat but I'm freezing. Every muscle is shaking.

I glance around. I'm in the living room of the Nightingale House, the Nightingale House I know. The pencil is still clutched in my hand, the point turned upwards towards my face. I'm gripping it so hard that it snaps in two.

I don't know if what just happened was real or if I fell asleep, but I've written something.

Among the angry scratches and looping swirls, two words stand out:

August 8th, 1900

    This will be the hardest entry to write. I am completely lost.

    Things are so much worse for Father than I had imagined. There is still no word from Carol. His drinking is getting worse. And now, vendors are beginning to send us notices of bills that are past due.

    This morning I woke up and went to check on Father. He was in bed, snoring loudly, and there was a bottle on the nightstand. I went to wake him, and the smell of alcohol was overwhelming. He told me he didn't feel well and that I would have to work by myself, again.

    I didn't argue with him. It wouldn't have done any good.

    I set off for the pharmacy and arrived to find more past due notices.

    A little past noon, a man walked into the pharmacy. He was tall with broad shoulders, and a bald head. He casually surveyed the shelves.

    "Can I help you find anything?" I asked.

    "Is Mr. Harker here?"

    The tone with which he asked about Father worried me.

    "No, he's not," I replied.

    "Do you know where he is?"

    "No," I lied, knowing he was probably at home, passed out drunk in bed.

    "Do you know when he'll be back?"

    "No."

    He eyed me for a moment. I don't know if he knew I was lying, or if he was trying to intimidate me, or both.

    "What's your name?"

    "Susan," I said, not wanting him to know that I was his daughter.

    "Well, Susan, you don't seem to know much about your employer."

    I was too afraid to speak.

    "When he does come back, can you give him a message?"

I tried to nod without letting the rest of my body tremble.

"Tell him Mr. Lloyd dropped by to discuss his delinquent accounts. Can you do that for me?"

I nodded again.

"Thank you." He gave one last appraising stare. "Good day."

He turned and walked out.

Once he had disappeared out of sight and I was no longer immobilized with fear, I ran to the door and locked it, fearing more visits from collectors. I went into the storeroom and began pacing. As bad as I had imagined things to be, they were so much worse.

I didn't know who to turn to, until I was struck by a thought: maybe Thomas would help. If he cares for me at all, maybe he would help a little. It would mean so much, and I wanted to see him. I wanted him to comfort me. I decided then and there that I would see him.

I went through the back to the alley, where the bicycle was waiting.

The sky was overcast and the morning was still cool. I rode out of town and tried to think of what I was going to say to him but by the time I reached Willow Lake, I hadn't decided.

I leaned my bicycle against the bushes, steadied myself, and walked to the front door. I wasn't going to use the key, in case his wife was home. I hoped that I could speak to him on the porch without anyone noticing. I pulled the chain and moments later, Thomas answered. He stood there, blinking at me as if I were some terrible illusion, but then became enraged. He looked around the yard, violently pulled me inside, and shut the door. He wrenched me with such force that I stumbled into the living room. I could see out the dining-room window into the backyard. Mr. Whitlock was standing in the middle of the grass with his hands over his eyes.

Thomas hissed at me to get away from the window and pulled me back so that I was hidden from view. It hurt so much that I gasped and tried to twist away but he held me firm.

"What are you doing here?" he asked.

I was so stunned by his actions that I momentarily forgot my entire purpose for coming to the Nightingale House.

"I—I needed to talk to you."

"We have nothing to discuss."

"But I thought—"

"You shouldn't be here! I told you my wife was becoming suspicious. My little shit of a daughter told her that she saw us on the Fourth of July."

I couldn't believe he used such foul language about his daughter. I didn't know this man.

"Is your wife here?" I asked.

"No, she's still in Boston, caring for her mother. Her health is deteriorating again, and she couldn't handle the brat while taking care of her."

This wasn't the man I thought I cared for. This was a monstrosity.

"And you need to leave, right now."

"I thought you cared for me."

"Don't be stupid, little girl."

I couldn't stop the tears from flowing.

From the backyard, I heard Mr. Whitlock call out, "Ready or not, here I come!"

Thomas threw open the front door. "You are leaving, now."

He dragged me to the porch, down the path, through the open gate, and into the road. Once we reached the bicycle, he spun me around to face him and gripped my shoulders. "Now, you listen to me; if my wife finds out this time, it's over. If she leaves me, it will cause a scandal and I'll lose everything. I will not let that happen. Do you understand me?"

I couldn't speak.

He shook me and said, "Say you understand me, you little bitch!"

I nodded, horrified.

He relaxed his grip but not his intensity. "Now, get on your bicycle, go away, and never come back."

He turned, walked back into the house, and closed the door.

I stood there, trembling, and choking back sobs. I leaned down and picked up the bicycle. As I did, I saw his daughter, Katherine, hiding in the bushes.

Her face. She had seen him yell at me. She heard what he called me. She looked terrified and furious at the same time. I understood. She lived with that thing every day. She was afraid of him the first time I saw her. So was Mrs. Carrington. I could leave and never come back. They were forced to live with him.

I saw her lips move but couldn't hear what she said. Shaking, I stepped over to the bushes.

"What did you say?" I asked.

"I said, 'Please go away. You make him mad,'" she whispered.

"I'm … I'm sorry."

"Please, go away," she whispered again.

"Katherine, where are you?" a voice playfully called.

I turned to see Mr. Whitlock come around the corner of the house. He saw me and stopped.

"Now, you've given me away," Katherine said, pouting and disappointed.

Mr. Whitlock and I stared at one another.

Without a word, I picked up the bicycle from the bushes and rode off.

I didn't return to the pharmacy. I rode around the countryside all day. When I returned home, Father was still in bed, asleep, and more whiskey from the bottle on the nightstand was gone.

I'm in bed now. I haven't heard him get up. I don't know what to do.

This journal is turning into nothing but sorrow.

25

"Hello, you've reached Dana Whitlock. I'm sorry but I'm unable to come to the phone, right now. Please leave your name and number after the beep and I will return your call as soon as possible. Thanks."

Beep.

"Hello, Ms. Whitlock. My name is Daniel Price ... I know this might sound crazy, but I'm actually calling to see if I could talk to your grandfather, Benjamin. I, uh, I live in Kingsbrook, in the Nightingale House where his grandfather used to work, and ... I had some questions about Katherine Car ... Well, I'll be able to explain better if I could speak to him."

I leave my contact info and hang up. I got their number by doing a ton of research on my phone and also paying some money to one of those 'stalker-services' online.

I try to do more research online, scrolling through the various links that lead to nothing of value.

I toss the phone onto the passenger seat.

This is infuriating. I need my computer but that's at the house, so it's out of the question, and unlike every other author I've ever seen at Starbucks, I don't own a laptop. I'll have to go to the library or a Kinko's or some other place that has computers that you can rent for an hour.

I start the car, put it in drive, and begin rolling forward, but slam the brakes.

What am I doing? I've got something so much better than the internet. Something that should be able to tell me everything I want to know, and he's right here in Kingsbrook.

*

"Mr. Price!" Mr. Howard waves cheerily from the porch of the Kingsbrook Historical Society as I walk up the path.

"Thank you for seeing me on such short notice," I reply, shaking his hand.

"My pleasure." He leans in. "Honestly, I can't remember the last time I got a phone call, asking me if I was open this late. It sounded urgent."

"It is. I need your help."

"Of course. What can I do for you?"

"I need to know everything you can tell me about the Nightingale House."

*

He leads me through the first floor, past the display cases, to what was once the kitchen, but has started morphing into an office/ storage room. Boxes rest on the counters, while papers and binders sit by the sink.

"Please, have a seat," he says, motioning to the small table by the window, overlooking the perfectly manicured backyard. "Would you care for some coffee?"

"Thank you. That'd be great."

He opens a cabinet and takes out two coffee cups.

"So, what is it you'd like to know?" he asks, taking a pot from a coffee machine that's so old, it looks like it would be perfectly at home with the displays out front and pours two cups.

"I'm trying to find out everything I can about the Carrington family. Specifically, about the disappearance of their daughter, Katherine."

His face lights up as he sets a cup in front of me and has a seat at the table. "Quite possibly Kingsbrook's darkest hour."

"Yeah. I'm surprised you didn't mention it when we were here that day."

He looks offended. "I wasn't sure you knew, and you were here with your daughter. I didn't want to upset her. Besides, why would I bring it up?"

I can respect that. "Okay, but I really need to know, now."

"Fascinating stuff, isn't it?" He's about to take a sip but stops. "Are you writing a book about it?"

I could tell him "no" and that my reason for asking is that last night, I saw a girl who has probably been dead for over a hundred years in my basement.

"Yep. Writing a book."

It's so much easier to lie when the person you're lying to offers the perfect cover.

His smile lets me know that I've come to the right place.

"Now, there's not a whole lot out there," I say. "I've found some newspaper articles online but they don't offer much beyond the fact that she disappeared from the train platform, no one found her, and then Thomas Carrington died of some sudden illness in the Nightingale House shortly after."

He gives me an amused, almost smug smile. "Well, that was the story that was printed. They would never publish what really happened."

"I'm sorry … What 'really happened'?"

"Thomas Carrington killed himself; he shot himself through

208

the head in the bedroom of his home. Well, I guess it is now *your* home."

"What?"

He shrugs. "That was the rumor."

"It was a hundred and twenty years ago. How could you possibly know that?"

"Mr. Price," he says, setting his cup down and regarding me as if I've now truly insulted his honor in some way. "My family is as old as Kingsbrook, itself. They've lived here since the beginning. However, since I don't have a family, I'm afraid the line stops here, which is why I started the Kingsbrook Historical Society." He holds out his hands to indicate the entire house. "My family has been witness to everything that has happened in Kingsbrook and that history has been my obsession for decades. I used to beg my grandparents, and especially my great-grandmother, Patricia Fleming, to tell me stories about the town, and in her lifetime, the disappearance of Katherine Carrington and the death of her father were *the* story of the town."

"Okay. I'm sorry. I apologize. I had no idea."

He relaxes. "No. I suppose you're right. It was only gossip."

"Please, tell me."

He runs his finger around the rim of his cup as he organizes his thoughts. "Well, as I was saying, my family has lived in Kingsbrook since the beginning. I was born here in 1952, well after all the era that Kingsbrook was a getaway from the wealthy came to an end, but I still loved Kingsbrook. I knew I never wanted to live anywhere else. The town, its people — even from a young age, I was obsessed."

I desperately need him to get to the point, but I don't want to interrupt. I wait for him to savor another sip of coffee before continuing.

"When I heard about The Carrington Affair—" he leans in "—that's what Gran-Gran called it, I had to know everything and she was more than happy to tell me. She was Kingsbrook royalty in her day. She was the daughter of the Mayor … and an unrepentant gossip." He smiles. "But that was fine with me. I loved hearing her stories." He chuckles. "Ironic that hearing about Kingsbrook's ghosts made the town come alive in my imagination." He picks up his coffee.

"So … what happened?"

"Oh, right, right, right. I'm sorry. There I go, again," he says, taking another quick sip before setting the cup down. "According to Gran-Gran, Thomas Carrington was not the most respected member of Kingsbrook society."

"Why not?"

"Well, there were things that were looked down upon, such as the fact that his own family had cut him off due to his behavior. 'Playing the field' was the polite term for his behavior at the time. Some said that he charmed Abigail into marrying him because of her family's wealth. That's what supported them. Gran-Gran said he was rude, arrogant, and he could be 'a very unpleasant fellow', which were harsh words, coming from her. According to Gran-Gran, everyone knew that it was an unhappy marriage."

"What about the daughter?"

"Gran-Gran never really knew her, but when she disappeared, the rumors swirled that he had something to do with it."

"Why?"

He shrugs, again. "His past. He was known to be a little violent. Gran-Gran had heard that after he was drunk with a young woman, Abigail forbade liquor in the house. Anyway, Gran-Gran said it all seemed so strange. As I said, there were rumors that he had something to do with his daughter's disappearance, but there was no proof."

"What about the rumor that he killed himself?"

"That one, Gran-Gran sounded more certain about."

"The paper said that he was found dead in his room."

"Of course it did. Out of respect for Abigail, it would never print that Thomas Carrington shot himself. That sort of thing simply wasn't done in those times. Afterwards, Abigail Carrington left Kingsbrook. She wanted nothing else to do with the town. She even left Nightingale House abandoned. She passed in 1927."

"Did your great-grandmother—"

"Gran-Gran."

"Yes, did your … Gran-Gran ever tell you if there were any rumors as to why Thomas Carrington killed himself?"

He rolls his eyes, not out of exasperation, but in a way I'm pretty sure his … Gran-Gran did while relating her narratives. "She sure did. The rumors ranged from a sense of guilt over killing his daughter to the absurd idea that he was murdered by a loan shark. Most of the people who believed he killed himself thought he did it out of grief."

"What did your Gran-Gran think?"

"She was certain he did it because he was caught in an affair and Abigail was going to cut him off."

"She was sure he was having an affair?"

"Yes."

"Did she say who?"

"Well, once again, rumors, but there was a whisper that he was carrying on with a young woman. She was the daughter of a pharmacist. The whispers really started flying around when she and her father disappeared from Kingsbrook right after he died, never to be heard from again."

"Did anyone know her name?"

He glances up at the ceiling as he searches his memory. "Gran-Gran told me once … Her last name was something like … 'Walker' or maybe 'Hooper', I think. I can't really remember. I do remember that her first name was 'Rebecca'."

The blood drains from my face.

"Mr. Price? Are you well?"

I stand up. I have to get back to the house.

"Thank you for your time, Mr. Howard."

"Of course … Is there anything else I can do for you?"

"No. You've been a great help."

*

The porch light of the Kingsbrook Historical Society goes dark as I get in the car and close the door.

I turn the key and the motor comes to life.

The Nightingale House is ten minutes away. I can do it in five.

I need to get to the Writing Room, because a whisper in that bookcase once told me, 'Rebecca's here'.

September 18th, 1900
No. Please. No.

26

The door to the Nightingale House slowly swings inward.

The lights are still on from when we left yesterday. I stand in the threshold, waiting and listening. There are no sounds of crying from the stairs and no dripping water.

I step inside, close the door behind me, and make my way to the kitchen.

The basement door is also still open. Without looking down into the darkness, I press it closed and go to the pantry. There, I find the small toolbox, tucked away on the top shelf. I bring it down and set it on the island counter. It's one of those el-cheapo tool sets you find at Walmart that only has the basics: a few screwdrivers, adjustable wrenches, a boxcutter, a leveler you'll probably never use. The only thing I'm interested in is the hammer.

I take it from the toolbox and carry it into the Writing Room.

I stand in front of the bookcase, hammer in hand. I'm about to do something that may necessitate some very costly repairs, but I don't care. I feel around the panels on the side of the book-case, where I had pressed my ear against the wood and heard the whisper. I start knocking on the panels, listening for anything that sounds hollow.

Right there. Third panel up from the floor. It's about waist-high.

I run my hand over it, trying to discern if there's anything different from the other panels. I can't really tell.

Thunk.

I quickly draw my hand back. I felt that. I felt the soft impact of something hitting the other side of the panel.

I steady myself, take aim with the hammer, and swing.

The panel cracks.

I swing again. Part of the panel bows in. There's empty space behind it. I strike one last time. The head of the hammer splits the wood and disappears into the bookcase. I have to work it back and forth to dislodge it.

I place the hammer on the floor and get out my phone. I turn on the flashlight app and peer into the space behind the panel through the hole I've created.

There's something in there.

I carefully slide my fingers into the opening, grip the panel, and pull. It comes away with a loud *crack*. The space is about the size of a shoebox.

I set the panel aside, reach in, and pull the object out.

It's an old journal.

The cover is a faded blue, and there are brass plates mounted to the front and back. A clasp connects them, binding the journal shut. There's an engraving on the front plate.

These Pages Hold My Thoughts and Fears
And the Dreams that I will Seek.
Wishes and Wonder You'll Find in These

Beneath the inscription is a circular indentation with three small holes.

I read the inscription again.

It's not complete. It doesn't make sense. It's missing the last line. I reread it, shaking my head. I'm just going to have to break it open.

Then it hits me.

'Wishes and wonder you'll find in these … the secrets that I keep.'

*

Climbing the stairs, I keep my eyes forward, but every now and again, I'll glance behind me, terrified of something appearing at the bottom of the stairs, cutting off my only route of escape. I reach the top of the stairs without incident. The door to the master bedroom is closed.

In Caitlyn's room, I walk around the bed, and over to the nightstand. The medallion is on the corner, face up. The engraving glitters in the setting sunlight outside the window.

I grab it and sit on the bed with the journal in my lap. I gently place the medallion in the circular opening, but it won't go in. I check the alignment of the pegs on the back of the medallion with the small holes in the circular opening and see my mistake. I try again, slightly rotating the medallion. The pegs slide home. I rotate the medallion. There's a light hissing sound as it slides against the rim of the lock.

The words align.

These Pages Hold My Thoughts and Fears
And the Dreams that I will Seek.
Wishes and Wonder You'll Find in These,
The Secrets That I Keep.

The clasp opens, and I gently lift the cover.

There's a photo of a young girl pasted on the first page. It's black and white, and fine cracks run across the surface. The girl's hair is braided behind her head. She looks to be about seventeen

216

or so. Underneath the photo are the handwritten words: *This journal is the property of Rebecca Harker.*

Where have I seen this face?

I've seen her somewh—

The Kingsbrook Historical Society. The photo from the Fourth of July Celebration. She was the girl that was sitting off to the side. The one who wasn't looking at the camera in the photo.

I turn the page and begin to read …

April 7th, 1900

I love it. I simply love this journal.

I've never kept a journal, but I will try to do so, especially because of who gave it to me, but more on that in a moment.

The party was fine but I'm really too shy for public gatherings. Besides, while it was my seventeenth birthday, the party wasn't really for me. It was Father's way of 'introducing' us to Kingsbrook …

September 25th, 1900

It's twelve-thirty in the morning.

Everything has fallen apart.

I don't know if I should go to the police or not. I have to tell someone but I can't, so I'm going to tell these pages.

I couldn't avoid it anymore. I've missed two of my cycles. I kept telling myself it was stress, but I know it's not. I'm with child.

I haven't told Father. He continues to drink. The bill collectors keep harassing us. The pharmacy is now open by appointment only. Whenever we work, we keep the door locked and stay in the store-room. If someone knocks, we'll peek out through the curtain. If we think it's a customer, we'll let them in. If we think it's a collector, we stay in the storeroom.

This morning, I told Father that I wasn't feeling well and that I couldn't work at the pharmacy. I spent the whole day sobbing in bed. Finally, I decided that I had to tell Father. I needed help. I didn't know how he could help me, but I had to tell someone.

Towards evening, I got up, dressed, and walked into town, carrying the spare key to the pharmacy that we keep in the house.

I opened the door to the pharmacy and found that it was empty. I went to the storeroom. Father was sitting with his head on the desk, not moving. I hurried to him and found that he was passed out. There was an empty bottle and a telegram from Carol. It said that he was to stop trying to contact her and that she was never coming back. She said that she was sorry for me, but that I was his daughter, and not hers.

I had nowhere else to turn.

I took the bicycle from the alley and rode through the town, cursing Kingsbrook, the pharmacy, Carol, Father, and Thomas.

But now, Thomas was the only one who could help me. He had to help me. I'm carrying his child.

The moon was bright and illuminated the countryside for my journey to the Nightingale House. I once again parked the bicycle by the bushes at the end of the path to the porch. I was already in tears and my hands trembled as I pulled the chain next to the front door. I heard footsteps descending the stairs.

Thomas had to have seen me from the side window because he threw open the door, quickly stepped onto the porch, and shut the door behind him.

"What do you think you are doing?"

"I had to see you."

"I told you never to come here! Do you know what will happen if someone sees you? My daughter is upstairs, asleep, for God's sake!"

"Please, listen to me—"

"No. You need to go, right now. Our valet will be back any minute." He then went to grab me.

"I'm pregnant."

He stopped. The rage that had been fueling him was replaced by panic.

"No …"

"I am."

For the first time, I saw fear in those blue eyes.

Then, he grabbed my arm and began violently dragging me off the porch. I screamed at him to let me go but he wouldn't. I was able to free my hand and struck him across the face. He went to grab my wrists, but in our struggle, grabbed the butterfly necklace. It came away from my neck in his hand. He hurled it towards the bushes and finally succeeded in grabbing my wrists. He held my hands at my side and pulled his face close to mine. I could smell liquor on his breath.

"Listen to me; you are not pregnant. There is nothing between us. There never has been. You delivered those items to my house and went home. That is all. If you say one word of us, or if anyone finds out, I will kill you, do you understand?"

I screamed at him to let me go.

"Say you understand me!" His face was contorted with anger. He was no longer in control.

"Daddy?"

We looked back towards the house. His daughter was standing in the open door, wearing a nightgown.

"I can't sleep," she said.

The fear, rage, and fury that had been building in him exploded. He hurled me to the ground with such force, my head struck the stone path. I was dazed. My vision swam. I was barely aware of him running away. I heard the girl scream as she fled back into the house. I pulled myself to my knees. My balance was thrown. I tried to stand but stumbled onto the grass. I had to get out of there. I crawled on my hands and knees to the bicycle. I heard the girl scream again. It sounded like it was coming from the backyard. Finally, I was able to get to my feet. Slowly, my balance returned enough that I started walking towards the road. I heard another cry from the girl but it was cut short. I picked up the bicycle and on the second attempt, I was able to throw my leg over the seat. I began to pedal but the road swayed beneath me. I crashed to the ground, picked myself up, and tried again.

I heard him roar my name from the side of the house.

I was able to gain speed. My head cleared and I quickly glanced over my shoulder.

He was standing in the road, watching as I hurriedly rode away.

I took the bicycle all the way home. I let myself into the house and went straight to my room. As I passed Father's room, I heard him coughing and retching on the other side of the door. Once I was in my room, I changed my clothes and sat in front of the mirror. There were scratches on my hands, knees, and shoulders. The spot on my head where I had hit the stone path was swollen and throbbed painfully, but it was hidden by my hair. Out of habit, I washed up for bed. The whole thing is a nightmare.

I tried, but I can't sleep.

I don't know what to do. I don't know what happened. I thought going to him was the only way out of this.

Now, it's worse.

So much worse.

September 29th, 1900

HE DID IT!

He did it! I know he did. I don't care what anyone says!

Forgive me. I need to start from the beginning.

I told Father yesterday that I still wasn't feeling well and stayed in bed all day. I figured it would give me time to think of how to tell him of my situation while also allowing my scrapes and bruises a little time to heal.

This morning, before he left for the pharmacy, he stopped by my room and asked if I was feeling better. I told him yes and that I would be into the pharmacy later. I couldn't hide in my room forever. I heard him leave through the front door, and I spent the next few hours trying to decide how to tell Father everything that had happened.

I waited until I knew Patricia Fleming and her little herd would have completed their walk and set out for the main square. I was so wrapped up in my thoughts, that it wasn't until I was almost at the pharmacy that I realized nearly everyone in the street was reading a newspaper. I went inside and Father was reading a newspaper, as well.

"Have you seen this?" he said, pointing to an article. "The Carringtons' daughter is missing."

I grabbed the paper and started reading. The more I read, the more my horror grew. The article stated that she had disappeared last night from the station in Dover where she, Mr. Carrington, and Mr. Whitlock were waiting on the train to Boston.

Father asked me if I had ever met his daughter when I made the deliveries to the Nightingale House.

I felt like I was going to be sick. Father helped me to a chair and asked if I was all right. I told him that I was fine and that it was the shock of reading the article, but that I probably should go home. He agreed.

I believe I truly was in shock. I couldn't conceive that he would do something to his daughter, but then I remembered that grip and those eyes, him throwing me to the ground, and running after her. That scream.

On the walk home, I did finally vomit into some bushes. Luckily, no one saw me. As the house came into view, I had a horrible thought—will Thomas come after me? If he was horrid enough to hurt his daughter, is there anything that would stop him? I worked myself into such a state that I raced inside, locked the door, and drew the curtains. I spent the rest of the day peeking out into the street until Father came home.

I skipped dinner and went to bed early. I've been in this room, worrying, and writing this entry ever since.

I still can't believe it. I know he's a monster, but his own daughter? She has to be alive. She has to. He's not capable of that …

But I still keep going to the window and checking the street.

September 30th, 1900

I'm alone in my room, trying to get the blood off my shirt.

I need to calm down. I need to think.

Yesterday evening, Father arrived home and asked if he could have a word with me. I feared it was more bad news about the pharmacy, but it was worse.

He showed me a telegram that had been delivered to the pharmacy.

It was from Thomas.

He claimed that he wanted to settle his account and would only deal with me. Father said he had gone to the Nightingale House himself, but Mr. Carrington refused to speak to him. He would only speak to me.

"I don't know why he insisted, but I need you to close the account." Father then grew very grave. "We need every cent, Rebecca. I've made a decision; we have to close the pharmacy. I'm going to have a fire-sale to get whatever we can for our inventory. Then, we'll close up the pharmacy and move on. We'll start over somewhere else."

The situation was plain; we were running away from the collectors.

It was too much and I began to cry. Father tried to console me, promising that it would all be all right. I couldn't tell him the truth.

All last night, I couldn't sleep. Somehow, I knew it was inevitable. I was going to have to confront him. I'm carrying his child.

I decided to go to the Nightingale House as early as possible to have it over and done with. I accompanied Father to the pharmacy and went back through the storeroom towards the back door and the bicycle waiting in the alley. As I passed Father's desk, I stopped. I can't explain why, but I grabbed the penknife he uses to open letters off the desktop and tucked it into my pocket. I went out to the alley and grabbed the bicycle.

It had rained the night before. The air was cold and the roads were wet, which slowed my progress. The closer I got, the more I was filled with dread.

As the Nightingale House came into view, I nearly fell from the bicycle. He was waiting on the front porch. I corrected my balance and continued on, finally reaching the stone path, but stayed on the road. He stepped off the porch, began walking down the path, and stopped in front of me.

For a moment, neither of us spoke.

I could no longer stand it. "What did you do to her?" I asked.

He glared at me and said, "You and I never had a relationship of any sort. You delivered the items from the pharmacy to my house. That was all."

"I'm pregnant with your child."

"Impossible. You must have been with some boy and are insinuating it's mine in order to extract some sort of blackmail from me."

The fact that this supposed pillar of the community wouldn't take responsibility for what he had done, that this man who I thought I was in love with was trying to deny the truth set my stomach on fire.

"Where is she?" I asked.

"I don't know what you're talking about."

"I was here. I heard her scream!"

"Keep your voice down," he hissed, looking over his shoulder. "Mr. Whitlock is inside."

"Where is she?!"

He drew himself closer and loomed over me. "Somewhere she'll never be found. Would you care to join her?"

I am not exaggerating. Those were his words. The man just admitted murder and threatened me with the same.

"She would have told my wife and that would have ruined me."

"Your wife must suspect that you're lying."

"My wife suspects I'm an unfaithful husband, but I doubt she believes I'm capable of what you're accusing me of."

"The police—"

"Also have no proof, which is why you're going to tell me, right now: have you told any of your friends about us?"

"I don't have any friends."

"Your father?"

"No."

"You haven't written any letters mentioning us?"

"No."

"You haven't written—"

His face went white.

"That journal …" he breathed.

"What?"

"That journal my insipid wife gave you at the birthday party. The first time I came into your shop, you told me you were writing in it."

I took a step back from him but he closed the gap.

"Have you written anything about us or your … situation?"

My silence told him all.

"You will bring me that journal."

"No."

He clenched his teeth. "I said, you will bring me that journal and I will destroy it—"

"No," I spat.

"Do you know what I'll do to you if—?"

"What? You'll kill me? You really think you'll be able to get away with murder twice? People know where I am, right now, and if I don't return, they'll come looking for me," I bluffed.

"Maybe I won't kill you here and now."

"Then I guess the best thing for me to do is show everyone the journal, right away." Then, I remembered. The thought struck me like a thunderbolt. "In fact, I don't have to … Somebody already knows."

"You're lying …" he said, but he knew I wasn't.

I shook my head.

"Who?" he asked.

"Patricia Fleming."

The panic in his voice grew. "No …"

"She knows. There's nothing you can do. You know what she's like. You killed your daughter and everyone will know."

In a blind fury, he lashed out and gripped my neck. His eyes bulged as he began to crush my throat. I struggled, clawing at his wrists, but he was too strong. He was about to choke the life out of me. I reached into my pocket, pulled out the penknife, and swung at his face. The blade sank into his cheek, under his beard. He released me, staggered backwards, reached up, and pulled the knife out. Blood poured onto his shirt. He dropped the knife onto the road and pressed his hand over the wound.

I took the opportunity and picked up the bicycle.

He was staring at me in horror as I rode away as fast as I could from the Nightingale House.

I went straight home.

Once inside my room, I changed my shirt. I found one that closely resembled it, and hoped Father wouldn't notice. I took the rest of the money Mr. Carrington had told me to keep from his cash purchases, which I would give to Father and tell him the account was paid. There was more than enough.

When I arrived at the pharmacy, Father was in the process of making and placing signs, advertising the new prices. Things that had been a dime were now a nickel, and items that were a nickel were now a penny. Some customers had even found their way into the store.

"There you are," he said, and gestured to the shoppers. "Busiest it's ever been."

I went behind the counter and handed him the money.

"Mr. Carrington's account is closed."

A wave of relief swept over him. Instead of depositing it in the register, Father stuffed the money into his pocket.

"Now, help me with these signs. I think my little plan is going to work."

I spent the rest of the day in a fog. I performed tasks without being aware of what I was doing. The attack felt as though it had happened in some distant nightmare.

It did seem that Father's little plan was working. As soon as the signs went up, people began wandering in. If it keeps up at the prices we were selling, it certainly won't be enough to save the pharmacy, but it might amount to enough to purchase a carriage and leave Kingsbrook.

Around one in the afternoon, among the handful of customers, I glanced out the window. I guess I had been unconsciously keeping a lookout, and sure enough, there they were: Patricia Fleming and her little herd out for their royal stroll.

She turned her head towards the pharmacy and we saw each other. Instead of her customary condescension, she actually appeared concerned, but it was only for a moment before she continued on.

Father and I worked the store for the rest of the day, which was indeed one of our busiest, but that is not very high praise.

Once we closed the pharmacy, we returned home. I went to my room and have been trying to scrub Mr. Carrington's blood off the sleeve of my shirt.

I assume Father is drinking down the hall.

I shall try to sleep, but I'm worried of what horrors tomorrow will bring.

Good night.

October 1st, 1900

I spent all of yesterday nervously glancing out the window, expecting Mr. Carrington to suddenly arrive and smash the glass, but he never appeared.

We were able to sell off a good portion of the store's inventory. It's all at a loss, but we're only accepting cash and all accounts have been closed so that we can have the money in hand.

The disappearance of Katherine Carrington is still all that anyone talks about.

Amid the bustle this afternoon, I happened to catch a glimpse of Patricia Fleming and her cadre walked across the square. However, this time, she stopped and looked at me through the pharmacy window. She was clearly concerned. She even made a step towards the pharmacy, but then continued on with her friends.

I thought it was strange but it only occupied my thoughts for a moment before I was forced to continue helping customers.

We stayed open later than usual in the hopes of selling more of our stock. Father's worried that the more days we stay open, the more likely a collector will eventually come calling.

We closed around nine o'clock after managing to clear out roughly a third of the storeroom. Father and I were both exhausted by the time we arrived home and went straight to bed.

October 2nd, 1900

This morning, Father and I walked to the pharmacy. I still haven't told him of my situation or of Mr. Carrington. I was hoping we could finish the sale and leave Kingsbrook before it became necessary.

As we entered the main square, we saw that everyone was either reading or carrying a newspaper. I assumed that there may have been a development in the disappearance of Katherine Carrington and was anxious to get to the pharmacy.

I opened the door and went inside while Father brought in the stack of newspapers, which he said was the last we would receive, as he had canceled the subscription. He set the bundled stack on the counter and cut the twine.

I was about to step into the storeroom to bring out more items to stock the shelves when I heard Father call out, "Rebecca?"

"What is it?" I asked.

He held up the paper and pointed to an article in the corner.

I stepped over for a closer look.

Thomas Carrington Found Dead

I braced myself against the counter. Father brought me a chair and a glass of water as I read the article, which didn't say much more than the headline. Thomas Carrington had been found dead yesterday in his bedroom at the Nightingale House. The article said that it may have been the result of a sudden illness, possibly brought on by the grief of his daughter's disappearance. I flipped through the paper to see if there was any more, but the article was all there was.

It didn't make sense. I considered that the wound I gave him may have become infected, but that would have taken weeks, not two days.

"Rebecca," Father said, "you look ill. Would you like to go home? I can run the store, myself."

I told him that I was fine, that it was just a bit of a shock.

I didn't want to go home. I wanted answers, and I hoped someone would have them.

There were more customers this morning than yesterday, which is no surprise when you're practically giving away the merchandise, but I made sure to keep my eyes on the window as one o'clock approached.

They arrived, right on time, strolling across the square.

Thankfully, we were experiencing a lull in the customers over lunch, and I told Father that I was stepping out for a moment.

I hurried out the door and across the street.

"Ms. Fleming?" I called when I was a few steps behind them.

They stopped and turned.

Patricia was surprised to see me.

"May I have a word with you?" I asked.

She regarded me briefly and then told her friends that they should go on without her and that she would catch up.

"What is it?" she asked, once they had moved away.

"I wanted to ask you about Mr. Carrington."

"Don't you mean 'Thomas'?"

"Please," I said. "You looked concerned, yesterday, like you were going to come to the pharmacy to talk to me. Do you know what happened?"

She paused again, and then her haughty demeanor fell. "Walk with me."

I obeyed and we began slowly strolling along the square.

"Is he really dead?" I asked.

"Yes. He was found in his bedroom. The police came and spoke to my father. I was listening on the stairs." She looked at me and sighed. "I guess I may have a bit of a habit of snooping."

I was still struggling to believe that he was truly gone.

"What illness?" I asked.

"I'm sorry?"

"The paper said it was a sudden illness."

She hesitated, as if weighing her words before answering.

"It wasn't an illness," she said.

"What?"

"It wasn't a mysterious illness. He killed himself in his room with a pistol."

She strolled on a few more steps before she realized that I had stopped walking and was no longer at her side.

"He killed himself?" I asked.

"So it would seem. You were on familiar terms with him. Any ideas why he would do that?"

By the way she was studying me, it was clear that she believed that I did, but my shock was unreadable.

"If he killed himself, why did the paper say it was an illness?" I asked.

"Because it's Kingsbrook. Their daughter's disappearance is enough of a scandal. It's out of respect for Mrs. Carrington and the rest of her family."

"Where is Mrs. Carrington?"

"I heard my father say that she's still in Boston. Their valet is on his way to join her."

I looked around the square, still unable to comprehend it all.

"Listen," Patricia said, stepping closer, "I don't know exactly what your 'business' was with Thomas Carrington, but if you want my advice, it's best that he's out of everyone's lives … Was there anything else?"

I shook my head.

"Well, thank you for the pleasant walk, but I'm going to rejoin my friends now."

She sadly smiled at me and walked off.

October 5th, 1900

Tonight we locked the pharmacy for the last time.

It took two more days, but we've sold almost all of the inventory. There were some items left on the shelves, but we're leaving those behind.

With some of the money we've made over the past three days, Father bought a horse and small wagon. Tonight, we're going to only gather the essentials from the house and leave first thing in the morning. I've already packed most of my clothes. It's all too much. I'm taking a rest to write this entry before deciding what else to bring.

I'm going to tell Father everything once we leave Kingsbrook. I don't know what I'm going to do. Maybe I'll be able to find a loving family to adopt the child. Maybe I'll try to raise it on my own to make sure it doesn't grow up to be like its father.

I don't know.

For now, I must decide how much of my life I want to take with me on Father's next 'adventure'.

October 6th, 1900

I'm sitting at Mr. Carrington's desk in the Nightingale House. I must be quick. Father is waiting outside. These are the last words I will ever write in this journal and I hope no one reads them, but I can't bring myself to destroy it. Destroying it won't erase the past.

Last night, while trying to decide what to take into our new lives, I decided that I did not want to take these memories. I want to leave them here, in Kingsbrook, in the Nightingale House, where so many of them were born.

I convinced Father to take us by the house as we left Kingsbrook. He was understandably confused but agreed to do it. We drove out through the bitter morning cold to Willow Lake. I knew no one would be here. Mrs. Carrington and Mr. Whitlock are still in Boston. I went to the porch and found the key under the pot on the table. I had to reassure Father to wait for a few minutes as I unlocked the door and went inside.

I walked around the house one last time, stopping in the master bedroom, and came down here, to his little sanctuary. I'm going to leave the journal in the secret compartment in the bookcase. I'm returning his gift. Then, I'm going out back and throwing the key into the lake.

I don't know what the future holds, but I know I want to let go of this past and bury it here in the Nightingale House, this house that holds nothing but sadness.

Farewell.

27

I close the journal.

I've been reading for hours and it's pitch black outside.

It happened here. It happened here in this house. Questions are tumbling in my head. What happened that night at the train station? Mr. Whitlock said Katherine was with them. I have to try the number for the Whitlocks again.

I take out my phone and stand up. It's stifling in here and I need air. I go to the window and am about to push it open but stop when I look down below.

Nicole is standing there on the lawn. She's looking up at me with a terrified expression.

"It's your fault ..."

The whisper to my left is coarse, like wet sandpaper.

I turn my head. Now Nicole is standing next to the bed, but it's the broken, shattered Nicole with the lifeless eyes. I stumble backwards. I momentarily look down at the floor to regain my footing. When I glance back, she's gone.

I don't see her but I can feel it. It's not over. There's still something here, with me.

In a panic, I run to the bedroom door and throw it open.

Instantly, I'm hit by a wall of black mist. It surrounds me and seeps into my skin. Then, in the blink of an eye, it evaporates.

Everything about the hall is different but the same.

Gas lamps line the walls of the hallway, giving off a rich, soft glow. It's like a dream and I never want to leave. This is a comfort I've never known.

The door to my bedroom at the end of the hall is open. The flickering light of the fire in the fireplace dances on the walls of the hallway, next to the open door.

I begin making my way down the hallway, running my hand down the wall.

This isn't me … but it is me. I'm seeing this. I can feel the wall but I'm not doing this. I'm not in control. It's like I'm locked inside myself, like before in the lake and in the living room.

The warmth of the fireplace fills the room as I enter. There's my magnificent four-poster bed. The settee sits next to the vanity. The ornate dresser is in the corner. On the mantle over the fireplace is a photo of myself, my wife, and my daughter.

That's not me. That's not me in the photo. That's not my family.

I'm never going to leave. We're never going to leave. It's so simple. I know what I have to do. The woman won't come in here. She got in once, for a second, but not anymore. I won't allow her in here.

With perfect calm, I walk over to the dresser. I run my fingers over the delicate carvings. I open the top drawer and pull out the derringer pistol. I open the drawer below and remove the bullets. I load them one by one and snap the cylinder closed, exactly as I remember it.

I go to the bed.

I can feel the gun in my hand. I can feel the weight but I'm helpless. I have no control. Stop! STOP!

I lie down on the bed and rest my head on the pillow.

I'm never going to leave this room. He's never going to leave this room and he's never going to find her.

I raise the gun to my head and point the barrel at my temple.

STOP! PLEASE!

I smile, close my eyes and begin to apply pressure to the trigger. This is not the end. Only the beginning of perfection.

"DAD!"

It was Caitlyn, from somewhere downstairs.

Rage courses through my body, searing, uncontrollable.

I'm in control again.

My eyes fly open.

The black mist is hovering above me, pulsating, roiling. It suddenly streaks out the door.

I'm lying in my bed. The fireplace is cold and dark. Dust has settled over everything. The only picture on the mantle is that of Nicole and I on our wedding day. I look towards the dresser. Both the top drawer and the one below it are open. I turn and see the gun in my hand, pointed at my head.

I drop the gun and spring from the bed into the hall just as the black mist goes down the stairs, out of sight.

I sprint down the hall to the stairs.

"DAD!"

Caitlyn is in the basement.

I make it down the stairs to see the black mist go through the living room and dining room into the kitchen.

It's moving too fast. It's going to reach her before I do.

I turn the corner into the kitchen. The back door is open, as is the basement door.

"Caitlyn!" I yell, racing down the basement stairs.

The light is on.

I reach the bottom of the stairs.

Caitlyn is kneeling on the floor in the exact spot where I saw Katherine.

The shadowy fog is behind her, like a beast waiting to strike.

Caitlyn stands, facing the mist. She slowly turns to me. Her eyes are filled with terrified tears.

"... Dad?" she chokingly whispers.

237

"Caitlyn, don't move."

"Dad, please. Don't let it get m—"

I take a step towards her.

The mist bursts outwards. A split second before it envelops Caitlyn, there's a brilliant flash of light, so blinding that I have to shield my eyes. I can feel the cold swirl around me.

Everything goes quiet.

I lower my arms.

The black mist is gone.

So is Caitlyn.

I'm alone.

"… Caitlyn?"

I spin around and search the shadows.

"Caitlyn?!"

She's not here.

I quickly check the corners and crannies, calling her name.

I run upstairs to the open back door, still calling her name, but there's no response.

She was here. I saw her.

I run through the dining room and living room. I look behind every bit of furniture and in every possible hiding place.

"Caitlyn?!"

I run up to the second floor and check all the rooms. She's here. She has to be here, somewhere.

I end up in her room, almost unable to breathe. It's like I'm having a heart attack and I'm still yelling her name. I can't keep my hands still as I look around her r—

There's condensation on the mirror of her vanity.

The air grows colder as I get nearer.

I stand in front of the vanity and look in the mirror.

My reflection isn't there.

But Katherine is.

She's wearing her soaked nightgown and her head is inclined towards the floor. Her wet hair hangs down, obscuring her face.

The condensation on the lower half of the mirror is growing. I can see my breath in the air.

"Where is Caitlyn?" I ask.

There's an excruciating silence.

Katherine doesn't move.

Then, in the condensation, a line appears, drawn by a finger I can't see, but can hear as it moves across the glass. The line become a letter, and then another letter, and another, written in a hand I've seen before on a whiteboard in a classroom.

The message becomes clear.

I start shaking my head and whimper, "No, no, no, no …"

My phone rings.

Shaking, I answer it.

"Hello?"

"Daniel? Hi. It's Mildred. I'm sorry to call so late, but is Caitlyn with you? I heard the door slam and it woke me up. I went to check on Caitlyn but she's not here. Please. Please tell me she's with you."

I can't tell her what happened. I can't tell her the truth.

"Yeah," I stammer. "She's here."

"Really?"

"Yeah. She got a little homesick." I pray the unsteadiness in my voice won't give me away.

She blows a sigh of relief. "Oh, thank God."

"She … uh … Yeah. Sorry she worried you. I told her she shouldn't do that, but she was really shaken up." I keep my eyes on the mirror.

"It's okay. I just wanted to know that she's safe."

"She's fine. She's getting into bed now."

"Daniel, are you okay?"

"Yeah. Yeah, she, uh, she startled me when she came home." I hate lying to Mildred but I have to.

"Okay. Her stuff is still here, if you want to pick it up tomorrow."

"I will. Thanks, Mildred. Again, I'm really sorry about that."

"It's fine. As long as she's safe. Good night."

"Good night."

She hangs up.

I begin taking in rapid gulps of air. I stare at the answer to my question, written in the fading condensation in the mirror …

in here

28

Morning sunlight streams through the living-room window as I lift my head out of my hands. From my spot on what's left of the couch, I glance around the room.

The place looks like a bomb went off. The whole house looks like this.

After hanging up with Mildred, I continued staring at the mirror in disbelief. Was I losing my mind or was I dreaming? I needed proof that what just happened had really happened. I went to the bedroom. The gun was there, lying on the bed, exactly where I had left it. I went downstairs. The back door was open, as was the basement. I checked the call log on my phone. There it was. Mildred had called me.

Yes. This was happening.

Uncontrollable terror set in.

I went to the basement and searched everywhere. No Caitlyn. I went outside into the backyard and called her name, but quietly enough that it wouldn't carry to Mildred's. I even waded into the water. She wasn't outside. I went back into the house and began turning the place inside out, double checking every corner and behind every piece of furniture. I took everything out of the closets and threw it on the floor. I cleared out the cabinets in the kitchen. The whole time, I kept calling her name. At some point, I wasn't just looking for Caitlyn. I was looking for any type of clue that would tell me where she was.

This went on for hours.

At last, I stood in the wreckage of the living room and was seized by paralysis.

I sank down on the couch and held my head in my hands, forced to accept a horrible truth.

Caitlyn's gone.

As much sense as it doesn't make, I have to accept it and I have no idea how to get her back.

I need help.

I have to call someone, but who? The cops? I know Caitlyn is here, somewhere in this house, but if I tell them what happened, they won't believe me. They'll just lock me up.

I could call Mildred. She can help me look but what if she comes over and sees this? She might call the cops anyway. I have to take that chance. She's the only one who might listen to me.

I take out my phone, unlock the screen, and pull up the recent calls. Mildred's number is right at the top. I'm about to hit 'dial' when my phone lights up with an incoming call. I don't recognize the number.

I hit 'accept'.

"Hello?"

"Mr. Price?" a woman's voice asks.

"Yes."

"I'm Dana Whitlock. I'm sorry to call so early, but you left a message yesterday. You wanted to speak to my grandfather?"

My mouth hangs open.

"… Mr. Price? Are you still there?"

"Yes. Yes, I did call."

"Can I ask what it's about?"

"Well … it's about his grandfather, Theodore Whitlock."

"Yes. You said that and that it has something to do with your house. Can you tell me more specifically what this is about?"

"It's … It's kind of a long story, but it has to do with something that happened in Kingsbrook concerning his grandfather's employers, the Carringtons."

"Yes, I understand that. It's just …" She's making no attempt to hide her frustration. "He wants to speak with you."

"Oh. Okay. Can you put him on the phone?"

"Mr. Price, he's ninety-five and very weak. He doesn't do phone calls. He said he will only speak to you in person."

There's no way that I'm leaving this house. Not now.

"I'm sorry. I can't do that."

"He said it was the only way."

"Then, I'm afraid—"

"He also told me to ask you a question."

"Oh. Okay."

"I don't know why, but he wouldn't leave me alone until I promised I would ask you."

"What's the question?"

"He wants to know, 'She still can't sleep, can she?'"

29

My knuckles go white on the steering wheel.

What am I doing? Why am I leaving the house? Caitlyn's in there, somewhere.

But where? I've taken the place apart. The only place she could be is in the walls.

I suddenly have a horrible vision of Caitlyn trapped in a wall of the house and I nearly swerve off the road.

No. The only way to get Caitlyn back is with answers and this guy sounds like he has them.

Still, the voices in my head are screaming at me to turn around and get back to the house. I grit my teeth, grip the steering wheel, and wait for them to pass.

I keep trying to rehearse what I'm going to say, but every attempt sounds more ridiculous than the last. When I see the exit for the town of Redmill, I have a crushing thought that causes my body to go limp; I lost Nicole, and now I'm going to lose Caitlyn.

The blaring horn of a semi-truck, barreling towards me as I drift across the yellow lines snaps me out of it. I wrench the wheel to get myself back into the proper lane. The butterfly necklace, journal, and medallion slide to the side of the passenger seat next to me. I punch the dashboard and take a deep breath through clenched teeth.

I can't give up. Until I hold Caitlyn's lifeless body in my arms, there has to be a chance. I have to believe that, or else there is nothing else but madness.

*

The Whitlock house is a simple, one-story ranch with a concrete porch on a lonely road, surrounded by fields, on the outskirts of Redmill. It has a sprawling, featureless front yard. The driveway is paved, but only just. I can feel every crack and depression as I drive over them. I park behind an ancient Ford Explorer and take a moment to check my reflection in the rearview mirror.

I look like shit. I'm worried that my appearance might scare the granddaughter off the whole thing, but what choice do I have?

I get out and walk up the stairs of the porch to the weathered screen door. The front door behind it is already open. Before I can knock or find the doorbell, I'm greeted by a petite woman somewhere in her forties. She has a sharp nose, thin lips, and wiry brunette hair that's pulled tightly into a bun. She peers at me through the mesh of the screen door.

"Are you Daniel Price?" she asks.

I nodded. "You Dana?"

"Yeah." She looks me up and down. "You okay?"

"It's been a long couple of days."

"I can tell."

She opens the door, steps out, and stands with her arms folded across her chest. "You mind telling me what this is all about?"

"I need to speak to your grandfather. I want to know if his grandfather spoke to him about something that happened a long time ago."

"He's old, bedridden, and not all together upstairs, if you know what I mean. I don't like any added stress for him and it sounds like that's all you are. So, why don't you ask me?"

"It's a long story and I think it's be better if I ask him."

"Well, you can ask me firs—"

"Please, I'm running out of time."

She cocks her head at me. "Until what?"

We have a momentary standoff.

"Please."

My gentle pleading reaches her and she sighs.

"I was so weirded out by your message that I wasn't going to tell him, but I let it slip last night. After that, he wouldn't shut up about it. He kept asking to hear it, so I played it for him. He was more stirred up than I've seen him in years. That's when he told me about the sleeping thing. What is he talking about?"

"It's something about my house. His grandfather used to work there."

"The Night-something house?"

"Nightingale House."

She looks out at the surrounding fields. "He hasn't spoken about that place in years …"

"I need to talk to him. It's important."

She gives me another appraising look. "I suppose I've got to or he won't ever shut up about it. Well, let's get this over with." She turns and opens the screen door but stops. "Fifteen minutes, then you have to go."

"I might need more time."

"That's non-negotiable. Fifteen minutes. If you're sixteen minutes, I'm calling the cops."

"Okay."

I consent because I have to talk to this guy. If I need more time, I'll figure something out.

Once inside, she leads me through the living room to a closed door at the end of a short hallway. She places her hand on the door and fixes me with a look.

"Fifteen minutes."

I nod.

She gently opens the door. "Pa-pa?"

The first thing that hits me is the aroma of antiseptic, plastic, and body odor; a nasal cocktail that I'll always associate with visiting my great-grandfather in a nursing home.

"There's someone here to see you," Dana says softly.

There's a mumble from somewhere in the room and she motions for me to enter.

The blinds are drawn, the carpet is worn, and the walls are covered in cheap wood-paneling. At the far end of the room is a hospital bed. Beside it sits a small steel stand, upon which rests a medical monitor and a pump attached to a breathing apparatus. Tubes run from the apparatus to the man lying in the bed: Benjamin Whitlock, the grandson of Theodore Whitlock.

The bed is inclined upwards, giving the illusion that he's sitting up, but there's no way he has the strength. I can see the outline of his frail and withered body under the sheets. The fine strands of hair on his head do nothing to hide his liver-spotted scalp. His eyes are small, bleary, and bloodshot, but they lock onto me as I step to the foot of the bed.

Dana comes over and gently takes his hand. "Pa-pa, this is Daniel Price. He left the message for you yesterday."

I register a slight nod from the old man.

"Thank you for agreeing to see me," I say.

"All right, Mr. Price," Dana says. "What did you want to talk about?"

I'm about to launch into my story, but Mr. Whitlock gently pats Dana's hand.

"Dana, can you please give us a few minutes alone?"

"But, Pa-pa—"

"It'll be all right."

She eyes me in confusion and mistrust, but respects her grandfather's wishes and leaves his side.

"Press the button if you need anything," she says. "Fifteen minutes," she whispers to me before going into the hallway and closing the door.

Once she's gone, the only sound in the room is the old man's rhythmic labored breathing.

The corners of his lips lift slightly in what I think is a smile. "I can only assume you're about to tell me some stuff my granddaughter, bless her, might not understand. Please, have a seat." He indicates the wooden chair next to the bed. I accept and sit down. It creaks as it takes my weight. "Now, my granddaughter usually gives my guests fifteen minutes so as not to over excite me, but I'm not sure I even have fifteen minutes left, so you'd better hurry up."

He starts to laugh, which sounds more like a quick succession of coughs.

"Well, again, thank you for seeing me," I say.

"You from Kingsbrook?"

"Yes. I live in the Nightingale House."

"How are you liking it?"

I don't answer.

He shrugs his shoulders by raising them a fraction of an inch. "I figured. What is it you want to talk about?"

"You told your granddaughter to ask me something: 'She still can't sleep, can she?' What did that mean?"

His sense of humor vanishes and he shakes his head. "You know damn well what I meant. Ask me what you called about in your message."

I took a breath. "Your grandfather was the Carringtons' butler, correct?"

"I wouldn't call him their butler. He was their valet. He didn't cook or nothing, but he helped around the house and the yard and he drove them around."

"Did you know your grandfather?"

"I did. He died when I was fifteen but I knew him. He lived with us for a while towards the end."

"Did he ever talk about the Carringtons?"

"Sometimes."

"What did he say?"

"Not much, but I guess he liked them enough ... well, some of them." He looks at me. "He loved the girl."

"Katherine?"

"Yeah. Katherine."

"What about Abigail?"

"Sure."

"And Thomas Carrington?"

"Not his favorite. Wasn't anyone's favorite, as far as I could tell. The Carringtons were long gone when he talked to me about them, and like I said, he didn't say much."

"Why not?"

"It was hard for him ..."

I decide to cut to the chase. "Mr. Whitlock, your grandfather was there the night Katherine disappeared."

He closes his eyes. "Yes. He was there ... Well, he said he was there."

"He told the police that he drove Thomas Carrington and his daughter to the train station in Dover."

"That's what he told them."

"Mr. Whitlock, did your grandfather ever talk to you about what really happened that night?"

There's a change in him—a resignation. Like a weight is sliding off his chest.

"My grandfather was a sad man ... At least he was when I knew him. He was broken. Towards the end of his life, he lived with our family. My parents and me. It was awful. He was going crazy. He would mumble all the time in his room. He kept shouting in his sleep. One night, I was outside the door, trying

249

to hear what he was saying and it sounded like, 'She can't sleep. She can't sleep.' Other times, he would just cry. The older he got, the worse it got. The littlest things upset him. It was like he would see something or someone who wasn't there and he would apologize, over and over. Finally, my parents decided that he couldn't live with us anymore. They made arrangements for him to stay at an asylum. The night before he left, I was outside his room, again, just listening to him mumble and cry. It got quiet, and then, all of a sudden, he opened the door, grabbed me, and pulled me into the room. I was scared out of my mind. He took me by the shoulders and kept saying, 'She wasn't there. She wasn't there.' I asked him, 'Who?' and he kept saying, 'Katherine can't sleep! Katherine can't sleep!' I started crying and that snapped him out of it. He said, 'I'm going to tell you something and you can never tell anyone.' I only wanted out of that room, so I said yes. He said, 'That girl was never there.' I asked him, 'What girl?' but he was so upset that he didn't answer. Then he said that Thomas Carrington had given him a thousand dollars to tell the police that she had been with them at the train station. Carrington said that if he didn't, he'd ruin him, but the daughter was never there."

He's been growing more and more agitated as he's been speaking. He releases a series of coughs and tries to calm himself. "Then, my grandfather reached under the mattress of his bed, pulled out an envelope, and stuffed it down my shirt. He told me to hide it, but never spend it. That it was cursed. He said she was coming to him in his dreams and that she couldn't sleep. I tried to get out of the room, but he grabbed me and told me that she's still in that house and that she can't sleep. I started shouting and crying. My parents came running. They hauled my grandfather off to the asylum right then and there. That was the last time I ever saw him. Later that night, when I was alone, I opened the envelope. It was full of money. I hid it and my parents never knew. At the time, I didn't know what he was talking about, but that night stayed with me. Nothing ruins a childhood like holding on to a dark secret. Years later, I started looking into what he meant. That's when I put it together. Thomas Carrington did something to his daughter and paid my grandfather to be his alibi. The guilt drove my grandfather crazy."

By the time he's done with his story, he's gasping for breath. I can understand why he didn't want his granddaughter in the room for this. I would have been escorted out long ago.

His breathing returns to what passes as normal and he looks at me. "The clock is ticking, Mr. Price."

"Did your grandfather tell you what happened?"

"No."

"What do you think happened?"

"Probably the same as you; Thomas Carrington killed his daughter. She never left that house."

"Why didn't you tell anyone?"

He's seized by another fit of coughing. "What good would it have done? By the time I put it all together, everyone was gone. I hated my grandfather for telling me. I wish he would have taken it to his grave."

"So, after all this time, why are you telling me?"

"Eighty-two years is a long time to hold on to something. You're not a child and it sounds like you need to know."

"One last question, Mr. Whitlock: do you have any proof of this?"

He motions just enough to indicate the closet. "Top shelf. Leather suitcase. My granddaughter doesn't know."

I go to the closet and open the doors. There are cardboard boxes on the floor and clothes that haven't been worn in years hanging from the rack. The top shelf is littered with shoeboxes and papers. In the back corner, I find a small, beat-up leather suitcase. I ease it down, trying to make as little noise as possible, because I'm sure Dana is listening in the hallway. I gently place it on the bed, next to his legs, press the latches, and open the lid.

It's empty.

"False top," he says in a raspy breath.

I find a loose corner of fabric and pull. It rips away.

Underneath the fabric, fastened with a pin to the underside of the lid, is a yellowed envelope. I pull it off and open it. It's stuffed with bills. They vaguely resemble dollar bills but these are bigger and feel like fabric rather than paper. Printed on them are words like "Gold Certificate" and "Silver Certificate".

"Proof enough for you?" he asks.

I nod.

The last piece is in place. Between his story and Rebecca's journal, I know everything now.

"I could never spend it. Never wanted to. It's blood money ... You want it?" he asks.

I return the bills to the envelope, close it, and stick it back to the underside of the lid. I secure the latches of the suitcase, and return it to its resting place on the top shelf of the closet. I close the closet door and turn back to him.

"Thank you, Mr. Whitlock."

"I thought my grandfather was crazy, the way he babbled about those dreams ... He was talking about her, wasn't he?"

"Yes."

He looks down at his feet. "When they took him that night, he just kept screaming, 'She can't sleep! She can't sleep!' I'll never forget that. I thought he was crazy but ... last night, I saw her. Saw her in my dreams ... She told me she couldn't sleep ..." He looks back up at me. "Can she sleep, now?"

"Not yet."

*

Sure enough, Dana backs away from the door as I open it. She's been listening.

"So, are you going tell me what this was all about?"

"He'll tell you, himself. I don't have time."

I walk past her, down the hall, through the living room, and out the front door.

I get in my car and start the engine. I back out of the driveway, slam it into gear, and stomp on the gas. The tires scream and the car lurches forward, carrying me off in the direction of the highway.

I know everything now and she's been trying to tell me from that first night. The drips. Seeing her in the lake by the pier when I lost Nicole's ring. The basement. Mr. Whitlock was the last piece of the puzzle that's made it all clear.

She was never at that train station.

The night Rebecca Harker told Thomas Carrington she was pregnant, he panicked. He worried that his daughter would tell his wife, and that would be the end. He'd be cut off. He chased her through the house to the backyard. That's where it happened. That's where he did it. He drowned her, and had to hide the body somewhere it would never be found. Like Thomas Carrington had told Rebecca Harker, "She was somewhere that she would never be found." Then, he paid Theodore Whitlock for an alibi.

The more I think about it, the more furious I become. Not only had Katherine been trying to tell me, but so had Caitlyn. She tried to tell me after the incident at school, and I didn't believe her.

Katherine was trapped. Her father won't let her leave because if she leaves, he has to go, too.

Just as before, he would lose everything.

*

I whip the car onto the exit before Kingsbrook, and drive to the hardware store on the outskirts of town. I park in a handicap spot, not caring about the scolding looks I receive. I walk up to the first person wearing a nametag, which happens to be the guy who helped me, before.

"Crowbar, sledgehammer, and shovels?"

"Oh … Did you lose something, again?"

I'm sure my appearance doesn't look good for someone asking for crowbars, sledgehammers, and shovels, but I don't care.

"Crowbar. Sledgehammer. Shovels."

"Umm … crowbars and sledgehammers are on aisle five and shovels are on aisle nine in the garden sect—"

I'm already off.

After finding what I need, I get some odd glances in the checkout line.

The girl scans the items while keeping her eyes on me.

"Sixty-three dollars and eighty-seven ce—."

I take four twenties from my wallet and drop them on the scanner. Without a word, I grab the tools and start walking.

"Sir, your change!"

I keep walking.

30

I pull into the driveway of the Nightingale House.

Midway down the drive, I hit the brakes, put the car in park, and kill the engine.

The sun is starting to set, casting an orange light over the gables and the Turret Room.

Caitlyn's in there, somewhere.

And so is he.

I know what I have to do and I know he'll try to stop me. He's almost made me kill myself, twice. I don't know how to keep him out. I'm not sure that I can. The only thing that saved me is Nicole.

I reach into my pocket and pull out her ring. I turn it over in my hand while keeping an eye on the house.

"Nicole … I don't know if you can hear me, but I … I don't know what's gonna happen … and I'm really scared. I know I've been scared before, like the night Caitlyn was born … and the time we took her to the ER because of that flu … I know you said you were just as scared as I was, but you always did a better job of hiding it. You were always that rock, through everything … I know we didn't have as much time as we thought we were going to, but even if we did … I don't think I could have said 'thank you' enough … Caitlyn and I really need you, right now … I don't care if I walk out, so long as our daughter's safe … I don't know if you can, but please, be by my side for this one …"

I pick up the necklace from the passenger seat. I slide the butterfly pendant off the chain and set it aside. Then, I thread the chain through Nicole's ring. I hang it around my neck, reach back, and tie the chain into a small, simple knot around the broken clasp.

Just to feel that small weight, again, pressing on my chest, fills me with calm. I close my eyes and I can see her. I see us — the moments we sat together at the kitchen table. The walks we would take. Playing with Caitlyn. I'm filled with a soft warmth.

I open my eyes. The Nightingale House waits.

I don't know if I'll walk out, maybe I'll be with Nicole again, but I'll be damned if he gets our daughter.

I tuck Nicole's ring into my shirt and step out of the car.

*

I open the front door. The house is already tense, waiting, and watching.

I step inside, close the door, and lock it behind me.

I stride with determination through the living room, dining room, and into the kitchen. I slowly open the basement door. The wooden stairs creak as I begin my descent. I don't bother with the flashlight app on my phone. I reach the bottom of the stairs, step into the darkness, and find the chain. I reach up and pull.

The glow from the light shows that everything appears as it should.

I go to the spot where I saw Katherine standing and where Caitlyn was kneeling. I drop the sledgehammer and shovel, but hold onto the crowbar. I take a deep breath, raise the crowbar, and ram the thin end into the space between the floorboards. I

256

pull against the crowbar with all my weight and I'm rewarded with a sharp *crack* as one of the floorboards comes free. I pry it up, rip it away, and throw it into the corner of the room. I repeat the process. The next board springs free. I continue until there's a hole large enough to stand in. I inspect the concrete underneath.

There's a patch in the old concrete that's noticeably different than the rest. It's uneven, and fine cracks stretch across the surface. I'm no contractor, but this was poured at a different time than the rest. I grab the sledgehammer and brace my legs against the sides of the hole. I raise it over my head, and swing. The impact sends shockwaves through my body. Bits of concrete fly in all directions. A few of the cracks become sharper and new cracks snake out in all directions. I raise the hammer again and bring it down with a grunt. Larger bits of concrete come loose, and more cracks appear. I swing again and again. To my relief, the concrete is only about half an inch thick, but it's still tiring work. Finally, I bring the hammer down with all the strength I can muster and the concrete shatters into large chunks. I can see the dirt underneath. I crouch down and clear out the heavy pieces of concrete, sweat pouring down my face and neck.

A few more swings and I have a big enough opening to the dirt below to start digging.

Suddenly, the air around me changes. It grows cold and more dense.

It's starting.

The skin on my arm ripples with goosebumps. There's a sound. Breathing. It's quiet but intense. I look around but it's only me down here. I clear more debris from the hole. The breathing continues to grow. I grab the shovel and drive the spade into the ground.

"… I can't sleep …"

The whisper comes from every corner of the room. I'm not going to look around. I don't want to. Whatever is going to happen, let's get it over with. All I care about is saving Caitlyn.

I ram the shovel into the hard earth, lift it out, and throw it onto the floorboards.

Another sound joins the tense breathing that fills the air — a slow heartbeat. I stop, but still refuse to look. She could be standing right next to me, but to look would slow me down. I continue plunging the shovel into the ground and throwing the dirt out of the hole. The disembodied breathing continues, as does the sound of the heartbeat. Both grow louder and more rapid.

"… I can't sleep …"

The whisper is right next to my ear — a child's whisper.

Katherine.

I quicken my pace.

The beads of sweat feel like ice sliding down my face. The hole is now about a foot deep.

"… Hurry …"

I try to go faster. The pile of dirt on the floor next to the hole is growing.

"… Hurry …"

The breathing quickens. The heartbeat grows louder.

She has to be down here. She has to be.

"… He's coming …"

The adrenalin that's been fueling my spent nerves and exhausted muscles gives way to blinding terror. I swallow down the bile that's rising in my throat. I can no longer tell if the pounding heartbeat I hear is in the air around me, or if it's my own heart slamming against my ribcage.

"… Hurry …"

I frantically dig. The hole is now about two feet deep, oval-shaped, and wide enough for me to stand in.

"… He's coming …"

The heartbeat sounds like thunder. I can hear the wooden shelves tremble with each thump. I feel like I'm about to burst into tears.

"… He's coming …"

I scream while continuing to frantically throw dirt onto the floorboards. I clench my teeth and keep digging. I'm three feet down into the dirt. The heartbeat rumbles. The breathing rages. I throw two more shovelfuls across the floorboards.

Suddenly, everything stops.

The heartbeat and breathing cease.

It's cold and silent.

"… Father …"

The whisper drifts away.

I wait, absolutely still.

Then, I hear it. It's faint, but the sound travels through the house—the sound of the door to the master bedroom opening.

Footsteps.

I look up at the ceiling.

They're moving down the hall, making their way to the stairs. They're slow, heavy, and deliberate. They descend the stairs, and methodically cross the living room … through the dining room … now in the kitchen. They stop at the top of the basement stairs.

I can't move.

The first footfall echoes on the top stair. I wait and watch, expecting the feet and legs to come into view but they don't. The footsteps come down the stairs, which groan under a weight I cannot see. They reach the bottom of the stairs, cross the floor, and stop.

Whatever it is, it's standing right in front of me, but I can't see it.

I know it's here, watching.

I'm waiting for something to happen, anything.

I can't take it any longer. I push the shovel into the ground. I lift the dirt out of the hole and look up to toss it onto the pile.

He's here. He's right in front of me.

Thomas Carrington.

He's standing exactly where the footsteps stopped. He looks as he did in the photos. Imposing. Intimidating. The only difference is his eyes. Instead of the clear blue eyes Rebecca Harker described, they now are milky and gray and stare lifelessly ahead.

He's not looking at me, but I can feel his awareness.

My feelings of dread and fear evaporate. This thing knows where Caitlyn is.

"Where's my daughter?"

He stares straight ahead.

"Where's my daughter, you son of a bitch?!"

No response.

"Answer me, Goddamnit! Where is my daughter?! Because I'm about to find yours."

His face lowers. Those eyes don't focus but he's looking at me — through me. His expression doesn't change but there's pure hatred emanating from him.

I wait, thinking I'll have to defend myself, but nothing happens. Fine.

I ram the shovel back into the dirt. I glance up. He's still there. I hoist the shovel, full of cold black dirt, out of the hole, and throw it across the floor.

He still doesn't move.

I do it again. No reaction.

I remove two more shovelfuls. I go to throw the last load of dirt and stop.

He's gone. The room is empty, but I can still feel his presence. He's still here. I don't know what to do … so I go back to digging.

Suddenly, I feel it: the cold. Not just on my skin. This is different. It's in my bones. It's a cold that's painful. It's the same cold I felt in the bedroom with the gun in my hand and in the living room when I almost stabbed a pencil through my eye, when *he* had taken over. It makes every movement feel like bits of broken glass are circulating in my veins, but I still keep digging.

I'm about to lift out another shovelful of dirt, when I'm shoved by unseen hands. I stumble backwards against the floorboards, but stay upright. I widen my stance, bracing myself against the sides of the hole, and slam the shovel into the dirt.

A roar begins to build like an oncoming freight train, but it's not in the air around me. It's in my head. It grows from a steady rumble to a skull-splitting roar. I keep digging. It feels like my head is about to cave in. Every fiber in my body is in agonizing pain.

I go to drive the shovel into the ground again, but the weight of it is unbearable, and my arms refuse to respond.

He's inside me.

I grunt, and with every ounce of strength I can muster, push the shovel into the ground. The pain is so intense, I scream. I lift it out of the pit like I'm lifting a truck.

"I'm not a little girl, you fucking prick," I rage. "You'll have to do better than that."

Just like that, it stops. I can breathe again. I frantically complete two more cycles of digging before all my limbs tense.

There's pressure in my throat. My airway is closing. I drop the shovel and pull at my neck. I fight, but it's useless. I can't stop him. I grab the shovel and keep going. The roar inside my head is back. The cold, penetrating pain has returned and now I can't breathe.

My efforts slow and became less effective, but I keep digging.

My vision fills with spots. My eyes bulge in their sockets. I can feel the pressure in my face as my lungs claw for air.

My consciousness begins to surrender.

Suddenly, I see Caitlyn. Images of her. Horrible images that I know *he* is putting there. They're the stuff of a parent's worst nightmare. Caitlyn dead in the car. Caitlyn floating face down in the lake. Caitlyn's broken body lying in a coffin. The images rush through me. I can't block them out.

Then, everything goes black.

I'm looking into a void. I can still hear the sounds of my

struggles and the digging, but it's miles away. I don't feel my screaming muscles, or my lungs clutching for air. The only physical sensation I feel is the light weight of Nicole's ring against my chest.

Another image appears before me.

Nicole.

She's standing before me in the void. She looks just as I remember her— beautiful, smiling. The most amazing woman I have ever known.

"Let go," she whispers.

"No. You're not her. You're not Nicole," I say, the sounds of my digging and gasping growing further and further away.

"We can be together, again," the thing pretending to be Nicole says and adds with a grin, "Just like you wanted." Her lips curl into a sinister, knowing smile. "Just like you planned."

My heart collapses from grief. The grief of knowing that deep down, on those lonely, depressing nights, I had thought about it. I had thought about ending it all to be with her. That's why I bought that gun—not for protection, but because I didn't want to go on, not without Nicole. I bought it so that one day, I could use it to blow my brains out and be with Nicole.

"You're not her! You're *him*!" I scream.

Nicole's face contorts in a flash of anger, but instantly returns to a caring expression.

Then, out of the darkness, Caitlyn appears by Nicole's side, holding her hand. She smiles at me, her face angelic.

"Let go, Daddy," she says. "And we can be a family, again."

This is too far. *He's* gone too far.

To be with Nicole again, is something that I would give almost anything for, but what keeps me from using that gun to end my life is Caitlyn. I could never leave her. Never. If I did make that terrible decision, whatever bridge I crossed, I know Nicole would be on the other side, and she would never forgive me for abandoning Caitlyn. I'll never let anything happen to my daughter.

In a flash, I see everything—every memory I have of Caitlyn. I see Nicole telling me she's pregnant. I see Caitlyn's birth. I see us taking Caitlyn home from the hospital. I see Nicole and I watching Caitlyn take her first steps in the living room of our apartment in Portsmouth. I hear Caitlyn's first words. I see her first day of kindergarten. The three of us celebrating birthdays. Every simple joy from making her breakfast, to kissing her good night, every night. All of it. Every moment of a love I didn't know could exist until Nicole and Caitlyn were in my life.

Suddenly, the black void around me is filled with light. I feel warm.

I'm released.

I can breathe. I can see.

I'm in the hole, shovel in hand, and air filling my lungs.

He's there, standing where I last saw him.

I can feel fear and uncertainty swirling around me, but they're not mine.

They're his. He's afraid.

I pushed him out.

I regain my senses, slam the shovel back into the ground, lift the dirt out, and hurl it away.

Almost immediately, it's back.

The previous roar, pain, and grip on my throat, are nothing compared to this. This is agony. This is desperation. This is Hell.

I'm going to vomit but can't because my throat is clenched shut. Tears pour down my cheeks. I keep my eyes focused on the hole below me. I can see drops of spittle fall from my lips and coagulate in the dirt.

The swirling spots before my eyes explode into pinpoints of light.

I weakly push the shovel into the ground. It hits something. I'm too weak to lift the dirt away. The shovel drops from my hands.

The darkness is coming, rushing at me like a wall of black nothing.

With one last speck of consciousness, I swipe my foot across the point where the shovel made contact. My foot wipes away the dirt, and through the hot stinging tears, and dimming vision, I see them—bones, small and spindly. Some have been shattered by the shovel's blade, but others are unmistakable. They're small fingers.

Blinding light flies up from the hole.

Again, I'm released.

I fall back against the floorboards, coughing and wheezing. A new rumble builds around me, shaking the shelves, floorboards, and walls.

He's still there, standing next to the hole.

The light continues to erupt from below me, filling the basement. It expands. Blinding. Pure. The figure of Thomas Carrington becomes a silhouette against it. The roar builds to a point that it threatens to tear the house apart.

An apex is reached. The silhouette of Thomas Carrington blasts apart, scattering like sand in a tornado.

I have to shield my eyes from the intense glare.

The roar stops.

I open my eyes.

Points of shimmering light drift through the air like ashes and stars.

There, standing before me, is Katherine. She is staring at the ground, her hair covering her face. Her head slowly tilts up and she looks at me with a quizzical expression. For a second, we stare at one another.

A form materializes next to her.

Nicole.

She's just as perfect as I remember her.

She looks at me, then at Katherine.

Nicole holds out her hand. Katherine carefully takes it. Nicole gives me that smile I've missed every second of every minute of every day since I lost her.

She looks back to Katherine, and something passes between them. They turn and begin to walk into the darkness, together.

I'm choking back sobs. I have so many things I want to tell her but I can't speak.

She glances over her shoulder. Her lips don't move, but I hear her voice in my head.

"I love you."

"I love you, too," I whisper.

With that, Nicole and Katherine disappear into the darkness, together.

The points of light fade and the darkness lifts.

I'm alone in the basement.

No sound. No unseen presence.

Just me.

I hear Caitlyn's weak voice call out from somewhere upstairs. "Dad?"

I scramble out of the hole and race up the stairs. I run through the kitchen and living room, and bound up the stairs, continually calling out Caitlyn's name. I throw open the door to her room.

"Caitlyn?!"

There's a sound from the closet. I open the door with such force that one of the hinges almost gives way.

She's balled up on the floor, still wearing her nightgown, eyes blinking as though she just woke up. I scoop her up and clutch her to my chest, not caring that I'm covered in dirt and sweat. She holds fast to my neck. Her skin is ice-cold. I carry her over to the bed and lay her down. I gently rest her head on the pillow, and pull the covers up to her chin.

"I had a bad dream," she mutters.

I rest my face next to hers, stroke her cheek, and whisper, "It's okay now, pumpkin. It's okay … It was just a dream."

31

Sheriff Watts chews the tip of his pen as he stares at the transcript of our interview. I sit in the chair on the other side of the table and wait. He's about to speak, but instead, he gets a pained expression, and uses the pen to scratch his head. He studies my words as though they might magically arrange themselves in some other order that makes sense.

"I … I just want to get this straight."

"Of course."

"You said you were …" He consults his notes, again. "You found these remains because you were installing a hot tub … in your basement?"

"Yep."

"Mr. Price, I'm no expert, but when it comes to hot tubs, most people put them outside."

"I guess I'm no expert, either."

No, it's not my best lie, but whatever.

Once things settled down and I knew Caitlyn was okay, I called the police and they took possession of the remains. They asked me how I knew that the bones were there. I told them I was putting in a hot tub. I'm sure they knew it was a lie but I don't care. I could tell them what really happened, and the hot tub story would still make more sense.

Sheriff Watts shakes his head. "Well, the remains have been there a long time, and even the person who put them there ain't around anymore, either. There's not a whole lot we can do."

"Okay."

He waits for a response I'm not going to give.

"Look, Mr. Price, we could open up a formal investigation, but I don't think it will do any good. Even if we could identify the remains, which I doubt, there's no reason to make this public. All it would do is pull resources from my office and state officials for a crime that can't be solved. I think it's best if you let us take possession of the remains, catalogue them, and we can forget all about this."

"Nope."

"I beg your pardon?"

"That doesn't work for me."

Sheriff Watts rubs his eyes. "Mr. Price, I understand what a shock this must have been for you and your daughter—"

"No, you *really* can't."

"—but I assure you, that if you go to the press, your house will become a tourist attraction."

"And, like you said, it would be a hassle for you."

"Well …"

"I won't tell the press on one condition."

"You have a condition?"

"Yep," I say, sitting forward in my chair. "You release the remains to me so that I can give them a proper burial."

He gives me a hard stare. "Why? Do you know who this is?"

"How could I?"

"Then why would you—?"

"What do you care?" I've been calm up until that point, but I'm tired and want this to be over. It was over the moment I had

Caitlyn back but this has to happen—for Caitlyn and myself. Sheriff Watts will have to deal with it. "If you allow me to give the remains a proper burial, I promise that no one will hear of it."

Sheriff Watts considers it.

"No one's gonna know?" he asks.

"Do whatever tests you want, take dental records, whatever, and then let me bury the remains. No one is going to come looking for this girl."

He peers at me. "How do you know it's a girl?"

I'm so tired and fed up that I lash out. "Because she told me. Does that work for you?"

His expression goes from baffled to insulted. He throws up his hands. "Fine! Fine, fine, fine. Just do me a favor, Mr. Price," he says, and stands up. "Next time, hire a professional to install your damn hot tub."

*

A week later, I'm looking at myself in the mirror next to the front door, adjusting my black suit and tie.

"You ready, pumpkin?" I call.

"Coming!" Caitlyn replies, and descends the stairs, wearing the black dress with the white trim she wore at Nicole's funeral. She insisted on wearing it.

We haven't talked much about what happened the night she disappeared. All I asked was why she came back from Mildred's. She replied that Katherine told her what was happening. That was the extent of our conversation.

"Don't forget your coat," I say, as she lands at the bottom of the steps.

"Dad, I was gonna get it."

As she goes to the closet, I look around.

This is a different house now.

A weight has been lifted. The presence is gone. Honestly, I'm not sure how to feel. I'm happy that whatever you want to call what was lurking in the house is gone, but also, for the first time since the accident, I know Nicole is also truly gone. I no longer feel her in the other room, just out of sight. She took Katherine across, which is one more thing I'll love her for, but now, there's only a scar that will never heal. She's gone, and even though Caitlyn and I live within the walls of the Nightingale House, it feels empty, like we're the ghosts, and the house wants to move on.

I'm snapped out of my thoughts by Caitlyn approaching, wrestling with her coat. The coat is winning. I help her get her arms through the sleeves.

"Ready?" I ask.

"Ready."

*

Elysian Fields Cemetery is a ten-minute drive to the outskirts of Kingsbrook. It sits on a hill, overlooking the town. The vast rows of gravestones have dates that range back to the 1700s and the landscape is dotted with sugar maples.

Caitlyn holds my hand as we walk through the granite and marble stones to the plot I've purchased in a corner of the field. The cold autumn air scrapes at our cheeks and makes our eyes water. Caitlyn doesn't complain.

There are no priests, ministers, or rabbis— only a small coffin containing the remains of what Caitlyn and I know to be Katherine Carrington, and a gravestone that's blank. There are two employees of the graveyard present, who don't seem to care about the circumstances. They've probably seen stranger. Having already dug the grave, they are sitting under a sugar maple thirty yards away, smoking cigarettes. I nod to them. They nod back.

Caitlyn and I stand before the grave. I lean down to her. "Is there anything you want to say?"

She thinks about it and steps over to the casket.

"I'm really sorry about what happened to you, but I'm glad I got to meet you. I'm glad you got to meet my mom. If you see her again, tell her I said 'Hi' and I love her."

She looks at me for approval, and I nod. Caitlyn returns to my side and takes my hand.

I motion to the workers. They put out their cigarettes and rise to join us.

They take the small casket off the pedestal, and slowly lower it into the grave. Once it reaches the bottom, I step over to the mound of earth. I take a handful, hold it over the open space, and let it fall from my hand. Caitlyn follows suit. Once completed, we step back.

The workers take over from there. They pick up their shovels and begin to fill the grave. Caitlyn and I watch, our hands still locked together. We don't move for the half hour it takes the workers to complete their task.

When it's over, the workers know their part, and quietly slip away. Caitlyn and I wait for a few more minutes, completely alone, staring at the blank headstone.

"Goodbye, Katherine," Caitlyn says.

A small breeze blows through the rows of headstones and sends dry, brittle leaves cartwheeling across the newly turned earth. Once the silence returns, I gently squeeze her shoulder.

"Ready to go?"

"Yeah."

In unison, we turn and begin walking away in silence.

Caitlyn finally speaks as we approach the gate leading to the parking lot. "Dad?"

"Yeah, pumpkin?"

"Can we move?"

32

"Let's go, let's go, let's go. Finish your waffles. The school bus is going to be here any minute."

My little pep talk has no effect. Caitlyn stares at the television and absent-mindedly keeps chewing.

"Pumpkin?"

Still no response.

I pick up the remote and turn off the television, which finally gets her attention.

"Chop chop!" I say, clapping my hands.

"I'm ready," she says with that sigh that every parent knows and loves.

"Got your math homework?"

"Yes."

"All right. Go get your book bag," I say, pouring myself a cup of coffee.

"Dad?"

"Yeah?"

"Can I have some coffee?"

"What? No, you can't have coffee."

"Trisha Carpenter's mom lets her drink coffee."

"Trisha Carpenter?"

She nods.

"Yeah. Well, it kind of shows. No coffee."

"You never let me do anything." She pouts, but doesn't really mean it. She hops off the chair.

"Yes, I'm a horrible monster for not— Hey! Young lady, where are your shoes?"

"They're up in my room." She shrugs.

"You are killing me this morning, sweetheart. You're absolutely killing me. Book bag. Shoes. Come on. Let's go!"

She rolls her eyes, grabs her bookbag, and dramatically stomps up the stairs.

I need to get her on that bus because I need to get to my writing. The novel is chugging along. It's late, to be sure, but it's shaping up to be that rare sequel that's better than the original. I've been working on it every day in the 'writing room' of our new three-bedroom house in a quiet neighborhood in the beautiful seaside town of Avalon in California, between Monterey and San Francisco. After everything that happened, we needed a change—a big one. The drive across the country with Caitlyn was an incredible adventure, and the perfect way to start a new chapter together. We marveled at the changing landscapes, tried to find the most interesting places to eat, played "I Spy", and listened to old radio programs. We'd stop at any roadside attraction that sparked our interest. My favorite was the Ice Caves in Wyoming. Caitlyn's was, of course, a famous candy store in Illinois, where we enjoyed milkshakes and stocked up on enough chocolate, licorice, and saltwater taffy to last us the rest of the trip and then some. After a week on the road, we were both sad to see it end, but I told her how big California is, and promised her a drive along the coast next summer. She immediately began counting the days. We finally reached Avalon and began our new lives.

We've been here for almost six months. The memories of the Nightingale House will always be with us, but they're fading, being overtaken by new memories and experiences. Caitlyn and I still don't talk about it that much. I don't think we ever will. There are some things we've held on to and other things we've left behind.

We both love it here. Caitlyn helped me pick out the house. It's smaller, but still charming. In other words, exactly what we were looking for. The town is great. Caitlyn loves her school. She's making friends, like the caffeine-riddled Trisha Carpenter, and Caitlyn's lying has stopped. Our lives are moving on.

I open the front door, step out onto the porch, and glance down the street.

Damnit.

"Caitlyn! The bus is almost here!"

"Coming, coming, coming!"

She descends the stairs, shoes on, backpack slung over her shoulder, and hanging from her neck is the medallion with the last line of the poem; *The Secrets That I Keep*. She wanted to hold on to it. I felt like it was kind of fitting. I had a small hole drilled in the top and put it on a delicate silver chain. She wears it every day, just like how I wear Nicole's ring.

I step back inside and meet her at the bottom of the stairs.

"Okay," I say, straightening her clothes. "Have a great day at school. Pay attention. And remember that I love you very much, Caitlyn Nicole Price."

I kiss her on the cheek.

"I love you too, Dad."

She kisses me on the cheek.

Then, she completes the second part of our morning ritual by turning to the small table, just inside the front door. There's a framed picture of Nicole. Caitlyn kisses the tips of her fingers and touches the photo.

"Bye, Mom."

She then looks at the framed black-and-white photo of a young girl, sitting next to it.

273

"Bye, Katherine."

With that, Caitlyn runs out the door as the bus pulls up to the end of the driveway. The doors hiss open. Caitlyn turns and gives me a quick wave. I send one back. She climbs in and I see her silhouette move down the bus and find a seat. The engine rumbles and the bus drives away.

I watch until it's a small speck in the distance.

I go back inside, close the door, and look at the photos on the table.

Caitlyn knows that they're gone. We both do. Even though we don't talk about it that much, we're both grateful for what they did for us. I kiss my own fingers and touch Nicole's photo. Then I do the same for Katherine.

I head to the kitchen, grab my cup of coffee, and go to the Writing Room, which is a little glass-enclosed porch that offers a spectacular view of the Pacific Ocean.

The notebook is open on the desk, ready to go.

I look out at the shimmering expanse of water under the blue sky.

I pick up the pen and begin writing.

It's a perfect day.

Acknowledgments

As a kid, I was obsessed with ghosts. I devoured stories about 'The Brown Lady of Raynham Hall', 'No.50 Berkeley Square', 'The Tulip Staircase', 'The Winchester House', 'The Bell Witch', etc. My favorite ride? The Haunted Mansion in Disney World, of course. So, I've always wanted to write a haunted house story, but I had a lot of help.

Thank you, Abigail Fenton over at HarperCollins/HQ for your guidance and patience on getting *Nightingale House* out into the world. There's no one I trust more with these stories.

Thank you, Sandy Comstock. I wanted to make Daniel's grief a form of haunting, because I feel that's what grief is, and you helped me put Nicole in the Nightingale House.

Thank you, Deborah Griffieth for Rebecca's voice. I can't imagine what this book would be like without your contributions.

And finally, thank you, Stephanie Frech, for reading me all those ghost stories when we were kids.

Dear Reader,

We hope you enjoyed reading this book. If you did, we'd be so appreciative if you left a review. It really helps us and the author to bring more books like this to you.

Here at HQ Digital we are dedicated to publishing fiction that will keep you turning the pages into the early hours. Don't want to miss a thing? To find out more about our books, promotions, discover exclusive content and enter competitions you can keep in touch in the following ways:

JOIN OUR COMMUNITY:
Sign up to our new email newsletter: hyperurl.co/hqnewsletter
Read our new blog www.hqstories.co.uk
🐦 : https://twitter.com/HQStories
𝐟 : www.facebook.com/HQStories

BUDDING WRITER?
We're also looking for authors to join the HQ Digital family!
Find out more here:
https://www.hqstories.co.uk/want-to-write-for-us/
Thanks for reading, from the HQ Digital team

ONE PLACE. MANY STORIES

Keep reading for an excerpt from
Dark Hollows ...

I'm standing in the basement of a run-down, abandoned warehouse, staring at the padlock on a heavy steel door. The walls are coated in grime and there is the sound of dripping water from somewhere in the darkness.

The padlock begins to tremble. It's subtle, at first, but then grows violent, as if some enraged, unseen force is trying to pull it open. The padlock rattles against the door.

"No … please … please, hold …" I whisper, my voice weak in pain and fear.

The shaking intensifies. It begins to infect the door and the walls, filling the basement with a low rumble.

"Don't … I'm so sorry … Please …"

The rumble grows into a deafening roar. It feels like the entire building is going to come down on top of me. Bile rises in my throat.

"No … no …"

Everything stops.

I know what's coming. I know what's behind that door.

Oh my God, what have I done?

The lock snaps open.

*

I sit bolt upright in bed. Sweat pours down my face and my lungs pull in rapid gulps of air.

In the dawning light of morning, I can see Murphy, my black lab mutt, lying in his bed in the corner of the room. He cocks his head at me.

I grip my side and hiss through clenched teeth. Sitting up so fast causes the old injury in my side to flare with pain, but it passes. I steady my breath and wipe the sweat from my eyes. I throw off the covers, hop out of bed, and head to the bathroom. The nightmare is nothing new. I've been having it for years, reliving the panic and shock of that night over and over, but I've learned to quickly put it out of my mind.

After throwing some cold water on my face, I pull on a pair of jeans and a shirt and head downstairs to start a pot of coffee. Murphy joins me in the kitchen, but instead of coming over to the counter, he sits next to his food bowl and gives me those big, dinner-plate eyes.

"What? Are you hungry?" I ask.

His tail thumps against the floor.

I feed him a little dry food from the bag in the pantry, and then go to the window over the sink and glance down the drive, past the pond, to the cottage sitting at the edge of the woods.

The Thelsons' car is gone. No surprise there. They said they were getting an early start back to Manhattan.

Coffee in hand, I walk to the front door and pat my leg as I step out onto the porch.

"Let's go, Murph."

Murphy inhales the last of his breakfast and hustles after me. I don't think I've ever seen him chew, even when he was a puppy. He springs off the porch and down the steps. We walk past the pond, towards the cottage. As we pass the truck in the driveway, I make yet another mental note to fix that damn taillight. Somehow, all the mental notes I make about it go unremembered.

I walk around the fire pit and note the wineglasses sitting next to the chairs. I step over to the front door of the cottage, take out my key, and open the door. Before doing anything, I go to the kitchen table and open the guestbook. I flip through the pages until I find the latest entry. The ink is so dark and sharp, it had to have been written not more than an hour ago.

We were in town from Manhattan to do some leaf-peeping and had a wonderful time. The Hollows is a beautiful little town. We loved the shops on Main Street and strolling through the cemetery at the Old Stone Church. What can we say about Jacob's cottage? So amazing! We began every morning with a walk through the woods to check out the hills and always stopped at 'The Sanctuary'. Jacob is the perfect host. The wine and the s'mores were just the right touch. And then, there's Murphy! Such a sweetie! Can't wait to come back!

~ John & Margaret Thelson

I snap the guestbook closed and look around the cottage. It never fails; whenever someone from Manhattan signs the guestbook, they always have to mention that they're from Manhattan. Hopefully, they'll post the review on Be Our Guest this afternoon, once they get home.

The Thelsons were standard New York City types; taking their yearly fall pilgrimage up north to see some trees. They were a wealthy couple who would call this quaint, one-bedroom cottage 'roughing it', even though it had all the amenities, a couple of bottles of wine, and a fire pit outside. Still, they were pleasant, and they've left the cottage in good shape. The turnaround should be quick, and I've got it down to a science.

Murphy walks through the open front door. He's done scouting the fire pit for any stray graham crackers or marshmallows left by the Thelsons, and goes right for the kitchen to see if there are any scraps lying about.

"Happy hunting, Murphy," I say. He deserves it. He's one of my best selling points.

I clap my hands and rub them together. "All right. Time to get to work."

First thing I do is bring in the wineglasses and wash them in the kitchen sink. Then, I collect the bedsheets and towels, put them in a bag, and carry it to the house. Murphy follows close behind. I take the bag down to the basement and pop the contents into the washing machine. Even though we've done this process hundreds of times, Murphy bolts as soon as I open the lid because to him, the washing machine is still some sort of monster. Once I get that going, I head back upstairs. Murphy's on the porch, waiting for me.

"Coward," I say.

He responds by letting his tongue flop out of his mouth and starts panting.

As we begin walking back to the cottage, Murphy spots the ducks that have settled onto the glassy surface of the pond. He pins his ears back and sprints after them.

"Murphy!" I shout.

He stops at the water's edge and looks at me.

"Nope. Come on."

He stares at the pond and then back at me as if to ask, "But do you not see the ducks?"

"Come," I say, with a forceful slap on my leg.

He runs to catch up, but instead of following me into the cottage, he lies down on the cottage porch to enjoy the cool New England morning.

I restock the complimentary toiletries and clean the bathroom. No disasters there. One time, I had a young couple from Los Angeles stay for a weekend and after drinking too much wine, they destroyed the bathroom. I almost left them a bad review, but they were in the "Elite Class" on Be Our Guest, so I held my fire. Thankfully, they left me a glowing review.

I finish scrubbing the tub and stand up a little too quickly. The pain in my side flares again, but it barely registers.

Time to tackle the kitchen. I clean the plates from the s'mores and refill the basket by the coffee maker with packs of Groundworks coffee. I wipe down the counter and sweep the floor. After that, I retrieve the vacuum cleaner from the hall closet. I have my routine down, working my way from the bedroom, then the bathroom, down the hall, and into the living room/kitchen area.

I push the vacuum around the bookcase, which is filled with some of my favorite books—a few thrillers, some Michael Crichtons, *A Christmas Carol*, et cetera. No one reads them while they're here, but they make for good pictures on the Be Our Guest website. There's also a row of DVDs no one watches: *Casablanca*, *When Harry Met Sally*, *Vertigo*, *Roman Holiday*, and *Dead Again*. As I glide the vacuum cleaner over the rug by the fireplace, my eyes catch the stick doll I made years ago, resting on the mantel. It's a crude figure made of twigs tied together with twine. It adds a nice, rugged touch to the place. In Boy Scouts, they taught us to use pine needles instead of twine, but those don't last long—

"For me?" she asked in mock flattery.
"Just something I learned in Boy Scouts."
She saw right through my bullshit.

"Well, I shall treasure it always," she said, clutching the doll to her chest, toying with me …
I'm pulled from my memory by Murphy whining.

He's sitting in the doorway. His expression is a perfect balance of wanting to enter the cottage but respecting the vacuum cleaner.

I flip the switch, and the vacuum engine whirrs to a stop.

"Done," I tell him, and put the vacuum back in the closet.

While in the closet, I rotate the stacks of towels, and accidentally knock over the small dish hidden on the top shelf, which

285

contains a spare key to the house and the coffee shop. I keep a spare key for both out here because I learned the hard way that I should when I locked myself out of the house about a year ago. I put the keys back in the dish, tuck it all the way back on the shelf, and close the door. I pull out my phone and take a series of pictures of the cottage. It's been a while, and I need to change the photos on the Be Our Guest website.

I head back to the house and transfer the sheets and towels to the dryer. Once again, Murphy stays by my side until I get to the basement stairs, because the dryer is the washer's evil twin. That accomplished, I head back down to the cottage to do one last spot check to make sure everything is perfect.

I normally wouldn't do an extra check, but tonight, I'm breaking a rule.

Here's the deal—a few years ago, my parents died. We weren't particularly close. In fact, we weren't close at all, which is strange for an only child, but there was history. They were the successful, wealthy, married couple who had done everything right, while I was nothing but one dumb decision after another. I could never get my feet under me and it was my own fault. I squandered every chance they gave me.

It got so bad that they finally cut me off after I screwed around my sophomore year in college. I had to find another way to pay my tuition, which I did. I told them I got a job, but not the whole story about what the job was. They were pleased that I had finally taken responsibility for myself and tried to reconnect, but for me, the damage had been done. I wanted nothing to do with them. There were obligatory phone calls on Christmas and birthdays, filled with awkward conversations. I was living in Portland, Maine, while they had moved to Hilton Head, South Carolina.

Their passing was quick. Mom became ill. I offered to come down and help out, because that's what an only child does, right, even if we hadn't really spoken in years? Dad declined my offer, claiming he could handle it. Well, he couldn't. The stress got to him and he had a heart attack. It was over before he hit the floor. I got the call from the nurse Dad had hired to look after Mom. On my way down to the funeral, Mom passed away. The nurse said it was from a broken heart. I didn't know how to feel. They hadn't been a part of my life for so long, it felt like they were already gone, but I did wish that I had maybe tried to patch things up.

The dual funeral was surreal. There were a lot of people there, and I didn't know any of them. When they found out who I was, they came up and commented on how painful and sad it must be for me, and what wonderful people my parents had been. I tried to be sympathetic, but I worried that they would be able to tell that I really didn't know my parents. The worst was having to give a speech. I felt like a fraud. No, I *was* a fraud. Thankfully, any question of my sincerity could be chalked up to shock and grief. I felt guilty for not knowing them. All those people were moved by their passing, and I was ashamed of myself. I pictured what my funeral would look like, and it was not a well-attended affair.

Then came the will.

My parents left me everything. There was no personal declaration in it—no directions as to what I was supposed to do with their life's savings. There was only the simple instruction that I was to receive everything. I assumed that it was their way of saying that I had shown myself worthy after making my own way. Maybe they were saying that they were sorry. Maybe they thought that some day, we really would be a family again. I don't know, but that's when I made the decision. I had made so many mistakes—the worst of which were only known to me. I decided then and there—no more messing around. It was time to straighten out my life.

I grew up in Vermont, and since I was looking at this as a reset, I decided to go back. I did my research, found The Hollows, and bought the property on the outskirts of town. The nearest neighbor was a half a mile away. The property was secluded, but not isolated. I loved the plot of land, which was nestled up against the woods. There was the main house, the pond, and the cottage. The cottage had been the main house when the land had been a farm, but around a hundred and fifty years ago, the land had been sold, the new house built, the pond dug, and the cottage was abandoned. The fact that the main house was old gave it a sense of maturity and responsibility that I now craved.

I also loved The Hollows. It had originally been settled by two French explorers in the early 1600s, who named it 'Chavelle's Hollow'. Then came the British, and after the French-Indian War, they decided to change the name to 'Sommerton's Hollow', in honor of the British General, Edward Sommerton. The problem was that the town was so small and located right on the border between the French and British territories, people called it by both names. Then the American Revolution happened, and Sommerton served in the British Army. After the war, the citizens of the newly formed country didn't want to have a town honoring their recently vanquished enemy, so they changed the name to 'Putnam's Hollow', in honor of Rufus Putnam of the Continental Army.

This all happened so fast, relatively speaking, that people were calling the town by all three names at the same time, depending on if they were French, British, or American. When the town finally got a post office, which is what makes a place an official town in the eyes of the government, the surveyor was so fed up with trying to determine the correct name for such a small town, he simply wrote down "The Hollows", and it stuck. The Hollows became one of those towns you see on travel websites—a charming New England town with a Main Street comprised of three-hundred-year-old, colonial-style buildings, a town green, an old stone church, and winding roads, hidden among the rolling hills and forests.

After purchasing the house, I moved on to the next phase of my plan—opening my own business.

I rented a storefront on Main Street and opened a coffee shop. Like the rest of the town, Main Street was a postcard. The centuries-old buildings that line the street each have a plaque identifying the year they were built and for whom. Instead of switching to electric lights, the town kept its old gas lamps. At night, it was a fairy tale.

My shop was a small, single-story structure just down and across from the church, which everyone called the Old Stone Church. My coffee shop's large front window gave the perfect view with the town green across the street, and the old cemetery next to the church, to the south. I named the place "Groundworks" and began my little endeavor. I quickly realized that I had bitten off way more than I could chew, but since there was no Plan B, I had put nearly all of my inheritance into the house and the shop, so I had to stick it out.

Little by little, I got it under control. I started by giving out free samples of Groundworks' signature coffee to the local hotels and B&Bs to put in their guestrooms. They jumped on it as a way to promote local business. That's what the fall tourist season is all about. The Hollows is a cottage industry. It also paid off in that everyone staying at the hotels and B&Bs came to the shop during their exploration of the surrounding hills and countryside. I slowly fought my way out of the red, and while things were looking up financially, it was really hard work.

One downside of moving to a new town and putting in so many hours was that I was lonely. On an impulse, I took a trip to the local animal shelter. Behind the shelter was a pen where they allowed the dogs to run and play. I told myself I was going to adopt the first dog who came up to me. I stepped through the gate and this little black ball of fur with oversized paws broke from the pack and came flying at me, ears and jowls flapping wildly. He charged and didn't stop. He simply plowed into my shins and careened across the ground. He instantly sprang up and repeated the process. After the third time of tumbling over my feet, he was going to try again but was so dizzy, he fell over.

I was laughing so hard, tears poured down my cheeks, and I had to sit down. The mutt leaped at me and attempted to lick my face off. That was that. I named him Murphy, and we've been inseparable ever since. I'm not exaggerating about that. In four years, we've rarely left each other's side. With the long hours I was putting in at the shop, I couldn't leave him at home, alone, so I brought him with me. Before long, Murphy was Groundworks' unofficial mascot.

I remodeled Groundworks to give it an "old-timey" feel and it started to pick up steam. I was there almost fourteen hours a day, seven days a week. Business continued to grow.

One morning two years ago, Maggie Vaughn, who runs the Elmwood Hotel a block away, stopped by to pick up her supply of coffee, and remarked that her hotel was so full, she was turning people away.

That sparked an idea to give myself a side project and make a little extra coin.

By that time, I had hired some staff to lighten the load and had some time for myself.

I had been using the cottage as storage for Groundworks, but I took out some money, and renovated it as a place to stay. I fixed it up into a charming, one-bedroom affair with a remodeled kitchen and bathroom. I even added the fire pit out front. At the time, Airbnb was starting to take off. I thought they might be too crowded, so I went with a rival start-up called "Be Our Guest". It marketed itself as a more selective and upscale version of Airbnb. They weren't going after people looking to save a buck. They were after wealthy people wanting a different experience. These were exactly the tourists who were coming to The Hollows.

Since Be Our Guest was new, they wanted unique properties. I contacted them with photos of the cottage, and they went berserk. A representative from Be Our Guest came out to inspect the cottage and loved it. We went through the formalities. I had to sign a bunch of papers, promising to comply with their policies, one of which was that I wouldn't become involved "physically or otherwise" with a guest during their stay at my property. I had to submit to a background check, which always makes me nervous. I was confident they wouldn't find anything, but still, I worry.

Once that was done, I was cleared for takeoff, and take off, it did. Be Our Guest ran the cottage as a featured property and immediately, the reservations filled up. It was great. I was charging $200 a night in the off-season and $300 a night in the fall. If I wanted to, I could have booked the cottage every night. It's the easiest money I've ever made. I usually only saw my guests once or twice. They were always polite—well, most of the time, and all it took was an hour or two, at most, to clean and reset the place after they left.

Some of the hotel owners in town were upset that I had gotten into the game, but not too upset. They were still operating at capacity. I think they were more worried that other residents with extra bedrooms might try to go the Airbnb route. Anyway, like I said—easiest money I ever made. I could set my own dates, and if I wanted to take a break from keeping up the cottage, I just blocked out a week or two here and there. People enjoyed their stay. I made sure to keep the cottage stocked with wine from local wineries and coffee—only Groundworks, of course. Once I put in the fire pit, I also made sure to have the stuff to make s'mores in the kitchen. Everyone took advantage of it.

And everyone loved Murphy.

I did have some rules, though. I didn't allow anyone to stay at the cottage who hadn't already written at least three reviews on Be Our Guest. That's one of the beauties of the site. Hotels have to let anyone stay at their place, so long as they have a credit card. With Be Our Guest, I get to vet who stays at my place. I can see what they've said about other places, and you can tell who's going to be a problem by their reviews. They're the people who are determined to have a bad time, no matter what. That's my rule—three reviews to prove that you are a reasonable person. It's my most sacred rule.

And tonight, I'm breaking it.

Two months ago, I received a request from a woman named Rebecca Lowden to stay in the cottage for one night only. I was going to reject the reservation request when I saw that she had no previous reviews, but I always check the reservation request to see where they heard about me to stay informed about where Be Our Guest is advertising. I clicked on her request, which took me to her profile page. She was undeniably beautiful, with brown hair and blue eyes, but it was her bio that caught me.

In the bio sections, Be Our Guest encourages you to list things, like your hobbies, favorite books, and favorite movies. As one of her favorite books, she listed *A Christmas Carol*. And in the "favorite movies" section? *Dead Again*, which is in my top five. Also, she had grown up in a town not too far from where I grew up.

So, out of simple curiosity, I broke my rule and accepted the reservation.

If you enjoyed *Nightingale House*, then why not try another gripping thriller from HQ Digital?

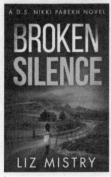

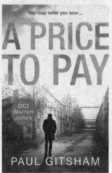

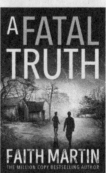